Bernard feels like an outsider in the gay community. Thirty-five, chubby, and hairy, he doesn't fit the image of the stereotypical gay man. Failed relationships in his past solidify the idea he is destined to be alone.

Rory is struggling with his identity. At thirty-five, he is still single. When he reunites with his childhood friend, his religious convictions and the desire to be with a man clash as he must choose between what the Church taught him is right and what his heart desires.

The two men are forced to face their fears and make a choice. Live alone and accept their fate or take a leap and challenge what they believe.

I0588151

LARGER THAN LOVE

Big Boys of Gilroy, Book One

Jole Cannon

A NineStar Press Publication

www.ninestarpress.com

Larger than Love

First Edition, July 2024

ISBN: 978-1-64890-785-2

Also available in eBook, ISBN: 978-1-64890-784-5

CONTENT WARNING:

This book contains sexually explicit content, which may only be suitable for mature readers. Depictions of homophobia, fat shaming, drug/alcohol abuse, deceased parent, and references to cheating and past physical and emotional abuse.

LARGER THAN LOVE

BIG BOYS OF GILROY, BOOK ONE

JOLE CANNON

A NineStar Press Publication

www.ninestarpress.com

Larger than Love

First Edition, July 2024

ISBN: 978-1-64890-785-2

Also available in eBook, ISBN: 978-1-64890-784-5

CONTENT WARNING:

This book contains sexually explicit content, which may only be suitable for mature readers. Depictions of homophobia, fat shaming, drug/alcohol abuse, deceased parent, and references to cheating and past physical and emotional abuse.

I would like to dedicate this book to my partner, Ken. He has always been supportive of everything I do. We are two bears living our best life.

Chapter One

Bernard

Friday, April 10, 1998

BERNARD SAT AT the bar with a glass of soda. Smoke blurred his vision as it wafted from machines. The scents of overpriced colognes, fruity drinks, and a hint of hair spray assaulted his nose. Thin twinks with platinum hair and gym bunnies in tank tops flooded the dance floor. The repetitive techno music pounded in his head as the dancers moved under the strobe lights. He couldn't tell when one song ended and another began.

Liquid Pearl was the nearest gay bar to home. It was a place Bernard believed he would fit in. His mistake. Close by these fitness gods sat a bear of a man. Him. Bernard was a few inches shy of six feet and carried a thick two hundred and seventy-five pounds. His round belly pushed against the bar as he attempted to find a comfortable position on the small bar stool. His once-muscular arms flexed as he lifted his glass, a shadow of his youth on the farm. Beefy calves strained against his jeans, the byproduct of years of milking cows. Short-cropped black hair matched his groomed beard. His plaid flannel shirt and blue jeans contrasted with the skinny jeans, muscle shirts, and salon-styled hair of the men surrounding him. The average age was twenty-five, and he was in his mid-thirties. Over the hill in the gay community. Odd man out was an understatement.

Bernard received a few looks and even had men approach him. However, every conversation revealed their true intentions. He never received more than a second glance or a chat because he didn't sleep around. They viewed him as a piece of meat, something to consume, rather than a person. He didn't accept their invitation. Bernard was not someone to conquer, and he wouldn't cave into the temptation of anonymous sex, no matter how strong the urge to touch another man became. He refused to settle for less than what he deserved. And he deserved happiness.

Regulars came in to unwind, dance, and have fun. Some men, like him, didn't fit the mold of Liquid Pearl but they didn't stick out the way he did. Friends surrounded them. Bernard didn't have friends here, and those who approached him didn't want his friendship.

While Bernard drank his soda, someone slid onto the stool next to him.

"Bartender, a Sex on the Beach," the man demanded.

What a rude way to order a drink. Doesn't he have any manners?

"Hey there, sexy." The newcomer's tone changed. He sounded less aggressive but still manipulative. Bernard shifted in his seat.

"I'm Chance," he said.

He shoved his hand in front of Bernard's face.

"Bernard." He gripped Chance's hand harder than he should have and refused to make eye contact.

Bernard recognized the name and voice. Platinum-blond hair, bright-blue eyes, and tanning booth skin. A hottie men fawned over, but not his type. Bernard returned to his drink.

"You look kind of lonely sitting here all by your lonesome," Chance said. "I see you here sometimes, but you don't talk to anyone."

Bernard glared back at Chance and caught him pouting. Clearly, he was used to a certain amount of attention and Bernard wasn't showing him enough.

"Why don't we go back to my place and get to know each other?" He caressed Bernard's shoulder.

"Thank you for the offer, but I'm here to drink and relax."

Bernard eyed Chance. He pinned him at twenty-one or twenty-two. There was no reason someone this young, a boy compared to him, would be interested in him except as a conquest. Chance's smile did not falter. His bleached teeth gleamed beneath the neon lights. *Does he think I'm so desperate I'll go home with the first person who shows an interest in me? I have standards, and this guy does not meet them.*

"Come on, I'm sure I can thrill you tonight." He lowered his hand below Bernard's belly. "I'm sure you could use a little attention. A guy like you probably doesn't get much. I can change that." His lips were close to Bernard's ear as his hand traced a path to Bernard's crotch. The stench of his cologne overwhelmed Bernard's senses. Chance's hand moved to find

Bernard's cock but appeared lost between his thick thighs.

Bernard grabbed Chance's hand and moved it off him. *Did he think that was a compliment? That I should take what I can get? Not a chance, Chance.* Heat warmed his cheeks.

"I said no, thank you."

"Oh, honey, I don't get told no." Chance placed his hand on Bernard's chest. The bartender placed Chance's drink on the bar and moved to the next patron.

"Well, there's a first time for everything." He removed his hand again. "Oh look, your drink is here. Now you can go."

But Chance continued his pursuit. "Sweetie, I know you want me, and I want you. There's no need to play hard to get. So, why don't we get out of here? What do you say?"

He slipped his hand into Bernard's shirt and stroked his chest. A flicker of disgust passed across his flawless face as he rubbed Bernard's chest hair. He composed himself, but not before Bernard caught him. *Does this guy have no shame? It's clear he isn't into me. What's he after?*

Bernard grabbed Chance's hand, rougher this time, and took it out of his shirt. He glared. "Touch me again, and I will break your hand, 'sweetie.'" He tossed his hand away.

"You fat bastard!" Chance yelled loud enough to drown out the music. Patrons closest to them turned. Chance stepped back and gestured at his body with a theatrical up-and-down sweep of his hands. "You have a hot guy right in front of you, willing to take your disgusting ass home to actually fuck, which I doubt you've had in a long time, and you turn it down? You're not only fat, but you're also fucking stupid! No one around here is going to touch your ugly, fat ass." He made a show of including the entire club. "You should get it when you can. You're old as shit and going to die alone!"

Silence followed the outburst. The music still thumped its rhythmic sounds while the dancers continued, oblivious to the exchange. Those nearby waited with bated breath for Bernard's reaction.

Bernard silently stood. His mass eclipsed Chance's frame. He closed his eyes and took two deep breaths then released them.

He spoke slowly and softly. "Listen to me, you egotistical, carbon-copy asshole. I may not have your looks, but I do have standards, dignity, and self-respect. You think I'm so desperate that I'll go home with the first person who talks to me? I am going to guess that you talked to me on a bet. I've seen your type. You're not interested in me. You don't want to have sex with someone like me." Bernard pointed out the musclemen who surrounded them. "Those are the guys I've seen you leave with. Either way, I wouldn't touch you with a ten-foot pole, so leave me alone."

Chance stood dumbfounded for a moment. He regained himself. "No! You listen to me, you—"

Bernard held up his hand to cut him off. He rotated it and flipped him off. Chance grabbed his drink and huffed away, mumbling to himself. Bernard's eyes followed Chance back to his table. Chance's face fell as he handed a bill to a broad-shouldered man. *Typical entitled kid who thinks the world owes him something for doing nothing but being born with the right body.*

Bernard drained his soda and set the glass on the bar. "I need to leave," he growled to himself. "I can't be the only bear who likes other bears." He stormed toward the door, past Chance and his friends.

"Honey, that big ol' prude has turned down way hotter guys than you." The broad-shouldered man laughed.

Fucking typical. I'm a joke here.

Outside, the warm California air filled Bernard's lungs. Fancy cars packed the parking lot. His truck, like him, stood out. The club stood on a lot alone, the nearest business a quarter of a mile away. His eyes adjusted to the darkness. The stars above shimmered with the near-full moon.

Bernard jumped into his truck and started it. The dash clock flashed 10:15. *It's only been twenty minutes? It felt longer.*

He pulled out and headed home. His water-filled eyes blurred the road ahead. He swiped at the tears under his glasses to clear the path.

Twenty minutes later, Bernard parked in his driveway. He meandered through his gate, into the house, passed through the kitchen, and stepped over the baby gate into the laundry room.

He opened the back door. A lush yard greeted him. A dilapidated greenhouse sat in one corner and a doghouse in the center.

A small brown-and-white corgi barreled toward him and leaped into his arms.

"Aww, did you miss me, Ginger?" He held his best friend tight against his chest as he fought back more tears.

Bernard took down the gate. He filled the dog's food and water bowls under the island. Ginger ran to her food.

"You hungry, girl?" He rubbed Ginger's ears. "Even though you don't understand me, you still love me."

He grabbed a pint of ice cream and a spoon, leaned against the counter, and ate from the tub. Tears mixed with the melted dessert as it dripped down his beard. Ginger sat and stared up at him as he sniffled.

"I know I'm not supposed to binge-eat, but it's been a long night."

Ginger barked at him.

"Okay, I'm almost done."

Bernard threw the empty carton away and walked to his bedroom, Ginger at his heel.

Ginger curled up on her bed next to the nightstand while he entered the adjoining bathroom and undressed.

He caught sight of his reflection in the mirror, recoiling at the ice-cream-splattered man in front of him. Disgust settled in the pit of his stomach as he turned on the tap, splashed his face with water, and scrubbed furiously at his matted beard.

After he dried his face, Bernard took in his naked body in the mirror.

"Who could love this?" He grabbed fat from his stomach and shook it. He closed in on the stretch marks hidden by his body hair. "This is…" He shook his head. Self-disgust writhed inside him. "Get a hold of yourself," he commanded his mirror image. "That is not all you are. You have a lot to offer. It's not your fault no one sees past your exterior."

He stepped into the shower and scrubbed. He paid close attention to the areas where the egomaniac rubbed against him. His skin became raw and pink. The hot water washed away the grime of the evening, along with fresh tears.

He lost track of time and glanced at his watch. It'd been thirty minutes. Stepping out of the shower, he mindlessly dried off before returning to the bedroom.

He stared with disdain at the CPAP machine on his nightstand as he filled it with distilled water. *Normal people don't need a machine to help them breathe at night.* He put the water away and dressed in a T-shirt and gym shorts.

Bernard plopped on his bed and stared at the blank TV screen. Leaning over, he rummaged through one of his nightstand drawers. He grabbed a VHS titled *A Bear's Day Work*, put it in, and laid back down.

The screen displayed two bearded, rugged, beefy men sensually undressing each other. They explored each other's bodies with the kind of raw and passionate desire that Bernard yearned for. He closed his eyes and envisioned a large man with him. The dream man desired him, touched him, and caressed him. This man loved him. It made him both hopeful and sickened. The men on the screen were muscle bears, not fat bears like him. They wanted each other, not him. These men were everything he wasn't. Men fawned over thin men like Chance or masculine men like them. He fell in the middle. Lost. Forgotten.

He shut off the tape and turned the channel. He lay there as a commercial boasted about a new weight-loss supplement that required one daily pill. Another described medication to help with depression and anxiety. Bernard stared at the ceiling; fresh tears clouded his vision as thoughts of a life without someone to love him filled his head.

Why does society shun those of us who don't fit their mold?

Ginger climbed up the stairs at the foot of the bed and nudged Bernard's side. He didn't respond. His unfocused eyes gazed into oblivion. Ginger prompted a few more times before she gave up. She curled up next to Bernard and whimpered softly.

Bernard rubbed the dog's head. "I'm sorry, girl, I didn't mean to ignore you."

Ginger sighed.

"You get me, girl. You love me. Is it possible to find someone who loves me as much as you do?"

Ginger barked.

"I know I need another human here. I wonder if I'm reaching too far."

Bernard rolled onto his side. Ginger nuzzled against his chest.

"What can I do to be noticed?" he asked. "Am I lovable?"

Chapter Two

Rory

Friday, April 10

RORY WORKED IN the graduate student workroom with his four colleagues. The team had developed a new method to gather solar energy. They designed it to work with multiple timers in a greenhouse. They discovered a way to increase the capacity of the solar generator, which allowed it to work for weeks without sunlight. This design was the apex of their device. They'd accomplished something no other graduate students had.

The small room held their spare parts, schematics, tools, books, and notes. Rory insisted they kept the space neat and clean. He organized it so everyone could find what they needed.

The adjoining room had a small greenhouse as their test area. They grew a variety of vegetables, including tomatoes and carrots. The team attached a small shed which housed the generator. Solar panels lay between the glass plates to absorb the sunlight.

At thirty-five, Rory was the oldest graduate student in the program. The team invited him out for drinks every Friday, but he didn't go. He didn't fit in. They all got along well, and Rory would mess up their dynamic. He needed to keep his work and social life separate.

"I can't believe we're almost done with school," Sophia said. She adjusted the ribbon at the base of her long, black hair.

Sophia was the youngest in the group and the only woman. She'd entered college at sixteen, and at twenty-two, was finishing her graduate program.

"Sophia, if you hadn't discovered that cross-wiring, we might not have finished in time," Jeff said.

Jeff was average in every way. He wasn't tall or short, fat or thin, and could blend into a crowd. He was, however, the most optimistic in the group.

"I'm sure I would have found it eventually," Nicolas said.

Nicolas was tall and wiry. He groomed his blond hair to perfection and kept his face clean-shaven. Nicolas became frustrated with himself when he didn't catch an error. He pushed himself harder than anyone else on the team.

"I'm sure you would have." Jeff smiled and patted Nicolas on the shoulder.

"I agree," Rory said.

"It's a fantastic feeling," Davi said. "What we've done here."

Davi was short and stocky with a strong Brazilian accent. His thick body threatened to tear his T-shirt. He kept his shoulder-length brown hair pulled back with a bandana. He was handsome, and Rory wanted nothing more than to emulate him. Davi was confident, attractive, kind, and had his life together. At thirty, he was the closest to Rory's age.

"How far are you with the slides for our presentation?" Sophia asked Jeff.

"They're almost ready. I'll have them done in plenty of time for us to review."

Jeff spent hours on the slides for the presentation. He'd taken courses in computer programming, which allowed him to make elaborate slides and images for their final project.

"I'll start creating notecards and get everyone's part ready after we finalize the slides," Nicolas said.

As the son of a politician, Nicolas learned to please a crowd. The group elected him to lead the presentation for their final project. Everything they'd worked for was riding on it.

"I've checked the battery power, and it's holding the energy we've stored longer than we could've imagined. It's been there for twenty days," Sophia said.

"That's perfect," Davi said. "It means Rory fixed the calibration we struggled with."

"Great job, Rory," Jeff said.

"Thank you." Rory's cheeks warmed at the compliment. "I couldn't have done it without Davi's wiring skills. I've never been good with the wiring portion of this project."

"Give yourself more credit," Jeff said. "You've been a valuable member of the team."

"Thank you."

"He's right," Sophia said. "You've pulled your weight on this project and we're lucky to have you."

Rory's heart soared. Warmth enveloped him as his team complimented his achievements. He was contributing to a major project, and they noticed.

"Well, I say we call it a day. We've done so much," Jeff said.

"Why don't we go for drinks?" Sophia suggested.

"That sounds great," Nicolas said.

"A nice Friday night at the club, sipping drinks and dancing. I'm in," Davi said.

"Thanks, but I'm going to grade some papers and head home," Rory said.

"That's right. The department has you teaching two lower-division courses. How is it?" Sophia asked.

"It's really not bad. It helps me pay for college and live on my own. I've started looking for work. Nothing yet, but I'm hopeful," Rory said.

"I wish you the best," Jeff said.

"I'd like to move out of my apartment and find a house. It'd be nice to have a yard and a garage to tinker in. I'd like a big kitchen too, so I can bake large cakes."

They all gaped at him. Rory shifted his feet.

"Why are you staring?" He averted his eyes.

"I think that's the most you've shared since we started the program," Jeff said.

"I'm sorry I'm not too open. I just…"

"We understand," Sophia said. "You grade those papers, and we'll take a rain check. You'll have to come out with us to celebrate when we finish."

"It's a deal." Rory smiled.

*

RORY STAYED ON the San Jose State College campus until five, then headed back to Gilroy. The half-hour drive was pleasant. He listened to the radio and relaxed.

Rory walked into his apartment.

"Home sweet home."

A small tabby cat trotted out of the bedroom, stretched, and leaped onto his shoulder from the couch.

"Hi, Mina." He scratched her chin. "Did you have a good nap?"

Mina purred.

"Such a good girl."

Mina jumped onto the back of the couch and curled up. Rory put his keys on the hook below the mail-filled slot next to the door.

Rory lived in a two-bedroom apartment alone. He had decorated it to his exact standards. He kept his apartment spotless. Family photos covered the plain white walls. A cross hung over his couch. Paintings handed down to him by his grandmother adorned the other walls. His favorite was a little girl in a field of yellow wildflowers.

His couch cover was a sea blue, matching the rug under his coffee table. A recliner sat next to the couch, the leather pristine. His coffee table held a basket for his remote control and a stack of coasters. In the corner of the room was a TV with a bookcase filled with novels next to it. The dining table had a pure white cover. His bedroom was bare except for his bed and a nightstand for his alarm clock and Bible.

Rory had converted his spare bedroom into a workroom. A computer sat on a desk in the corner with an old chair. In the middle of the room was a table with blueprints, wires, metal pieces, and a toolbox. Everything had a place.

The red light flashed on the answering machine as he walked into the kitchen.

He pushed play. "Hey, Rory, it's João Silva. I'm having a barbecue next Saturday and thought you'd like to come. Haven't seen you in a few years. Hope you're doing well."

João always thinks of me. I think it'll be nice to finally take him up on his offer.

Rory picked up the phone and called.

"Hello?" Mr. Silva asked.

"Hello, Mr. Silva. It's Rory."

"Rory, you're an adult now. You can call me João."

Rory found Portuguese pronunciations difficult but tried his best. João was a kind man, with a heavy Portuguese accent. He'd moved to the States from the Azores in the fifties.

"Okay, João."

"How are you?"

"I'm doing good. I just got your message, and I'd love to come for a barbecue. What time?"

"Oh, great to hear. We'll be starting at about twelve. If you want to come by early to help, that would be fine too."

"Great. Do you need me to bring anything?" Rory asked.

"Well, if it's not too much trouble, could you bring some of your pies?"

"Sure, can I use your kitchen?"

"Of course." There was a pause. "Are you going to bring someone? A girlfriend, or anyone?"

Rory furrowed his brow. He'd never had a girlfriend. He'd been single his entire life. Thirty-five and he had no one.

"No, it's just going to be me."

"All right, I'll put that down for a head count."

They said their goodbyes, and Rory hung up. He was a little nervous. Mr. Silva had invited him to a barbecue a few times over the past six years, but with work, church activities, and grad school, he didn't have time to socialize. It'd be nice to get out of the apartment and relax a little.

Rory made dinner. He steamed vegetables and rice, and baked chicken. He poured a glass of Merlot and took his meal into the living room. Mina was still asleep. He turned on the TV.

"Oh, *Not Without My Daughter* is coming on at six. We made it in time to see it, Mina." He settled in and watched as Betty, played by Sally Field, realized her husband had no intention of going back to the States from Iran. He cheered Betty on as she planned her escape.

Betty made it over the border and was on her way to freedom.

"Oh, that movie gets me every time."

Rory carried his dishes to the kitchen. He cleaned them along with the rest of the kitchen. It sparkled by the time he'd finished.

Settling on the couch, he pulled out his knitting set. He'd just got into a nice pace when the phone rang.

He sighed and put the knitting to the side to answer the phone.

"Hello?"

"Hello, Rory." His mother's voice came through.

"Hello, Mother," he said.

"How are you doing, dear?"

"I'm doing okay. How is everything at home?"

"Oh, everything is fine. I just wanted to check on you."

"Thank you."

"So, how's the new diet? Have you lost weight?"

Rory groaned. They attended two services a week together, and he ate lunch with her and his father every Sunday. She still brought up his weight every week. He'd been the same size since he was twenty-five. Six feet and three hundred pounds. He wished she'd leave his weight alone. He loved himself at this size. No one would make him ashamed of his body, which included his mother. He wanted to tell her to stop but decided against it.

"No, I haven't lost any weight since last month."

"Hmm," she said. "Well, I'm sure you're trying."

"Thank you, Mother."

"So, how's school going? Are you done yet?"

Another thing his mother brought up. She believed he should have finished his degree within eight years of starting. It took Rory twelve years to complete his bachelor's and master's. His parents gave him enough for full-time tuition, but he wanted to live alone. He used the rest to rent his apartment.

"I finish in May," he said.

"Oh, finally. Now you can get a proper job," she said. "Well, I'm glad we could catch up. I'll see you at the service tomorrow night."

He had a proper job. He taught two classes at the college. It wasn't extravagant money, but it paid the bills. It was work he enjoyed.

"Yes, ma'am."

"Good night." She hung up before he could say he loved her.

Rory sat on his couch, knitting a sweater for his niece. She loved lavender, and she'd love anything her Uncle Roro made for her.

He left the TV on the American Movie Classics channel while he worked. The background noise helped him focus.

An hour had passed when Rory warmed up one of his brownies. He put a scoop of ice cream on top and took it into the living room.

His mother's voice interrupted him. *Is this really the way to lose weight? You'll never find a nice girl looking like this.*

He turned on *Jeopardy* and ate his brownie.

Is my mother right? Am I going to be alone if I don't lose weight?

He cleaned up his dish and headed to the bedroom, Mina trailing behind.

Rory dressed in his pajamas and lay in bed. Mina found her way to the open area between his legs and curled up. Rory grabbed his Bible and read passages for thirty minutes. Same as every night.

Once he finished, he held the Bible to his heart and said his evening prayer.

I don't know where my life is going. How do I become the son my mother wants? How do I make her proud?

Chapter Three

Bernard

Monday, April 11

MONDAY MORNING BERNARD picked up his friend and coworker, Sarah.

"You look down today. What's wrong?" she asked.

Bernard could always confide in Sarah; they'd been close friends since high school. She was the first person he'd ever come out to, and one of the few friends who'd stood by him afterwards. She'd met her husband John at college, where she'd been on a tennis scholarship. Bernard had even acted as groomsman at their wedding two years later.

Her husband, John, was an amazing man. He was big, burly, hairy, and compassionate. John ticked all the boxes Bernard looked for in a man. He never told Sarah he found John attractive, but she knew.

"Well," Bernard said. "It's about what happened Friday night."

He described the night's events. Sarah did not interrupt his story. She allowed Bernard to express his pain.

After he finished, Sarah placed a hand on his shoulder.

"I'm so sorry, Bernard. I can't believe he would say those things. How awful."

Bernard fought back tears as his chest tightened. He struggled to breathe. He pulled over as he hyperventilated.

"It's okay. Deep breaths, deep breaths." Sarah rubbed his back. "It's going to be okay. Did you take your medication this morning?"

Bernard forced a nod. He'd been on the same anxiety medication for seven years. He'd started taking it after he broke up with his last boyfriend, Tracy. It was supposed to relieve anxiety attacks and depression. Nights like Friday proved it didn't always work.

"How much did you drink last night?"

Bernard shook his head. "No"—breathe in—"drinks." Breathe out.

"Okay." She continued to rub his back.

With his breathing evened out, he balled his hands into fists. He looked at Sarah, tears threatening to release. Her green eyes gleamed back at him.

"Why are these guys so nasty?" He choked on the words. "They wanted to fuck with me. I'm just a joke to them. None of them actually want me."

Sarah sat speechless.

"Even guys my size don't want a guy my size. They want thin, athletic, hairless, toned, or muscular men. They want everything else, but they don't want me!"

The tears fell. Sarah grabbed tissues from the glove compartment and handed them to him.

"I'm meant to be alone. That's it. I have to face facts, or I'll implode." He blew his nose. Bernard removed his glasses to wipe his eyes.

"That place is no good for you, Bernard," she said. "You like to sit and read. Play video games. You prefer a good sappy movie over a dance club. You don't like those places."

"But I can't meet people at home. It's the only gay club within twenty miles."

"You need to take a break from the bar scene."

"I can't do this anymore," he said, ignoring her comment.

"That place has changed you." Her face screwed up in a grimace.

"What do you mean?"

"You used to be happy sitting at home, watching a movie with Ginger curled up at your feet. Now—" she looked at him. "Now you want to push your limits to see how much you can torment yourself before you collapse."

"I…"

She cut him off. "You have to face the fact the club scene is not for you. You need another route."

"Like what?"

"I don't know. We'll think of something."

"Or I live alone."

"Bernard, you're a wonderful person who deserves to be happy. There has to be a bear out there for you."

She reached over and hugged him. He smiled at her use of the term bear. He didn't know what he'd do without her. Sarah was his rock, confidant, and biggest supporter. She even set him up on dates multiple times. When the dates ended with the guy never contacting him again, he couldn't face her. He asked her to stop setting him up two years ago. She obliged and stopped. He'd told her he didn't want to date, and he just needed time alone.

He'd had a single date in two years, but never told Sarah about it. His coworker, Mark, set him up with his brother-in-law, Sean. She'd be upset if she'd found he let someone else try to find him a boyfriend. That date didn't end well, and he couldn't admit to Sarah that he'd failed again.

"Maybe I should give in to what the gay community wants. I'll lose weight, get in shape, and become the stereotypical gay muscle bear they all want. It would make everything easier, wouldn't it?"

"Seriously?" She pulled away from the hug. "No, it wouldn't be easier. You're fine the way you are, and I know you better than anyone. You're not one to give in to the pressures of beauty standards." She punched him on the shoulder. "You're a strong, intelligent, and independent person. You're a great catch. Anyone who doesn't see that is missing out."

"Thank you." He smiled.

"Now get driving, or we'll be late for work."

"Yes, ma'am."

Bernard cleared the rest of his tears from his face and got back onto the road.

*

BERNARD AND SARAH walked into a three-story office building. It had an empty shop on one side and a drugstore on the other. The Haggarty

Insurance Corporation sign occupied the area above the door.

"See you at lunch?" Sarah asked.

"Let's get sandwiches at Carrie's."

"Sounds good to me."

Sarah walked down the hall while Bernard walked past the information desk.

"Good morning, Alice," he said to the receptionist.

"Good morning, Bernard." Alice smiled.

Bernard took the elevator to the third floor, entered the breakroom, waved to Sharon and Mark, and grabbed a cup of coffee on his way to his office.

A desk, filing cabinet, computer, chair, and two shelves crowded the small office. Bernard lit two vanilla candles and pulled out a folder from a cabinet. He pored over spreadsheets, entered data, and performed mathematical calculations. He used risk analysis to help his company turn a profit. His job wasn't glamorous, but he enjoyed it. Bernard became absorbed in his work. Everything else took a backseat when he focused. He required an alarm clock set at different times to ensure he took breaks, ate lunch, and didn't stay too late. Sarah joked if he didn't have the clock he'd be there overnight.

His break alarm sounded. He stood, stretched, and shut it off.

His bladder ached for release. He rushed to the restroom to relieve himself.

After a break, Bernard strolled back to his office with fresh coffee, an empty bladder, and plenty of paperwork on his desk.

When his lunch alarm sounded, he headed downstairs to meet Sarah. They walked across the street to Carrie's.

Carrie's Sandwich Shop had a homey feel to it. The scent of their fresh bread, roast beef, and caramelized onions enveloped the shop, tantalizing Bernard's nose. Two arcade games sat in the back of the shop; their screens called to people to play.

Bernard squeezed into a booth. "I wish they'd get bigger booths. I feel like an adult trying to fit into a child's car seat."

"I'm sure it's not that bad."

Bernard pointed to the table, his gut a mere inch from the booth. "No?"

"Okay, let's grab a table."

They ordered and sat at a table with their drinks.

"So, what are your plans tonight?" Sarah asked.

"I'm going to stay in, put on a movie, have a nice dinner, and just relax for a change."

"That sounds amazing. After the night you had Friday, I couldn't imagine anything better."

"Yup. You're right. That place is toxic. I don't need it in my life."

"It's definitely not your scene."

"You're right."

A server dropped off their sandwiches with a smile.

Bernard bit into his pulled pork sandwich. "These are amazing. I would eat every meal here if I could."

"Tell me about it." She took a bite and swallowed. "So, there's someone I want you to meet."

"Are you trying to set me up?"

"No, not at all. John's cousin moved to town after saving up to leave Washington. He's…" She hesitated. "He's not in a good place and could use friends. He's gay and got out of a relationship a few years ago. He's still recovering from it. I don't want to say too much, but I think you two could be friends, nothing more."

"Wow. It must be hard to pack up and move to another state."

"He's a great guy and doesn't have any gay friends here. So, of course, I thought you two could at least meet. He's a bit shy, but a kind man. Even if you don't become friends, he'll know another gay man in the area and not feel overwhelmed or alone."

"You are the sweetest person I know. You always think about others."

"Thank you. I just want to make sure everyone in my life is happy, or as happy as they can be."

"In that case, yes. I'd like to meet him."

"Great, we'll plan a dinner party."

*

BERNARD DROPPED OFF Sarah after work and drove home. He let Ginger in and started dinner.

While the vegetables steamed, the phone rang.

He answered the kitchen phone. "Hello?"

"Hey, son, how are you?" Bernard's dad asked in Portuguese.

"Hi, Dad. It's good to hear from you. I'm doing well. How are you?"

"Oh, not too bad, not too bad. I was hoping you could come by for lunch on Saturday. I want to barbecue some burgers and hot dogs. It's going to be a small gathering. Just some family and a few friends."

"Yes, I'm in."

Bernard had not visited since Christmas. It'd be good to see his dad, brother, and the family again.

"Perfect grilling weather," his dad said.

"Sounds great."

"So, anything new in your life?"

"Same ol', same ol'."

"So, you won't be bringing anyone to the barbecue?"

"I could ask Sarah and John to come along," Bernard said.

"No, I mean, a boyfriend." Bernard couldn't help but catch the coyness in his father's voice.

His father was being his father. He asked every chance he got if Bernard was dating. He meant well, but Bernard didn't have the heart to tell his father that his last boyfriend, Tracy, had hurt him. He wanted to find love again, but the memory of Tracy loomed in the back of his mind.

"Probably not. I'm not seeing anyone."

"That's a shame. Well, I look forward to seeing you on Saturday."

"Thanks, Dad. Love you, and I'll see you Saturday."

"Love you too, son." They both hung up.

What is with everyone's sudden obsession with my dating life?

Bernard grabbed his dinner and walked into the living room. He pulled out a tape and showed it to Ginger.

"Let's watch *In & Out* starring Kevin Kline, playing the part of a lifetime. A straight actor playing a gay man struggling with his sexuality." Bernard laughed at his joke.

Still, the public finds men like Kevin Kline attractive. He's not fat like me. So, he's what both straight and gay audiences want.

Bernard ate dinner while Howard Brackett's former student outed him on national television.

"Ginger, do you think I need to find a man like everyone says?" He placed his empty plate on the coffee table.

Ginger barked and jumped into his lap to curl up.

"I didn't think so."

They finished the movie and watched the end credits. "Well, even the newly gay teacher can find love," he sighed. "First man he meets, and bam. Ah, the magic of a rom-com."

He put the tape away and took the dishes into the kitchen. He cleaned the dishes, then headed to his bedroom.

After a hot shower, Bernard dressed in his nightclothes and moved to his bedroom window. He looked out at the backyard. Rain fell into the yard.

"Maybe this is a sign," Bernard told Ginger. "The rain is washing away the past, and my future is bright." He smiled. "You know what? I need a snack."

He walked to the kitchen to grab cookies and poured a glass of milk.

"You know, Sarah's right," he said through a mouthful of cookie. "That place is not good for me. I was fine until I saw all those men. I've been happy with myself before, and I can be happy again."

The dog pawed at his leg. "Aww, do you want a doggie biscuit?"

Bernard gave Ginger a biscuit while he finished off his cookies.

"Well, we should get to sleep. I can't wait for Saturday. I'm sure you'll love to run around and have fun on the farm."

Ginger barked at him.

"You know, I am happy, but I still feel something is missing. I'm sure I'll meet someone one day when I'm not expecting it. That's how it works, right?"

Ginger cocked her head.

"They could be right under my nose, and I'd never know it."

Bernard ignored the comment. The last time he got his hopes up was with Sean. He'd had one date with Sean a year ago, and it didn't work out. Sean wasn't to blame for what happened. It was a miscommunication on Bernard's part. Right now, he needed to focus on himself. He had to figure out his life before he could share it with someone.

Chapter Four

Bernard

Saturday, April 18

BERNARD AVOIDED LIQUID Pearl the entire week. He and Sarah sang along with the radio on the drive to work. He walked Ginger after work every day. Ginger played at the dog park while he read.

The phone rang Saturday morning as Bernard finished the dishes.

"Hello?"

"Hey, son," his dad spoke in Portuguese.

"Hi, Dad. How are you this morning?" Bernard replied in Portuguese.

"Doing all right. I wondered if you could pick up a few things on your way out here for the barbecue?"

"Sure thing. What do you need?" He grabbed a piece of paper and a pen.

"Two bags of ice, twenty pounds if you can get them, and some soda. Any type, just grab three twelve-packs."

"Not a problem. I will grab those and be there around noon."

"Thanks, son. See you soon. Love you."

"I love you too, Dad."

*

BERNARD PULLED INTO his dad's driveway at noon. Dust enveloped his truck on the dirt road. His dad lived alone on two acres of land. He had a three-bedroom farmhouse with a small barn. The farm housed chickens, a few milking goats, and a Queensland heeler named Bonnie. His dad also had a stubborn ram who disliked everyone except his dad and Ginger.

Bernard parked and let Ginger out to run. She made a beeline for Bonnie. Bernard lifted the cooler out of the bed of his truck.

"Long time no see, Bernard," a voice called out from behind him.

Bernard turned around. A man taller and stockier than him strolled up the dirt path. His short chestnut hair danced in the breeze. His jeans and T-shirt hugged his curves.

"Rory Sinclair." Bernard put his cooler down and hugged him. "It's been way too long, my friend."

His soft beard rubbed against Bernard's cheek.

Bernard's heart skipped a beat. The hint of Rory's cologne took him back in time. They were teenagers again, hanging out in the food court at the mall. He took a deep breath, savoring the scent. Rory's cologne was the only brand that didn't make him nauseous.

"It's good to see you, Bernard." Rory broke the hug. His family moved from Scotland when he was ten and he still held a subtle Scottish accent.

"You as well," Bernard said. "How are you doing?"

"I'm doing all right. I'm finishing my master's degree in electrical engineering in a few months."

"That's fantastic. Congratulations."

"Thanks. And what have you been up to?"

"I'm still living the dream at Haggarty Insurance Corporation as an actuary."

"Fancy." Rory grinned.

"Oh yeah, so exciting." They both laughed.

Rory vanished when he started grad school six years ago. He didn't have time to spend with his friends. Bernard didn't blame Rory for the distance. He suspected Rory's mother had something to do with it.

They hauled the supplies to the backyard where a few people had gathered. Bernard recognized his brother, Emilio, Aunt Antonia, and her son, Carlos.

"Dad. Where do you want this?" Bernard grunted.

His dad stood at the grill, cigarette in his mouth and beer in hand. The man always had a beer and cigarette nearby in his waking hours. Bernard and Emilio told him to stop drinking and smoking so much, but he refused.

The aroma of burgers and hotdogs wafted outward. Bernard's mouth watered; he loved his dad's cooking.

"Just put them on the porch. There are a few coolers inside. Can you fill them with ice and soda?"

"No problem."

"Oh, and there's beer in the fridge. If you can put them in a cooler by themselves with ice, that'd be great. Thanks, son."

Bernard and Rory filled the cooler, and Bernard took a soda. Rory grabbed a beer, and they made their way to the grill.

"These look fantastic, João," Rory said.

"Thanks. The secret is in the spice." He smiled.

"Which you've never taught us," Bernard said.

"If I taught you, it wouldn't be a secret." His dad looked up at him and winked. He stood five feet tall. Bernard got his height from his mother's side. His great-grandfather had been six feet tall.

"Fair enough," Bernard conceded.

"I'm going to check on the pies," Rory said.

"All right, we'll talk later," Bernard said.

A dozen people milled about the yard. All the guests had a drink and someone to talk to. Bernard gave Antonia and Carlos hugs and said hi. Carlos was talking with a few people Bernard didn't recognize. Antonia discussed Avon or Mary Kay with a few women, so he left them to it.

Bernard walked up to his brother.

"Hey, Emilio."

"Hey, Bernard. How is everything?" Emilio hugged him.

"Taking it one day at a time."

Emilio was the polar opposite of Bernard. Emilio was two years younger and had inherited their father's appearance. He was four inches shorter than Bernard, lean and muscular, with jet-black hair, piercing blue eyes, and suntanned olive skin. Bernard's skin was a pale olive from years of being indoors. Emilio possessed a sense of confidence Bernard lacked. Their father's confidence. Bernard gained their mother's insecurities.

"So, how are you doing, really?" Emilio asked.

"I'm doing okay, I promise. I've stopped drinking, I'm taking my medication. I have a great job, and a fantastic friend who keeps me on the straight and narrow."

Bernard didn't tell him about his experiences at the club. His brother would worry. It was his burden, not his brother's.

"Good." Emilio smiled.

"How are Camila and the boys?"

"They're doing well. Camila is visiting her parents in Nebraska for a week with the boys before they have to be back in school. To be honest, it's good to have a little time alone."

"I'll bet. Alone time is necessary to stay sane."

"Hear, hear." Emilio held up his beer.

"Wait? Why aren't they in school?"

"We transferred, and they attend a year around school. They are out in, let's see—" Emilio paused. "April, August, and December."

"How do holidays work?"

"They get the usual holidays off. Fourth of July, Christmas, Thanksgiving, same as we did," he said.

"Not like when we were kids. Summer was it," Bernard said, "but I wouldn't give it up for rotating months off."

"Same."

"I'm going to grab another soda. We'll catch up some more."

On his way back to the cooler, his dad stopped him.

"Bernardo, come here."

"Dad, can't you call me Bernard?"

"No, I named you Bernardo, and that's what I'll call you," he said. "Anyway, how are you and Rory getting along?"

"Fine," Bernard said. "Why?"

"Oh, just wondering." He shifted and looked down at the grill. He wouldn't meet Bernard's eyes.

Bernard narrowed his gaze. "Why?"

"No reason." He held up his hands. "You two haven't seen each other in a while, so I just wanted to check."

"Dad, are you trying to set me up?"

"Not set you up. I just remember how well you and Rory got along at school, and he was one of the few people who stuck around after you came out. You guys had great times. I just thought—"

"Dad, I love you, but your taste in men isn't the same as mine."

"I don't have a taste in men," he protested.

Bernard laughed. "Okay, let me rephrase it. What you think I like in a man differs from what I like in a man."

"Except, you forget I've met the guys you date. Rory checks all the boxes. He's your age, he's handsome, he's a sweet boy, he's got a large build like you, he's single, and he's employed. What more could you want?"

"For starters, someone who's actually gay."

"Rory's gay," his dad insisted.

"I'm sure if he was gay, I would know. I'm sure he would have told me."

"Would he tell you?" His dad raised an eyebrow.

Would Rory tell him? He hadn't told Rory right away. He'd been out to Sarah for two years before he told Rory.

"Of course he would. We're friends."

"Even friends keep secrets if they're scared."

"I'm sure he's not gay."

"I wouldn't be so sure."

"Dad, why are you trying so hard?"

"Bernardo, I love you, son. I see how you look at Emilio and his family. I know you want someone in your life. I care about you, and I want what's best for you. Your mother wanted it for you too. She would have found someone for you if there had been more time."

"She was wonderful," Bernard said. "She never got to know I was gay. I know she would have accepted me, loved me, and helped me find love." Tears welled up in his eyes.

"She knew. We both did. Neither of us wanted to force it. We knew you'd come to us when it was time." He put his arm around Bernard.

"Thanks, Dad. That means a lot." He wrapped his dad in a hug.

Bernard wiped away the tears and walked to the cooler to grab a soda.

He went over to Bonnie's fenced-in area for her house and play area. Ginger and Bonnie chased each other. Two carefree dogs.

Rory walked up next to him. "It's wonderful to see them play."

"It sure is," Bernard said. "We need to hang out more now that you're done with college."

"I'd like to hang out again. It's been lonely the last six years."

"I've missed you," Bernard said. "You and Sarah are the only ones I've kept in contact with from high school. I haven't seen you since you started grad school."

"I've missed you too. I'm almost done, so we can pick up where we left off."

"I'd like that. I don't have many friends these days."

"Why do you think that is?" Rory asked.

"I didn't think most people would accept me when I came out. So, I pushed most of them away for fear of being hurt. I'm sorry I did that to you."

Bernard put his face in his hands. He'd pushed one of his best friends away. He'd come back after a year. It was great, until Rory left for grad school. He'd missed his friend for six years.

"I understand why you did it. I know my family doesn't approve of our friendship."

"I'm glad you came back," Bernard said.

"I'm glad I did too."

Bernard turned. Rory stood there, a handsome man. His father was right. Rory was his type.

Rory's cologne wafted into Bernard's nose. He closed his eyes and smiled.

"So, how are you after…you know?" Rory asked.

"Tracy?" Bernard said. "I'm doing okay. I haven't dated since."

"I know it was hard on you," Rory said.

"It was. But I needed time, and it turned into seven years."

Bernard swallowed a lump at the memory of Tracy. He pushed it aside, refusing to allow his ex to occupy his mind again.

"I'm sorry to hear that."

"Thank you," Bernard said. "What about you? Do you have a special lady?"

"No one in my life. I don't have many friends either. It's been hard."

"I'll always be your friend."

"Thank you, and remember, you will always have me by your side." Rory patted Bernard on the back.

"So, did my dad say anything to you when he invited you here?"

"He just told me he was having a barbecue. He's invited me a few times, but I couldn't make it. Why?"

"Well, he thinks you and I would make a handsome couple."

"Wait, your dad thinks..."

"That you're gay, yes." Bernard finished the sentence.

"I mean, why would he think I'm gay? Is there something..." Rory sputtered.

"I don't think you're gay," Bernard said. "I'm sure as much as we hung out, you would've told me."

"You didn't tell me at first." Rory's face fell. He muttered under his breath.

Can he be? Is this his way of seeing how I'll react? If he is gay, could I be his type?

"Rory, I–"

"We were close, Bernard. Real close. But you didn't tell me." Rory wrapped his arms around himself.

"I'm sorry, Rory. Because of your family's connection to the Church, I didn't know how you'd take it." Bernard reached over and wrapped his arms around him.

"I understand. You told me as soon as you felt comfortable," he said. "But then you didn't want to hang out anymore."

"The Church excommunicated me. Being around you reminded me of what it cost me to come out. But not having you in my life was worse than anything I could have imagined."

When the Church excommunicated him, his father, brother, and sis-ter-in-law refused to attend anymore. They stood by him.

"I'm sorry you went through that. I'd never hurt you. You know I'll be by your side, no matter what."

Bernard pulled away. "I know, and that's why I reached back out to you, and you helped me at my worst. I'll never let you go again."

Rory stared off into the distance. Tears formed in his eyes as he turned to face Bernard. Bernard didn't take his eyes off him. Rory wiped away the tears.

"I'd like to think if I was gay, you'd support me the most," he said.

"Of course I would."

"My parents wouldn't," he said under his breath.

"I would accept you if you were gay, bi, or anything in between, Rory. No doubt."

"I...I'm happy to hear that." Rory smiled.

Bernard wrapped his arms around Rory again. This was what a rela-tionship is. Love, understanding, and compassion. This was the relationship Bernard never had with Tracy.

Bernard pulled away and looked into Rory's eyes. His beautiful green eyes.

"We're going to hang out more, Rory."

"Thanks." Rory smiled.

The sun set behind the field, producing an orange shimmer on the lawn. Ginger and Bonnie had curled up in a patch of grass.

Bernard and Rory stood in silence until the sun disappeared over the horizon.

Bernard got a pen and wrote his number on his business card and had Rory do the same.

"I'll call you soon to hang out," Rory said.

"I look forward to it." Bernard hugged Rory.

Bernard squeezed hard against Rory's chest. The heat of Rory's body warmed him inside.

Bernard said his farewells to his family and headed home with Ginger.

"Ginger. It's been a great day," he said as he undressed. "Tomorrow, I'll sleep in and we'll go for a walk in the park."

Ginger barked.

"Do you think we should invite Rory? He might enjoy a walk in the park with us. Although he said he'd call me. What should I do?"

Will he want to walk in the park with us? Or was he just being nice when he said he wanted to hang out more?

Feelings flooded back. He'd fallen in love with Rory when he discovered he was gay at nineteen. He told Rory he was gay in hopes Rory was too. His stomach churned at what he'd done when Rory never admitted he was gay. Bernard pushed him away, unable to see him. A man he was in love with who'd never love him back. That's when he chose to date Jason. A man no better than Tracy. Bile boiled up in his throat at the thought of the two men who ruined him.

Chapter Five

Rory

Saturday, April 18 / Sunday, April 19

RORY ARRIVED AT his apartment the evening after a day at João's barbecue.

"Mina, I'm home," he called out.

The little cat rushed in and leaped to his shoulder. He scratched her under the chin.

Rory walked into his kitchen and filled Mina's self-watering and food bowls. He placed the leftovers João gave him in the fridge. There was enough to last him a week.

As he put the food away, the phone rang.

"Hello?"

"Hey, Rory, it's Bernard."

"Hey, Bernard. What's up?"

"Well, I'm taking Ginger to Edgewater Park tomorrow and was wondering if you'd like to join us. We could make a day of it. Take a nice walk around the park and have lunch. It'll be great."

"Oh, I can't do it all day. I can meet you there for lunch though. I have mass at eight in the morning, and then I have lunch with my family, but I might be able to leave lunch early."

"I understand." There was a hint of disappointment in Bernard's voice. "Maybe another time?"

"No, we can," Rory said. "I can meet you at the park around noon. Then we'll have the rest of the day to hang out."

"Oh, that sounds great then."

"Do you need me to bring anything?"

"No, I'll bring a small cooler with drinks, sandwiches, and some chips. It'll be fine."

"Okay, see you tomorrow."

"See you tomorrow."

I'm so happy we reunited. It will be great to have my best friend back. I want to be friends again.

Six years apart, and he and Bernard jumped back into their friendship. They were hanging out, laughing, and having a great time. His feelings came back.

He remembered their conversation about Bernard coming out. Rory found men attractive. Or he thought he did. He never had anyone he could talk to about it. Bernard would understand, but how would it affect their friendship? He found Bernard attractive. He couldn't tell him; he had to figure this out himself.

As he sat there contemplating, the phone rang.

"Hello, Rory." His mother's stern voice carried through.

"Hello, Mother."

"Where were you tonight?"

"I'm sorry, Mother, I was at Mr. Silva's barbecue this evening. I lost track of time."

"You missed Saturday evening service."

"I'm sorry, Mother, I won't let it happen again."

"Good, we will see you at service tomorrow and then for lunch."

"I'm meeting a friend for lunch and a walk in the park tomorrow after services," Rory said.

"Oh, really? Sounds nice." His mother's voice turned sweet. "What's her name? Do we know her?"

"It's Bernard Silva."

Rory waited with bated breath. His mother and father hadn't spoken to or about Bernard since he came out. It took Bernard a year to reconnect with Rory after coming out. The last time he spoke to Bernard was six years ago, when he pushed Bernard away. He blamed it on grad school, but that wasn't the whole truth. He couldn't tell Bernard why.

"You're spending time with that Silva boy?"

That Silva boy? He has a name.

Rory decided it was better to keep his thoughts to himself. His mother's wrath was nothing to tempt.

"Bernard and I have been friends for years. We reconnected at Mr. Silva's barbecue and he asked if I wanted to hang out."

"That Silva boy is going to fill your head with some nonsense."

"Mother, he's not going to fill my head with nonsense. We're friends. That's all. I need more friends. I don't have many."

"You have the church. That's all you need," she said.

"Mother—"

"Don't you 'Mother' me," she snapped. "His younger brother, Emilio, is a fine young man. He attends Saint Catherine's Catholic Church every Sunday, has a beautiful wife, and lovely children. He's a proper man. But you will not spend time alone with Bernard, do you understand me?"

"Yes, ma'am."

"Good. We'll see you tomorrow."

He stood at the table. His mother denied him the pleasures of a friendship outside the church. What was he going to tell Bernard?

I better call him now, before it's too late.

"Hello?" came Bernard's voice.

"Hey, Bernard. I'm sorry. Something came up and I'm not going to make it tomorrow."

"It's okay. I understand. It was last-minute," Bernard said. "What about next Saturday?"

I can't keep avoiding him. It's not fair to him. He hasn't done anything wrong. I can go and not tell my mother. What she doesn't know won't hurt, right?

"Yes, next Saturday works great. We can meet at ten? Then make a day of it."

"I'm looking forward to it. I'll see you next Saturday."

Rory hung up. His heart sank. He'd let his friend down.

He got into bed and read his Bible. He read the story of Sodom and Gomorrah. How Lot attempted to save the angels. He'd been taught it was a cautionary tale against sodomy and homosexuality.

I don't see it the way the church taught it. This story is about greed and hatred. Is homosexuality actually a sin?

Rory knew there were more passages, but he didn't care to read them again right now. Pressing the Bible against his heart, he prayed for strength against the temptations of the flesh.

I must resist these urges. I must resist these urges. He let the phrase play over in his head like a mantra.

*

THE NEXT MORNING at mass, Rory found himself sandwiched between his mother and father in the pews. His younger brother, Duncan, sat on the other side of their father with his wife, Catherine, and their four-year-old daughter, Penelope. The pews weren't comfortable for a man of Rory's size. While his father was taller than him, Rory had more bulk. His dad's family had always been large, but Rory was at the extreme end of the family.

Everyone around was dressed in their best suits and dresses. Pearls and watches adorned their bodies. They all attempted to one-up one another. His mother was no different, but his father had worn the same suit for twenty years.

Rory went through the motions of the service. Sit, kneel, stand, sing, repeat. He didn't follow the service. His mind wandered to Bernard. How wonderful it was to spend time with him. Bernard never judged him. Bernard joked with him and cared about him. He had invited him to the park with his dog to hang out. He cared about Bernard and there was no reason they couldn't be friends.

At the end of the service, Rory's mother walked over to a couple two pews behind them.

"Hello, Mr. and Mrs. Jenkins. So lovely to see you again," his mother said.

"Hello, Mrs. Sinclair, it's a pleasure to see you too. How's your family?" The woman had a thick Southern accent. Rory had heard this accent on television but hadn't heard anyone talk like this. She was lean and wore a full-length flowery dress.

"They are well, thank you," his mother said.

"You remember my husband, Andrew."

Andrew was lean and muscular. His black handlebar mustache shimmered with oil. His hair was slicked back with a large amount of grease. A single strand stuck out to the side.

"Yes, of course. Nice to see you, Andrew," his mother said. "And you remember my husband, Ronan."

Andrew and Rory's father shook hands. They shifted their feet. This meeting wasn't accidental.

"You remember my son, Rory." His mother moved Rory in front of her with surprising strength.

"Maeve, what are you doing?" his father cut in.

Rory's dad was built strong and muscular. A few inches over six feet tall, he intimidated most men, but not his wife. She was the polar opposite. Short and petite, but a fire burned inside her. When she wanted something, she got it.

"Nothing, Ronan. I just want to make sure everyone is acquainted, that's all," she insisted.

"Hello, Rory." Mrs. Jenkins held out her hand. "It's nice to see you again."

He shook hands and made eye contact, as his parents taught him. "It's nice to see you as well, Mr. and Mrs. Jenkins."

"The pleasure is all ours, Rory. Such a fine young man," Mrs. Jenkins said.

Rory held in a sigh. He was thirty-five and his mother talked about him like he was still a teenager. He continued to be the good son he was raised to be. No questions, do as your parents ask, no matter how old you get. That's what a well-behaved son does.

"Isn't he though," his mother said.

They continued to talk. Rory, his father, and Mr. Jenkins moved aside, so the women could talk. Rory shifted his feet. His stomach twisted into knots. His mother only talked to another woman this long if she knew she had a daughter she could set him up with. His mother planned this interaction. She'd find the right words to draw out their daughter.

"And of course, Duncan and his wife have a beautiful little girl. She's just the sweetest thing. I hope Rory gives us grandchildren someday."

"Oh, that reminds me." Mrs. Jenkins turned. "Missy, come meet the Sinclairs."

A young woman glided over to stand next to her. She had fair skin, silvery-blonde hair, a row of freckles across her button nose, and a build similar to Mrs. Jenkins.

"This is my daughter, Missy."

How did mentioning grandchildren remind her of her daughter?

"It's a pleasure to meet you all." Missy shook hands with everyone. When she got to Rory, her hand lingered for a few extra moments as she gazed into his eyes. She smiled and batted her eyelashes. He felt nothing.

"It's nice to meet you," Rory said.

"What a lovely young lady," his mother said, "and so polite."

"Thank you, ma'am," Missy said.

"So, is your husband or boyfriend here?" his mother asked.

"Oh, I don't have a beau, ma'am. I'm a proper lady waiting for a proper gentleman."

This was the opening his mother needed. She wasted no time and swooped in.

"We must have you over for lunch. We have Sunday lunch every week after morning services. Why don't you join us sometime?"

"That sounds absolutely charming," Mrs. Jenkins said. Mr. Jenkins and his father exchanged knowing glances. Rory stood there, unable to speak.

"Wonderful. We will keep in touch." The two women exchanged numbers and parted ways.

"Let's head to lunch, shall we?" his mother asked with a satisfied smile.

*

THE FAMILY SAT around the dining table his brother built for their parents for their thirtieth wedding anniversary. Duncan never failed to show how much more skilled he was than Rory. A skill his parents praised. His mother frowned at Rory's insistence on knitting and baking.

Rory pushed food around his plate. His family talked around him while he stared at his uneaten food. He'd disappointed Bernard. Bernard wanted to be friends, and because he was gay, his mother refused to let him see his best friend. It'd been too long. Why couldn't they pick up like they did when Bernard came back to him after coming out? He owed it to

Bernard.

"So, what do you think, Rory?" his mother said.

"Huh, what do I think about what?"

His mother sighed. "About Missy."

"I don't really know her," Rory said.

"Well, you'll get to know her when we have them over for lunch," she said.

"Mother, why do you insist on me meeting a girl and getting married?"

"Because you are over thirty and should have been married by now."

Rory continued to dwell in his thoughts. Where he could be himself, explore his own needs and wants, and not placate his mother's every wish. The hint of desire he had for men. Something he fought against.

His mother chose his friends, his dates, his everything. His apartment and his career were the two things he chose for himself, and she did not approve of either. She believed he should have a stable job and own a home by now.

"Rory, let's go for a walk after lunch. Clear our heads and talk man to man," his father said.

Rory was taken aback. His father hadn't asked him to go for an afternoon walk before. His walks were his father's time to reflect and decompress.

"Yes, sir," Rory said.

Rory and his father put on light jackets and headed out of the house.

"We'll be back in a little bit," his father said.

Rory and his father walked in silence down the street. Every house was a clone of the one before. White houses, manicured lawns, trimmed hedges, and little white fences stood in a neat row. The sidewalks were clean of debris. The trees along the path were equal distance, surrounded by iron, and trimmed to match. The neighborhood was out of *The Stepford Wives*.

A wrought iron fence surrounded the park. The gate closed and locked. The park was only accessible to residents of the neighborhood. It covered an entire block. Benches and grills surrounded a small duck pond. Swings, sandboxes, jungle gyms, and seesaws covered a corner of the park. Basketball courts, a tennis court, and a small grassy area filled the remainder of the space.

His father sat on a bench facing the pond. He motioned for Rory to join him. The sun reflected off the clear water.

"Thank you for inviting me, Father," Rory broke the silence.

"Just call me Dad," he said, "your mother isn't here."

"Thanks, Dad."

"So, you reunited with Bernard." It wasn't a question.

"Mother must have told you."

"She did."

"Yes, and I want to hang out with him again. He was my best friend for so many years. We had a few ups and downs, but that's the past."

His father looked at him for a moment. "Your mother does not approve of him."

"I know, but I'm a grown man. I should be able to make that choice myself." His voice was defiant. He'd never spoken to his father like this. "I'm sorry, that came out wrong." Rory lowered his head.

"You have every right to be upset," his father said.

"I do?"

"Of course. You were told to stay away from your best friend. The one friend who no matter what, you've stood by. Someone I know would stand by you no matter what. I've never seen you so determined to hold on to a friend. You shouldn't have to make that choice again."

Again? His father knew he'd distanced himself from Bernard, but he never told him why. He didn't want to make the choice. He cared about Bernard and wanted him back in his life. No matter what the cost.

"But Mother said—"

"As you said. You are your own man. You make your own decisions. That decision is between you and Bernard. No one else should make that choice for you, including me or your mother."

Rory nodded; a lump stuck in his throat.

His father leaned over and hugged him. "No matter what happens, remember I will always love you, Rory."

Does he know my feelings for Bernard? Would he approve? Or am I reading into this too much?

They returned to the house. Rory's mother insisted he take leftovers.

"It's still early. Maybe you need another walk to clear your head." His father winked. His mother appeared oblivious to their exchange.

Chapter Six

Bernard

Sunday, April 19

BERNARD WOKE UP early Sunday morning. He gathered his things and packed a lunch for one.

"Okay, Ginger," Bernard said, "it's just you and me."

He got dressed in a polo and shorts. After packing up his backpack and the cooler, he got Ginger into the truck.

Bernard drove to Edgewater Park, a popular spot for small gatherings, quiet afternoons, and lunch on the grass. The park, adorned with trails, flower beds, trees, and lush grass, covered a square mile around a manmade duck pond. A chain-link fence divided the parking area from the park, to preserve the natural environment. The sun glistened off the pond as ducks bobbed on the water, dipping down to eat.

He filled his lungs with warm air. The fragrance of blooming flowers titillated his nose. Bees buzzed around the flowers, while squirrels ran up and down trees.

Bernard pulled a large blanket out of his backpack and settled it on the ground after he checked for unwanted messes. He placed the cooler next to the blanket and set rocks at the corners to keep it still. He pulled out a few sandwiches, soda, and chips.

"It's going to be a wonderful afternoon, Ginger."

After lunch, Bernard sat against the tree to read. Ginger curled up beside him.

The sun moved across the sky as people wandered through the park. Couples relaxed in the grass, kids played on the swings, and a few people sat on the benches at the lakeside.

"Is there room for one more?" It was Rory. He walked toward him.

Bernard jumped to his feet and embraced Rory. "I thought you couldn't make it?"

"Well, after lunch with my family, I thought I'd surprise you."

"It's a pleasant surprise. Thank you."

Ginger sniffed at Rory.

"Hello, Ginger." He rubbed her ears.

She barked and rolled onto her back for belly rubs.

They sat on the blanket and enjoyed the sounds of nature. Ducks swam through the lake while blue jays called to each other in the trees above. Bernard took in the aroma of fresh-cut grass.

"It looks like Ginger needs to potty." Rory pointed at her sniffing the grass.

Bernard grabbed her leash and doggie bags to take her to the designated area. Rory followed behind.

"I wanted to ask you something personal," Rory said.

"What is it?"

"I knew Tracy, but I really didn't know Jason. What happened?"

Bile built up in his throat. Jason was his first boyfriend. They'd started dating when he was twenty-two, right when he'd come out. They'd lasted three years, but Rory didn't get to know him. The real him. Bernard left him when he was twenty-five, when he and Rory rekindled their friendship.

"He…" A lump formed in his throat. "He was similar to Tracy. Tracy never verbally abused me, but Jason did. Often. I felt like I was worthless, and I didn't deserve love. I found him a few times with some thin or athletic guy. He apologized each time and said it wouldn't happen again."

He averted his eyes. He couldn't meet Rory's gaze. His stomach churned at the memory of Jason.

"I'm so sorry. I only knew the end. I didn't know it'd gone on so long."

"You gave me the courage to leave him."

"Me?"

"Yes, knowing you were back in my life helped me realize I could do so much better."

"Then, there was Tracy. I remember him."

"He only lasted a year. I learned he was the same as Jason when he cheated. I left the first time I found him with another man."

He blocked the memory of what happened afterwards. He couldn't relive those events.

"I wish I'd have told you I was gay sooner," Bernard said.

"You do?"

"Of course I do. You were my best friend, Rory. I knew you'd accept me."

"I'm glad you told me," Rory said. "I know it was hard, but we're friends again and that's all that matters. And I'll always be here for you."

Bernard wrapped his arms around Rory. "Thank you, my friend."

Rory squeezed back.

"What the hell are you two doing?" An angry voice pulled them out of their reverie.

A red-faced man stormed over to them.

"This is a public park. There are kids around. Who do you think you are, showing this disgusting display?"

The park had more than a dozen couples, all straight.

"What are you talking about?" Bernard broke their embrace and stood in front of Rory, shielding him from the man. Heat swelled in his cheeks as he calmed his breathing.

"This." He waved over them. "Hugging in public. You should be ashamed of yourself."

"Oh, I'm sorry. Are you going to go to that couple and tell them to stop kissing?" He pointed to a young straight couple on a blanket. "Or that couple holding hands?" He indicated a straight couple walking around the lake.

"That's different," he yelled.

"How?" Bernard's voice was calm.

"They're normal. You two freaks are out here flaunting your…whatever you call it."

"First off, *sir*." Bernard emphasized the last word. "I was comforting my friend who has had a rough time. Second, your judgmental attitude needs to come down a bit. We're not doing anything illegal or indecent. So, I suggest you go back to your family."

"Who do you think you are, telling me what to do?" the man shouted.

"If you look around, you seem to be the only one who has a problem with us."

"Fucking queers. Think they own everything," he mumbled as he walked away.

Bernard moved forward, but Rory grabbed his elbow and wrapped his other arm around him.

"He's not worth it. Let him go."

Bernard closed his eyes. Rory's touch stirred a warmth inside him.

"I just…I can't stand people like him," Bernard said.

"Thank you. I think you made your point clear to him." Rory spun him around and smiled.

"What does he think? You're not even interested in men. So, he just made an assumption."

"There are judgmental people who will jump to conclusions to ease their own biases."

"Thank you for calming me down. I appreciate it."

"Anytime."

Once Bernard cleaned up after Ginger, they made their way back to the blanket.

"We still have time for a walk around the lake if you'd like," Bernard said.

"That sounds nice."

They walked along the lake trail. Joggers, families, couples, and dog walkers passed as they conversed about recent movies. *U.S. Marshals* was in theaters.

"I'd like to see it," Rory said.

"Well, maybe we can see it together."

"That'd be fun."

Bernard felt Rory's hand brush up against his. A chill ran up his spine. *Stop thinking about him that way. Rory is your friend, and he's straight. At least, he told me he's straight.*

Rory didn't appear to notice, or at least didn't react to the touch.

They finished their walk and made it back to the blanket.

"Oh, I brought some snack cakes and milk if you'd like some. I have plenty."

Rory cocked an eyebrow. "Snack cakes and milk?"

"Look, I can cook basic food, but baking is not my forte. So, we get snack cakes and milk."

"Okay." Rory giggled. "If it's what you have."

They ate and discussed the books they were reading.

"I'm reading *The Hobbit*," Rory said.

"Wait, you haven't read it yet?"

"No, give me time. I've had a busy life," he joked.

"Okay, no judgment," he said, "but it has been out for over fifty years."

"I feel like you're judging me a little."

"Okay, a little. Not much though."

"So, what are you reading?"

"*Sole Survivor* by Dean Koontz."

"Well, that sounds like something I'm not sure I'd read, but I hope you enjoy it."

"Thank you."

Rory helped Bernard pack up the blanket and food.

They walked back to the parking lot. Rory unlocked his Toyota Camry.

"This has been one of the best days I've had in a long time," Bernard said. "I'm so glad you made it today."

"I'm glad I made it too. It's been wonderful hanging out."

"I have to thank you as well," Bernard said. "Sarah said I needed to get out more and away from the club scene. You helped."

"I'm glad." Rory went in for a hug. Bernard squeezed back. Rory's cologne lingered in his nose. Rory squeezed harder.

"We need to do this again," Rory said. "I never want to lose you."

Bernard broke their hug. "You won't lose me. You can't lose me."

"Thank you."

"I'm happy to be your friend."

"So, can we do something next weekend?"

"Yes, I'd love that. What if we take a day trip to Santa Cruz? Then we can watch *U.S. Marshals*."

"That sounds fun."

They parted ways after one last hug.

*

BERNARD MADE IT home and took in the disorganization his living space came to. He'd not cleaned in two weeks, and he needed to get something done.

"I better clean while I still have the energy."

Bernard took two hours to clean his house from top to bottom.

"There, it looks much better, right, Ginger?" Ginger had curled up on the sofa and fell asleep. "Such a carefree life. Well, all that's left is to vacuum."

Bernard opened the closet. Above the vacuum was a box.

"I think this is my old gaming console?"

He opened the box to find his game system and a dozen games.

"Vacuuming can wait," he said.

Bernard set up the system and played *Resident Evil.*

The next two hours flew by as he explored the mansion as Chris Redfield. Fighting zombies and discovering the mysteries hidden within. He saved the game and shut off the system.

"I need to play more often," he said.

He vacuumed the house.

After cleaning, Bernard shambled to his bedroom and collapsed on his bed. Ginger made herself comfortable at his feet.

"This has been a fantastic day, Ginger. I got to spend time with a dear friend, cleaned the house, and even got back into video games."

He stared at the ceiling. *You know what? I'm going to call Sean. Maybe he'll want to hang out and I can increase my circle of friends and not worry about dating.*

Bernard picked up the phone on his nightstand and dialed Sean's number.

"Hello?" came Sean's husky voice.

"Hey, Sean, it's Bernard."

"Hi, Bernard. It's great to hear from you. What's up?"

Bernard noted his cheerful voice.

"I thought we could hang out sometime."

"I'm glad you called, man."

"I'm just looking to reconnect with friends."

"So, we're okay then?"

"Of course. I already told you what happened wasn't your fault. It was just the wrong time. I needed some space afterward and I'm sorry it took this long."

"It's just…I tried calling for months, but you never picked up. I didn't know what to think."

He and Sean went on a wonderful date. They'd spent the day in San Francisco. They walked the shops in Castro, ate at a cozy cafe for lunch, then had dinner at The Stinking Rose. Sean rented them a room, and they had a night of passionate sex. The thought of sex made Bernard hard again. Sean was amazing in bed.

It all came crashing down the next morning when they returned home. Bernard had parked his car at Sean's house. When Bernard got into his car, the neighbors whispered. They all stared at him. Bernard called Sean the next day to set up another date, but Sean said he wasn't interested in dating anyone. It was hard on him. He didn't know if he would ever find love.

"I'm sorry for that. I was in a terrible place. I expected more than was there, and it's something I had to work through. I think we can be friends now. At least I hope we can."

"I understand," Sean said. "I'm glad you took the time to work through it. I wish you'd told me though. I think we both made some assumptions we could have resolved by talking."

"You're right."

"So, about hanging out. What are you doing on May 30th?"

"I don't think I have any plans. Why?"

"I have two season tickets to the San Francisco Giants games. I know you're not a huge sports fan, but I remember you enjoy live games. Wanna go?"

Bernard smiled. *He remembered what I said a year ago. That's sweet.*

"That sounds like a fun time. I'm in."

"All right, I'll call next weekend and we can make plans to meet up. Sound good?"

"Sounds great. Talk to you soon." Bernard hung up the phone.

Well, this is exciting. I now have two great friends I can spend time with, without worrying about complicated sex or wondering if we're right for each other.

Bernard sighed a breath of relief. He knew he wouldn't find love, and so this was the best thing for him. *Don't think about it, and just enjoy the friends you have.*

Chapter Seven

Bernard

Monday, April 20

BERNARD PULLED INTO Sarah's driveway on Monday morning. She wasn't waiting for him on her porch. It wasn't like her to be late. He walked up and knocked on the door.

John answered the door. Bernard hadn't seen him in a few months, and he appeared more muscular than the last time he'd seen him. His tight shirt showed off his pecs, while his belly still protruded outward.

"Hey, John. Is everything okay?"

"Oh, yeah. Sorry, Sarah tried to call, but you'd already left the house. She's running a little late. Do you want to come in and sit?"

"Yes, thank you."

Bernard sat on their couch and waited. Sarah and John had eccentric taste. They filled their house with the most colorful pieces of artwork and mismatched furniture. A rug adorned the center. It appeared to be made with every color of thread known to man. Every open outlet had a plug-in air freshener.

They lived in a two-story house with four bedrooms. Sarah and John wanted kids someday, so this house was perfect for them.

A bulldog charged in and jumped into Bernard's lap. The dog attempted to lick his face. Bernard avoided the tongue.

"Gross, don't lick my face," he said.

"Chester, down," John said. "He's excited."

"When did you get a dog?"

"He's not ours," John said.

As if on cue, a man walked in. The resemblance to John was apparent. The man had auburn hair and beard, which contrasted John's black hair and beardless face. This had to be Kelly.

"Hey, John. I'm heading to the store to buy groceries today. Is there anything specific you need?" He stopped. "Oh, I didn't know you had company." He turned to go.

"Oh, sorry," John said. "Kelly, this is our friend, Bernard. Bernard, this is my cousin Kelly."

"Nice to meet you." Kelly smiled and extended a hand. He had a warm smile. His voice was soft and low. It didn't match his large build.

Bernard stood and took his hand. His hazel eyes scanned Bernard, but never made eye contact. Kelly's strong, calloused hands trembled ever so slightly. Kelly stood level with Bernard. His T-shirt and tight jeans accentuated his thick body.

"It's nice to meet you," Bernard said.

Sarah chose this moment to come downstairs. "I'm so sorry I'm late. We'll get out of your hair, Kelly." She kissed John. "Thank you, babe. I'll see you tonight."

*

BERNARD AND SARAH got on the road. They sat in silence for five minutes.

"What was that about?" Bernard asked.

"What was what about?"

"Oh, please." Bernard rolled his eyes. "I've known you since high school. You've never been late for anything in your life. You 'happen' to be late the one day John's cousin is there?"

"He's staying with us while John helps him find a house."

"Okay, fine," Bernard said. "But you promised no setups."

"Whatever are you talking about?"

"Sarah, what's going on?"

"Fine, I just wanted you to meet him. Naturally. He didn't know you were going to be there either."

"I wish you would have warned me."

"I promise it's not a setup. I just couldn't wait for you two to meet."

He sighed. "I just got myself out of the rut I was in. I haven't been back to Liquid Pearl, I haven't thought about a date, and I just got Sean and Rory back in my life."

"Sean?" she asked. "Who's Sean?"

Damn. Bernard hadn't mentioned his one-day and one-night stand with Sean. He'd thought it better not to admit Mark had set him up after he'd told Sarah not to do it anymore.

"A guy I went on a date with about a year ago," he admitted.

"You went on a date a year ago?"

"Yes, I did."

"Why didn't you tell me?"

"I didn't know how you'd feel after I told you not to set me up."

"Did you sleep with him?"

"Well…yes."

He didn't sleep with someone on a first date. Sean was different. Bernard wanted him. It was a combination of Sean being hot, and Bernard not having sex since Tracy.

She smacked him lightly. "You dog, and here I thought you hadn't had sex in like seven years."

"What can I say," he said. "A man has needs."

"How was it?"

"Oh, it was incredible," Bernard said.

Sean was an amazing lover. Bernard melted in his hands. The way Sean pounded his ass sent shivers up his spine. It'd be hard to tell Sean no if he asked again.

"Spicy," she laughed. "So, what happened to him?"

"It didn't go anywhere. He wasn't looking for a relationship. So, it came crashing down like it always does."

"I'm sorry to hear that."

"Thank you."

"So, you're friends again?"

"I think so. I called, and he seemed happy to hear from me."

"That's great." Sarah smiled. "So, who set you up?"

"Mark."

"Mark from your office?"

"Yes, Sean's his brother-in-law."

"Wow, I wouldn't have thought that of Mark."

"He's very progressive."

Mark was one of the few people who knew he was gay. Bernard didn't trust most of the people in the office. Conversations he'd overheard warned him against saying anything.

"That's good to hear."

"Either way, Sean and I are friends now and we're going to a ball game at the end of May."

"Are you going to have sex after the game?"

"Sarah," he laughed. "No, it's just friends hanging out."

"Friends can have sex."

"Sarah."

"Okay, fine. So, it's not a date?"

"Right, it's not a date."

"Good, you need to take care of yourself."

They agreed to meet at Carrie's Sandwiches for lunch, and he headed up in the elevator.

Bernard grabbed his usual coffee and a few donuts in the staff break room someone brought and headed to his office.

He shut the door and lit his candles. The scent filled the air and surrounded his desk. He took a deep breath and got to work.

Bernard was working on a file when Mark called out to him.

"Huh?" Bernard asked.

"Someone's got a date," Mark sang.

"What are you talking about?"

Mark leaned against the doorframe. He had a grin on his face. Mark was short and lean. His solid body from years of the gym filled out his suit.

"Well, I talked to Sean, and it seems you two are going to a ball game at the end of May."

"He just asked me to go last night. How in the world did you find out?"

"Because I called right after you did to see if he wanted to go, and said he was already going with you."

"He has season tickets. It's odd that you asked about the same day he's going with me."

"I asked what days he had free, and he said all except that Saturday and he told me he was going with you."

"Mark, we're just friends. I've already told you he isn't interested in dating. He wants to stay single," Bernard said.

His heart ached. He hit it off well with Sean. There was a connection. Sean was a guy he'd see himself spending his life with. If only he wasn't in the closet.

"Not what I've heard."

"What has he said?"

"Well, Melissa said Sean might be getting lonely and might want to open up more about himself. Not that he'll come out at work, but maybe find someone to spend his life with. I thought of you."

Here it was. Mark knew exactly two gay men and thought they were destined to be together. He was unaware of a wider world and the fact Bernard met at least a dozen gay men at college. He wasn't wrong though.

Bernard could give him that much.

"He didn't say anything to me," Bernard said.

"Well, maybe he's waiting. Either way, this might be a chance for you to find love. You guys would be handsome together."

"Thanks for the heads up, Mark. I'll keep my eyes open."

Mark headed back to his office, and Bernard sat at his desk. His vanilla candles soothed his mind as their scent filled the space again.

Was this why Sean was eager to invite him to the game? Did he want a serious relationship with Bernard? He wanted to hang out and had wanted to for a while. He'd mentioned having tried to get hold of him for months before he gave up.

Was he waiting for me to reach out to him?

*

BERNARD AND SARAH sat across from each other in Carrie's.

"So, what did you do this weekend?" Sarah asked.

"Oh, it was great. I went to my dad's barbecue, met up with Rory," he said, "then we spent Sunday afternoon at the park."

"Wait, slow down. You ran into Rory?"

"Yes, I told you I got him back in my life."

"I was more concerned with Sean. How did you meet back up?"

"Yes, my dad invited him to his barbecue, and we started talking," Bernard said.

"You haven't talked to Rory in like six years," she said.

"I know it's been a long time."

The last time he'd hung out with Rory, they were at the Round-Up Saloon. Rory had just turned twenty-nine and was off to grad school. Rory's cologne lingered in his memory. A Hint of Pine. The night lived on in his dreams. Rory was excited when he received his acceptance letter to San Jose State for electrical engineering. That was six years ago.

"So, how's he doing?"

"He's doing great."

Bernard went into detail about their talk at the barbecue, their walk in the park, and even the man who confronted him.

"Wow, you really get the worst of the worst out there, don't you?"

"He wasn't that bad," Bernard said. "I've run into much worse. At least this guy backed down quickly when I confronted him."

"So, why would he assume you and Rory were gay?"

"Probably because I gave him a hug, and in his macho mind that is only something gay men do."

"I will never understand people," she said.

"So, he finishes his degree this semester and then he'll probably look for work."

"That's great. Does he have a girlfriend?"

"No. He said he hasn't found anyone. Come to think of it, I don't think he's ever had a girlfriend."

"Well," Sarah said. "If I remember correctly, his mother is pretty overbearing. She might not want her special man to be with the wrong woman."

"It was something he said at the barbecue that gave me pause. Don't repeat what I'm about to tell you."

"Of course not."

"He said he'd trust me to be there for him if he was anything other than straight and then whispered to himself that his parents wouldn't be supportive."

"So, you think Rory might not be straight?"

"I get that feeling," Bernard said. "But I didn't press him. I'm going to let him discover who he is on his own and I'll be there for him."

"He's thirty-five. Shouldn't he know by now?"

"Not always. His devotion to his religion can suppress some emotions. I came out at twenty-two. It was hard."

Bernard remembered coming out. He had a supportive family behind him. Rory wouldn't have the same. He would have Bernard as a support, no matter what.

He took a bite of his burger. Rory might be gay, or bi, or anything in between. He'd support him. He couldn't say the same about Rory's family. The church would excommunicate him and his family might disown him. There was no way to know.

"So." Sarah squinted. "Is this why you're waiting? You might have a chance with Rory?"

"No, he's my friend," Bernard said. "And besides, he could find someone hotter than me."

"If you say so." Sarah smiled.

"What's that mean?"

"You need to stop with this self-doubt. It's getting old. You're an attractive man. It's time you see that."

"I don't know."

"Take a good long look in the mirror one day and point to the things you like about yourself. Then you'll see it."

Bernard left it at that.

*

AFTER WORK, BERNARD dropped Sarah off at home.

"Hey, you should come over for dinner on Friday," she said. "John's going to make roasted chicken, roasted potatoes, steamed veggies, and some amazing bread pudding."

"Is this a setup?" he asked.

"No, I promise." She crossed her heart. "We just haven't had you over in a while. Now that you're feeling better, we need to spend time together. And stop being so paranoid."

"Dinner sounds wonderful, thank you."

"Great."

On his way home, Bernard rehashed everything that had happened with Sarah that day. He was well aware how sneaky she could be, and he was positive she was plotting something. Kelly seemed great, but Bernard didn't know him. He had already done something similar with Sean, but it'd be worse with Kelly. If it didn't work out with Kelly, he'd still have to see John and Sarah. Kelly would also be around. He wouldn't risk it.

Bernard took Ginger for a walk. He breathed in the warm evening air. It soothed him as they went on their way that evening. He took in the familiar sights of the neighborhood. Ten years he'd been here. Ten years. Where had all that time gone? Working his fingers to the bone, that's where. After college, he'd bought his house from his Uncle Jorge and spent the last decade paying it off. Now, the place was all his.

He walked around the block three times before he ran out of energy. The walk invigorated him. He was proud of making it around three times.

After showering off the sweat, he warmed up leftovers from the barbecue and put on *Sleepless in Seattle*.

"Are these rom-coms giving me unrealistic expectations of finding love?" he asked Ginger.

She snuggled up to him and sighed.

"Well, I think they are. I'm not going to find Mr. Right sitting at a coffee shop or a diner. That might be why I'm not good at dating. I expect too much."

Was Sean an option for dating? They hit it off and, according to Mark, he might be looking for a relationship. Sean lived on the other side of town. They could keep it secret. He didn't want to jump to conclusions and would let Sean make the first move.

Bernard went into the kitchen and cleaned his dishes.

He decided to play through *Resident Evil* again, this time as Jill Valentine. He made it a quarter of the way through before saving and shutting off the system.

He headed to his bedroom, Ginger at his heels. He slipped into his gym shorts and T-shirt, and plopped onto the bed. Ginger opted for her dog bed on the floor. She curled up and fell asleep.

"Ginger, things are starting to look up for me."

Bernard wanted more in his life, but he needed to be happy with himself first. Walking every day would be a step in the direction he needed. The walks allowed him to decompress. He didn't care about weight loss; he wanted something fun to do with Ginger, and this was a start.

Chapter Eight

Rory

Friday, April 24

RORY HAD MADE the most of the cramped, closet-sized office the engineering department had given him as part of his payment for the two courses he taught.

He'd placed his desk so that he could look at the beautiful garden below, covered in red, yellow, and white roses.

A bookshelf sat against one wall filled with books on basic engineering and texts he needed for more advanced courses. He'd even managed to fit a small table and chair opposite the bookshelf for meeting with students. Like his home, it was well organized and neat.

Rory stood, stretched, and walked down the empty hall to the staff room for a cup of tea.

While his water boiled, he idly wondered if someone had left any cookies or snacks lying around.

He opened the fridge to find it empty except for a sports drink, left-over cake, and a few lunch boxes.

A clearing throat from behind him stopped his search through the cupboards.

"Mr. Sinclair."

Rory turned around. Dr. Yosef Sanchez, the department chair, stood in the doorway. Dr. Sanchez was a short man in his mid-fifties who'd opted to shave his head rather than show his bald spot.

"Oh, hello, Dr. Sanchez, I was just looking for a snack to go with my tea," Rory said.

"No one is around, you can call me Yosef," he said. "I think Dr. Montgomery leaves his cookies in the cupboard next to the fridge in the box labeled ginger root."

"Thank you." Rory found the box, took a few cookies, and replaced it. "To what do I owe the pleasure?"

"Well, it's about your application," Dr. Sanchez said.

"From when I applied for graduate school?"

"Yes, and we've decided to take another look at it."

Rory's heart stopped. He'd received his acceptance letter six years ago. Were they going to revoke his diploma now? He was so close. Wouldn't they have pulled it before now if they were going to? What had happened? Six years of research and work down the drain. No one would hire him. Would he be able to apply to another school? He couldn't do another six years of graduate school.

"Oh, is something wrong?" Sweat built up on his face. He swiped at it with a paper towel from the roll.

"Nothing bad," Yosef said. "We want to meet with you to interview for an adjunct position."

"Wait, what?"

"You've been teaching the lower division courses for three years now. You have the experience and education needed to be successful."

"I...I don't know what to say."

"We'd like to meet you on Monday to discuss it," Yosef said. "But if you feel it's not for you, I completely understand."

"Thank you, sir. I'd be happy to meet you on Monday."

"Well, enjoy your cookies and tea." He turned around. "Oh, and don't work too hard. Those papers will still be there next week."

Rory sat at the small breakroom table and had his snack. It was five, so no one except the janitors and the few professors who taught evening classes were in the building. The sweet chocolate cookies mixed well with the tea. Rory always enjoyed tea and cookies with his mother.

"I would like to share this quiet time with someone special." The words slipped out. He imagined Bernard here, having tea with him.

Rory returned to his office and pored over papers. His students impressed him with their grasp of his lessons.

"I thought I'd find you here." A voice came from the door.

Rory turned around.

"Oh, hey, Sophia," he said.

"I see you're hard at work as usual."

"The end of the semester is coming, and I have to make sure all my grading is caught up so when I give the final, I can grade them and be done with it."

"Sounds like fun." She smiled.

She had a beautiful smile. Sophia treated him with kindness. It was like having a little sister. Their relationship couldn't be any other way.

"So, we're going out tonight," she said. "I know you don't usually go out with us. But I wanted to ask anyway."

Dr. Sanchez's words echoed in his mind. He needed to relax and enjoy some time away from work.

"That actually sounds like fun," he said. "I'd love to go."

"Really?" Her eyes widened and she grinned. "That's wonderful."

"Yeah, I should get out of the house and this office once in a while."

"Fantastic, we'll meet you at Shaffers at six-thirty?"

"I'll be there." He smiled.

"Great, see you there," she said, turning to go and sounding genuinely happy he would be going with them.

In the three years working with the team, Rory had been out with them only once or twice. They meant well and he needed to get over the age gap. There was no reason they couldn't hang out.

*

RORY WALKED INTO Shaffers at a quarter till seven. Patrons occupied every table. He tried to find his colleagues, but too many people blocked his path.

"We're over here." Davi's voice rang out.

Davi stood near a table. He waved his arms to get Rory's attention.

"Sorry I'm late," Rory said, sitting between Jeff and Sophia.

"We're just glad you're here," Jeff said.

"Where's Nicolas?" Rory asked.

"Oh, he's at the bar getting a drink," Sophia said.

Rory ordered appetizers for the table and a gin and tonic for himself.

"It's nice that you finally decided to hang out," Davi said. "We like hanging out with you."

"Thank you," Rory said. "I'm just not used to going out."

"Well, you should try it more often." Davi smiled.

Davi was genuine and honest. He had soft hair—a fact Rory only knew because he had the team touch it when he changed shampoo. Rory's fingers had slid right through the strands. While not as large as Rory, he had a robust build.

"I'm going to get another drink, this round's on me," Rory said. "What would you all like?"

Sophia ordered a tequila sunrise, Jeff ordered a whiskey and coke, and Davi ordered a vodka soda.

Rory stood at the bar as the bartender made the drinks.

"Bartender, a Sex on the Beach," a man demanded.

"Just a moment, sir, I'm getting drinks for this gentleman," the bartender said.

"Oh, hello there." The man spoke in a condescending tone. Rory ignored him. "I said hello," he said. "I'm Chance."

"Sorry, I just want to get my drinks and get back to my friends," Rory said.

"Well, I'm sure they won't miss you too much."

Rory turned to him. Platinum-blond hair, dancer's frame, and eyeliner accentuating his blue eyes.

"What?" Rory asked.

"You're adorable. Why don't we get back to my place?"

"I'm sorry, I'm not into guys."

"No one says no to Chance." Chance winked at him.

"Well, I'm saying no because I'm not interested in men." Rory turned back to the bartender.

"Why are the ugly ones so picky?" Chance said.

"What did you say to my friend?" Nicolas appeared next to Rory.

"Who are you and why do you care?" Chance said.

"I care because that's my friend you just insulted." Nicolas twisted his hands into fists.

"I was just leaving," Chance said.

"Right, get your drink and go. No need to linger here," Nicolas said. His face reddened with each word. He'd never looked this angry.

Rory and Nicolas made it back to the rest with the drinks.

"Wow, Nicolas. You're scary," Rory said.

"I'm not going to stand around while some asshole insults my friends."

His friends. Nicolas thought of Rory as a friend. He smiled. His colleagues over the last three years viewed him as a friend. Why didn't he spend more time with them? He'd have built strong friendships with amazing people.

Rory told the others what happened at the bar.

"Why would he assume you're gay and interested?" Sophia asked.

"I honestly think he didn't care," Rory said. "I told him I wasn't interested, and he said everyone is interested in him."

"You're out of his league anyway," Nicolas said.

"What?" Rory laughed.

"I mean, if you were interested in men, you could do better than some wannabe like him."

"I agree," Davi said. "You're a bright, sweet, wonderful man. You need someone who isn't as two-dimensional as a guy who literally asks someone to go home with them without even knowing their name."

"It was kinda gross to watch," Nicolas admitted.

"I've never had anyone flirt with me before," Rory said. "I didn't know how to respond."

"I mean, I wouldn't call what he was doing flirting," Nicolas said. "He was trying to get into your pants."

"Isn't that a type of flirting?" Rory asked.

"I mean, it can be," Jeff said. "But not if you're interested in something more than a one-night stand."

"What do I look for?"

Rory's isolated existence under his parents showed. His colleagues showed support. They didn't judge him on his lack of knowledge in social situations. They were teaching him. His body warmed. He had friends.

"Little things," Sophia said. "A light touch, a smile at the right moment. You'll know when it happens."

"Thanks," Rory said.

Had anyone ever flirted with him? A few young ladies from church giggled at his jokes. One brushed his arm. Were they flirting with him? Bernard came to mind. He and Bernard had been friends for years. Did Bernard flirt with him? Bernard was gay, but he wasn't interested in Rory. Bernard couldn't be interested in him. He liked guys that were... He stopped. Jason was larger than Bernard and Rory. He had short hair and a beard. *Just a coincidence.* What about Tracy? He was similar to Jason in size and build. They both had similar builds to him and Bernard. Bernard had used a word a few times to describe the men he was attracted to. Bears. Was he a bear? Would Bernard be attracted to him as well?

"I saw Dr. Sanchez leave the staff room right before you," Sophia said. "Did you talk to him?"

Rory came back to the present.

"Um, he wants to interview me on Monday for an adjunct professor position."

"What? That's amazing," Sophia said.

"Congratulations, man," Nicolas said.

"You'll do great," Jeff said.

"Thanks, I'm a little nervous though."

"It'll be great." Nicolas held up his glass. "To Rory."

Everyone cheered for Rory. Rory's face warmed at the attention. His friends cheered for his success. He'd never had many friends outside the church aside from a few in his high school group. His parents didn't know he spent time with anyone other than members of the church.

They finished up their drinks and said their goodbyes.

*

THAT NIGHT RORY lay in bed. His friends—yes, he could call them that now—thought he deserved love. They treated him with kindness and respect. They hoped for his success in everything he did. He wanted love. Could he have feelings for Bernard? No, he couldn't, because he couldn't be gay.

Why couldn't I be? My religion says so, but Bernard's gay. I love him, and I don't condemn him for it. Why am I condemning myself for these feelings? How do I know what is real and what is just sinful lust?

Chapter Nine

Bernard

Friday, April 24

BERNARD AND SARAH pulled into her driveway on Friday evening. He'd brought a change of clothes, so he didn't have to go home.

Sarah and John lived in a two-story home in Oakwood Estates. Each home came with a well-manicured lawn, a two-car garage, four bedrooms, three baths, and garbage collection included. John was a real estate agent and got their home with a low interest.

"Honey, we're home," she called out.

"Hi, dear," John said.

He walked into the living room with an apron on and kissed her.

"Hey, John," Bernard said.

"Hey, Bernard." He hugged Bernard. John had limited boundaries. He loved to hug, fully confident in himself. Bernard respected him for it. It could be off-putting to others, but Bernard didn't mind.

"Can I use your bathroom to change?" Bernard held up his overnight bag.

"Of course," Sarah said.

Bernard undressed and looked at himself in their full-body mirror. He didn't have a full-body mirror. They'd always made him uneasy. He rubbed his hands over the hair on his chest and belly.

I like men who look like me. Why can't I like myself?

Taking Sarah's advice, Bernard searched his image for things he liked about himself. He smiled as he saw his soft brown eyes looking back at him. Eyes that cared. Eyes he loved.

He pulled on jeans and a polo for dinner, stuffed the rest of his clothes in his bag, and opened the door.

Kelly stood on the other side.

"Oh, sorry, Bernard." He backed away. "I didn't know you were in here."

"I'm done. It's all yours."

They skirted around each other in the hall, and he made his way to the dining room.

When Kelly rejoined them, John put out plates of roasted garlic chicken, roasted potatoes, and steamed veggies. He gave everyone except Bernard a glass of red wine, instead placing a glass of water and soda in front of him.

Bernard took in the combined aroma of all the food. His mouth watered. John always cooked everything to perfection.

"John, this looks amazing," Bernard said.

"It is my specialty." John smiled.

"He doesn't make it often," Sarah said. "But when he does, it's always fantastic."

"Remember when we were kids, we'd sneak into the kitchen to cook something?" Kelly asked with a chuckle.

"We got into so much trouble." John shook his head fondly.

"We also made nothing that tasted good." The men laughed. Kelly had a pleasant laugh. Genuine.

Bernard savored each bite of the meal. The chicken melted in his mouth. He inhaled the scent of the potatoes. John covered everything in fresh Gilroy garlic. Although John came from Washington, he'd acclimatized to the Gilroy way. The garlic capital of the world. Each summer the town held its garlic festival. Bernard's family attended every year when he was a kid. He hadn't gone since he was a teenager. It wasn't the same without his mother.

"Kelly, do you want to share your good news?" John said.

"Huh," Kelly said. "Oh, yeah. John helped me find a house today."

"That's great," Sarah said. "Where is it?"

"It's down on Newport Ave, next to Wish Street," Kelly said.

"That's just a few blocks from me," Bernard said.

"Great. I'll know someone in the neighborhood."

"It's a nice, quiet neighborhood. I'd be happy to introduce you to the people I know."

"That'd be nice," Kelly said.

Bernard caught Sarah's eyes. She smiled at him and nodded toward

Kelly. Bernard shook his head and mouthed "no". She just grinned at him and took another bite.

Bernard shifted to face John, who averted his eyes. Sarah had pulled John into her scheme. John found the perfect house for Kelly near him. John had multiple listings as a real estate agent. Bernard paused. John didn't sell houses in his neighborhood. Did John give up a commission to help find Kelly a house near his? They were going through a lot of trouble to set him and Kelly up.

John cleared the plates and brought out his bread pudding. Bernard took in the decadent cinnamon and custard. He dug in as soon as the food hit his plate. *Delicious.*

"Will you need help?" John asked.

"Yeah, most of my stuff is in storage. I should be able to move in the first week of June," Kelly said.

"We can plan a weekend to move your stuff," Sarah said. "I'm sure Bernard would love to help."

"Of course, I'd be happy to help," Bernard said. "I have a truck. It's small, but I can haul a few things."

Bernard looked over at Sarah. She smiled and winked at him. He didn't like her plans. He'd made it clear what he wanted, but Sarah wouldn't give up. Bernard was happy now. He'd reunited with Rory, reconnected with Sean, and just met Kelly. He didn't need to muck up the waters by dating any of them.

"I'm going to go wash up the dishes and get everything put away," Sarah said.

"Would you like help?" Bernard asked.

"No, you gentlemen can go into the living room and have a pleasant conversation," she said. "And I'll bring some drinks."

"I insist." Bernard stood and followed her into the kitchen.

Bernard helped Sarah put the leftovers into containers and get them into the fridge. She ran the water and rinsed off the food. She handed the dishes to Bernard to put in the dishwasher.

"So, what are you up to?" Bernard asked.

"Not much. John and I might head to the tennis courts tomorrow."

"Not what I'm talking about. I mean, with me and Kelly?"

"I don't know what you're talking about."

"I met him accidentally last week, then John got him a house in my neighborhood where I know he doesn't work, and you asked me to help him move? I agreed to make friends with him, but this seems like you're trying to get us to be more."

"I just thought you guys could become friends," Sarah said. "You said you wanted more friends."

"Sarah, I know you're trying to help me," Bernard said, "but I need time. I don't want to rush into anything, especially with someone so close to friends of mine."

"Fine, I'll tell you why I'm going about it this way," she said. "Kelly is extremely shy, has a past I won't get into, and from what John has said, has trouble making friends now. I just want to help him. It has nothing to do with dating him, although that's what it might look like. I promise."

"That makes sense," Bernard said. "I'll do my best to be friends with him. However, I don't know if I'd date him. He's too close to you, and if it didn't work out…"

"Bernard." She put her hand on his shoulder. "It's been seven years since, well, you know. You need to move forward. I know it's scary."

"How do you even know I'm his type?"

"I don't," she said, "but I know he likes husky men. I may have seen one of his videos while I was changing his bed linens."

"You snooped?"

"No, I just opened the drawer, and there it was."

"Okay."

"And the cover had men that look like you. I don't remember the title, but I think the word bear was there."

Kelly watched bear porn? Bernard's heartbeat increased. Kelly, lying on his bed naked, jerking off to porn. Damn, that would be hot.

"Okay, so he's attracted to guys like me," he said. "Physical attraction is only part of it. How do you know we'll hit it off?"

"Well, I only met Kelly a few times when we went to visit John's parents. He didn't make it to the wedding…"

"Why'd you stop?"

"I can't say why, I promised," she said. "Anyway. John talks about him a lot. So, from what I've gathered, you might make a good pair. He's so sweet."

"I need you to trust me to know when I'm ready," Bernard said.

"Okay, I'll stop pushing." She hugged him.

"I know you want to help," Bernard said, "and he is attractive."

"Right," she said.

They rejoined John and Kelly in the living room. John cued up an episode of *Unsolved Mysteries*.

"Oh, I love this show," Bernard said.

"Me too," Kelly said.

They sat through the episode. Sarah, John, and Kelly enjoyed a glass of wine while Bernard drank his soda. He loved how Sarah and John never pressured him to drink. He found it hard at first. Seeing others around him drink while he had soda or water. Kelly didn't mention him not drinking. How much had Sarah and John had told Kelly about his past? He didn't want to think about what Kelly would think of him if he knew.

After the show, Bernard said his goodbyes. He hugged John and Sarah. Kelly held out a hand to shake, and Bernard took it.

"Thank you for a wonderful evening," Bernard said. "I had a lot of fun."

He walked to his car when Kelly called out his name. Bernard closed his eyes. *What did Sarah tell him?*

"What's up, Kelly?" He turned around.

"I know what Sarah and John are trying to do," he said.

"Ah, I thought you'd figure it out," Bernard said. Sarah and John were not subtle.

"I chose the house because it was perfect for me," he said. "I didn't even know it was near you."

"I'm not blaming you for anything. Sarah has done this before," Bernard said. "Her heart's in the right place. I'm just not in the right place."

"Then we agree."

Bernard stared into his hazel eyes. Kelly smiled.

"I'm not looking to date," he said. "I had…" He wrapped his right arm around his left. His eyes shifted downward.

"You don't have to talk about anything that you're not comfortable with."

"Thank you," Kelly said. "I don't think I'm ready to talk about it yet."

"If you ever want to hang out, let me know."

"I will."

They shook hands and Bernard headed home.

Bernard walked to his backyard. One of the neighborhood teens came by once a week to mow his front and backyard for twenty bucks. The greenhouse sat, unused. It came with the house, but Bernard hadn't done anything with it.

He thought it might be time to put that greenhouse to good use. He'd always wanted to learn to grow vegetables. No time like the present.

Chapter Ten

Rory

Saturday, May 2

RORY GRABBED THE gift he wrapped for his niece. He used lavender wrapping paper with a pink bow. He'd finished the sweater the night before. It took him two weeks to knit it and he loved how it came out. He knew Penelope would love it.

He packed a box of ingredients for a cobbler so he could make it fresh for her birthday. It brought him joy to create whether baking or knitting. Creating was an easier way to show he cared than trying to put things into words.

Rory arrived at his brother's at noon. Catherine scheduled the party to start at two, but he always arrived early to help.

Penelope opened the door. "Uncle Roro!" She jumped into his arms. He caught her with one arm, holding her gift in the other.

"How's my favorite niece?"

"Is that for me?" she asked, pointing at the present.

"Yes, it is."

"What is it?"

"You'll see when you open it later."

She tightened her grip as Rory carried her into the living room.

Duncan and Catherine kept a neat house. They'd decorated the living room with off-white furniture, a glass-top coffee table, white bookshelves, and a white TV stand. It baffled him how they kept it so clean with a five-year-old running around.

"Hello, Rory." Catherine walked into the living room. "We're so glad you could make it."

"How could I miss my niece's fifth birthday. It's a big day." He kissed Penelope's cheek and she giggled.

He let her down to run to the backyard.

Catherine hugged him and he followed her to the table with gifts. He placed his gift among the others and followed her outside to the back porch.

Catherine and his mother decorated the backyard with lavender and pink streamers. Two tables stood in the center, one with a lavender tablecloth and the other with pink. The place settings were of the opposite color from the tablecloth. Each table had a flower arrangement with tulips and violets.

A bounce house and a variety of games filled the yard, all in the same lavender and pink scheme. Would Penelope outgrow these colors? He hoped not. They were a wonderful combination.

"Can I help with anything?" Rory asked.

"Do you have time to make one of your amazing desserts?" Catherine asked.

"It just so happens I brought the ingredients to make a peach cobbler."

"That sounds amazing. We have ice cream to go with it too."

"Fantastic."

Rory busied himself in the kitchen preparing the cobbler. Penelope insisted on helping, so he had her mix the peaches with the glaze to bake after he'd sliced them.

"Shouldn't you be spending time with the men?" Rory turned to see his mother.

"Catherine asked me to bake something for the party," Rory said.

"Well, why don't you let the women take care of the cooking?"

"I enjoy baking," he said. "Besides, Penelope's helping me. She's such a big help."

He didn't understand his mother's insistence on what men and women should and shouldn't do. She criticized his hobbies. She insisted he needed to do something more masculine. She suggested woodworking, fishing, or repairing cars. None of those appealed to him. His father loved to repair cars and fish, but never forced it on him or his brother. Duncan took on woodworking and made some beautiful furniture. He'd built a TV stand and nightstand for Rory.

"If you insist." She pursed her lips. "I'll be outside."

"Why does Grammy not like you baking?" Penelope asked. Children didn't miss a beat.

"I don't know," Rory lied.

"I like when you bake," Penelope said. "It tastes good."

"Thank you."

Rory picked her up to taste the peach mixture.

"Yum." She smiled.

Rory loved his niece. He'd been told he'd make a wonderful father, but his heart sank at the idea. He hadn't found a woman he connected with. He didn't even know if he liked women romantically. Maybe one day he could adopt.

Party guests began to arrive at a quarter till two. Rory had put the cobbler to cool to be ready to eat after gifts.

"That smells amazing," Duncan said, coming into the kitchen.

"Thank you," Rory said. "I altered the recipe in the cookbook. I hope it tastes as great as it smells."

"I'm sure it'll taste wonderful," Duncan reassured him.

Once everyone had arrived, the kids began playing with the bounce house, puzzles, cornhole, and the variety of games set up in the yard. The adults sat around talking. He didn't know most of the people there who were mainly the parents of Penelope's friends.

"Uncle Roro," Penelope said. "Come play."

Before he could answer, he found himself dragged to the yard to play cornhole with Penelope and a few of her friends. He didn't try too hard and allowed the kids to win. The kids enjoyed his company. He chased them around the yard, making them laugh and scream.

"Okay, everyone, time to sing happy birthday and open gifts," Catherine said.

Penelope unwrapped gifts from her friends. She got picture books, puzzles, dolls, and a set of building blocks.

She thanked each person after she opened the gift. Her parents raised her to be polite when you receive a gift, even if you didn't like it.

Penelope opened her gift from Rory. She squealed with delight and ran to him.

"Thank you, Uncle Roro, I love this color," she said.

Rory wrapped his arms around her. "I thought you'd like it."

"Did you make it yourself?"

"I did. I wanted to make sure it was perfect for you."

"Thank you," she said, putting the sweater on before going back to her gift pile.

She opened the gifts from her parents and grandparents. She received some toys, a few books, and a new dress from her parents. Her grandparents got her a few collectibles. Rory didn't think a five-year-old needed porcelain dolls, but his mother had insisted. He wasn't going to argue with her.

Catherine handed everyone a plate with chocolate cake and a scoop of vanilla ice cream. The children scattered. The adults left them to it while they converged into the living room and dining room to talk.

Duncan introduced Rory to a few people he hadn't met. Two men sat with Catherine at the dining room table.

"Eddie, this is my brother, Rory," he said.

"Eduardo Perez, but everyone calls me Eddie." Eddie stood and extended a hand. "Nice to meet you."

"Nice to meet you too," Rory said.

Eddie stood a head shorter than Rory. Mahogany hair and beard, square jaw, and deep-brown eyes. His shirt hid a beer belly, and Rory wanted a peek. His eyes lingered a few seconds longer than needed on his broad chest.

"That's my son, Parker." Eddie pointed to a dark-haired boy who was unmistakably his son.

"He's adorable," Rory said, sitting down. He'd been on his feet since he arrived and took the opportunity to sit.

"Duncan tells me you are finishing your degree and working at the college in San Jose."

"Yes, I'm earning my master's in electrical engineering. I work part-time as an instructor at the college."

"That's amazing. I didn't get a chance to go to college, but I did an apprenticeship for a landscaper. Taught me everything I know. Now I own my own landscaping business, so if you're ever in the market for an upgrade to your front or backyard, I'm your man."

"I don't own a house yet," Rory said. "I'm not sure if I want to stay in Gilroy or move to San Jose to be closer to work."

"Oh, I can do either for you. I have offices in Gilroy, Morgan Hill, and Hollister. I don't do much of the work myself outside of Gilroy, but for a friend, I'll make an exception," Eddie said.

"Great, I'll keep you in mind."

Next, Duncan introduced him to Catherine's brother-in-law, Thomas Jones. Thomas stood to shake hands.

"It's nice to meet you," Rory said.

"Nice to meet you too," Thomas said.

Thomas was half a foot taller than Rory. He didn't look up to talk to people often. He was thick and muscular, and his tight shirt revealed six-pack abs. This man worked out. His shoulder-length blond hair hung loose.

Pale-blue eyes rounded out his features.

Thomas didn't say much and preferred to keep to himself. Rory didn't know what to make of him.

Rory grabbed another piece of cake and ice cream. He sat in the living room. He needed some quiet time.

"Is that your second piece?" his mother asked. Rory stopped mid-bite.

"Yes," he said.

"I thought you were trying to lose weight?" Her nostrils flared.

He'd lied to her. He had no intention of losing weight because he loved the way he looked.

"It's a party," he said.

"Still, just a little bit of fun will ruin your diet," she said. She took the plate from him. "There's a veggie platter. Why not have some of those?"

Rory walked to the table and grabbed a plate of veggies.

He sat on the front porch alone. He took bites of carrots. He'd hoped to have a piece of the cobbler he'd made. His mother wouldn't approve.

"Why are you out here alone?" Eddie sat next to him.

"Oh, I just needed some fresh air," Rory said, looking at him.

"Why didn't you finish the piece of cake you got?"

Rory hesitated. "I really should work on losing weight. I shouldn't have gotten a second piece."

"It's a party," Eddie said. "You can have a little fun."

Rory agreed. His mother insisted otherwise. She decided what he should and shouldn't eat and he didn't want to disappoint her.

"I also heard what your mother said," Eddie said, turning red.

"Oh," Rory said. "She's just worried about my health."

"I see," Eddie said. "I wanted to check up on you. You seemed upset."

Eddie had that right. His mother upset him. He hated how she controlled his life.

"I understand what you're going through," Eddie said. "My mother was the same way. She even decided who I should marry. Didn't matter what I wanted."

Eddie placed a hand on his shoulder. Rory's stomach fluttered at his gentle touch.

"My mother is trying to do that. But I'm not interested in any of the women she has tried to set me up with."

"My advice," Eddie said. "Do what makes you happy."

"Thanks."

Eddie got up to leave. "Oh, and Catherine said you made the cobbler."

"Yes."

"It's amazing." He smiled. "I grabbed a piece and sealed it in a container for you."

"You didn't have to do that."

"No, but I thought you should get a piece of the cobbler you made."

The party wound down and everyone said their goodbyes. Rory stayed to help clean up.

"Be sure to eat healthier. No more baking. I knew it was a mistake for your grandmother to get you interested when you were younger," his mother said.

"Yes, Mother." Rory hugged her.

Catherine presented him with a warm piece of cobbler and ice cream while he cleaned the kitchen.

"You've earned this," she said.

"I…I don't know if I should."

"Mother's not here to scold you," Duncan said. "Have a piece of the cobbler you worked so hard to make."

Rory smiled and took the plate. The warm cobbler mixed with the ice cream to create an explosion of flavors. He'd outdone himself this time. It was the best cobbler he'd ever baked.

"So." Catherine smiled at him. "You and Eddie seemed to hit it off."

"Yeah, he's a great guy."

Duncan and Catherine shared a look.

"What's going on?"

"Well," Duncan said. "Eddie has been alone for a while. It's nice that he's making friends. He rarely hits it off with people so quickly."

"Oh," Rory said. "I'm glad I could make him comfortable enough to talk to me."

"He's raised Parker for the last four years by himself," Catherine said.

"What happened to Parker's mom?" Rory asked.

"She was in a car accident," Duncan said. "He and Isabella married when they were twenty. She had Parker at twenty-four. They didn't think they'd be able to have children. It was wonderful when they did. But then she passed away on Parker's second birthday."

"That's awful," Rory said. "That poor man. And his son, losing his mother so young."

Eddie raised his son alone for four years and ran a business on top of it. He must be exhausted.

"Yeah," Catherine said. "I tried to set him up a year ago. But he said no woman could replace Isabella."

"I'm sure it must be hard to move on after something so tragic."

"He did say no woman," Catherine said. "We knew he was bisexual. But we didn't know what kind of guys he'd be interested in."

Eddie mentioned his parents forced him into the marriage. He might be looking for the right man now.

"Oh," Rory said, "I get what you're saying."

They wanted him to set Eddie up with Bernard. Bernard said he wasn't ready to date. He'd introduce them after he got to know Eddie better and see what happens.

"We're glad you see it," Duncan said. "So, we'll leave it at that."

Rory needed to breach the subject with Bernard. He didn't want to just come out and say it.

He said his goodbyes and headed home with an extra piece of cake and a piece of cobbler. He was going to enjoy this food, no matter what his mother thought.

Rory put his desserts in the fridge and sat on the couch.

"Mina, what am I going to tell Bernard? I'm not sure if Eddie would be right for him. But what if they hit it off?"

Bernard deserved to be happy, but what if Rory's feelings for Bernard were more than friendship? Rory wanted to understand these feelings before it was too late. He didn't know if he should tell Bernard about Eddie. If Bernard and Eddie hit it off, then where would that leave him? Would he find love? Rory needed to sort this out. He had some choices to make.

Chapter Eleven

Bernard

Saturday, May 16

BERNARD WRAPPED THE gift for Sarah. It wasn't the best-looking wrap job he'd ever seen, but the ribbon was cute. He smiled at the memory of his mother teaching him to take the edge of scissors and scrape it across the ribbon to make a curl.

The telltale sting of tears stung the back of his eyes. It had been twenty years since he held his mother's hand, hugged her, or heard her voice.

He picked up the phone and called his dad.

"Hello," his father said.

"Hi, Dad," Bernard said in Portuguese.

"Hey, Bernardo. How are you, son?"

"Just wanted to check on you."

"I'm doing all right, how are you?"

"Just thinking about Mom."

After his mother's death, Bernard and his father became closer. He'd wanted to spend as much time with him as he could. They talked often. He went to visit and sent cards for his birthday and holidays. And he worried about his father's health.

"Dad…" Bernard hesitated. "Have you been to the doctor lately?"

"I'm fine," his dad said. "My doctor said everything's good."

He was lying. His dad drank a case of beer a day and smoked at least two packs of cigarettes. No doctor told him he was fine. Bernard didn't call him out on it.

"Okay, Dad," Bernard said. "I'm just calling to check on you."

"Is this about your mother?"

"Yes. I just don't want to lose you too."

"Son, you don't need to worry about me. I'm doing fine."

"I'm glad to hear that. I love you and I'll talk to you soon."

"I love you too, son."

Twenty years of drinking and smoking had to take its toll. He didn't know how much time he had left with his father, but he'd make every moment count.

Bernard made sure Ginger had everything she needed and headed out to Sarah's.

The party was in full swing when he arrived.

"I wish I'd known to be here earlier," Bernard joked when John answered the door.

"Nah, you're right on time." John hugged him.

Rory was decorating Sarah's cake as Bernard headed through the kitchen.

"That looks fantastic."

"Thank you," Rory said. "I'm almost done, then I'll join you all in the backyard."

He gave Bernard a hug. Bernard held tight and took in Rory's cologne. His heart swelled as Rory squeezed him.

Why do you have to be straight? You'd be perfect for me if only you liked men.

"See you soon," Bernard said.

A dozen people mingled in the backyard.

Kelly swam in the pool with his shirt on. It looked similar to the suits worn by surfers. Black and tight, it hugged his thick body. Blue swim trunks completed his outfit.

"Happy birthday, Sarah." Bernard hugged her from behind.

"I'm so glad you made it." Sarah turned around and hugged him back.

"You know I wouldn't miss it for the world."

"The food should be ready soon. Go have fun."

Bernard grabbed a cup of punch labeled non-alcoholic and stood by the snack table, watching everyone enjoy the party.

"How do you know Sarah?" a woman asked.

"We went to high school together and now we work together."

"Sorry, I'm rude." She held out her hand. "I'm Jeanine. I'm in a book club with Sarah."

"I'm Bernard. It's nice to meet you."

Bernard racked his brain. Sarah mentioned her book club, but not anyone in it.

"What book are you reading now?" Bernard asked.

"*Little Women.*"

"That's a great book."

"You've read it?"

"Yes, a few years ago."

"Maybe you should join our group. We could use a man's perspective on it."

"Oh, thank you, but book clubs aren't my thing."

"I'm sure us ladies could make you feel welcomed."

She flipped her blonde hair and giggled. Had he made a joke? She placed her hand on his arm. She moved it up and down. He shivered. Did Sarah mention him to her book club? What did she tell Jeanine?

"Has Sarah ever mentioned me?"

"She may have," she said. Her smile broadened, and she batted her eyes. "But I don't think she mentioned how cute you were."

She was flirting with him. Bernard shifted his feet.

"Did she mention how gay I am?"

"Oh." Her smile stayed in place. "It just takes the right woman to change that."

He closed his eyes and counted to ten, trying to quell the anger stirring inside him. This phrase came up with family members who disagreed with homosexuality. How he needed to find the right woman. No right woman existed for him. He didn't know if a right man existed anymore, but there had never been a chance for a right woman.

"I'm sorry," Bernard said. "That's not how it works. I'm gay and I've never been interested in a woman in my life."

"Aww, that can't be true." She pouted her lips.

Bernard removed her hand from his arm. He took a deep breath. Jeanine wouldn't leave him alone unless he made it clear.

"I'm sure you're a lovely woman, Jeanine. But I'm not interested. I don't want to make a scene, so please walk away and don't talk to me again unless you're willing to accept that I'm not interested in you."

"You're an asshole," she said.

Bernard winced. This was Liquid Pearl and Chance again. She couldn't take no for an answer. She made a scene.

"What's going on?" Sarah walked over.

"Your friend here insulted me," Jeanine said.

"Bernard?" Her eyes widened. "Bernard's never insulted anyone in his life."

"Well, he just did." Jeanine crossed her arms.

"Tell her exactly what happened," Bernard said. "And let her decide."

"I shouldn't have to explain myself."

"Fine, I'll tell her."

Bernard told Sarah about the series of events. Jeanine didn't contradict or interrupt him. When he finished, Sarah glared at Jeanine.

"I only invited you because you overheard me inviting the other members," Sarah said. "I don't even like you. You hit on every man you see and won't take no for an answer. Bernard is gay. Got it? He doesn't want to be with a woman, and he especially doesn't want to be with you. Now, I'm going to kindly ask you to leave my home and I'm talking to the others about having you removed from the book club."

"You can't do that." Jeanine threw her arms into the air.

"I can and will. Now, leave."

Jeanine stormed out of the backyard. Bernard watched as she slammed every door on her way.

"I'm sorry about that, Bernard," Sarah said.

"I think it's funny that someone thinks I'm straight," he laughed.

Jeanine hit on him because she hit on all men. She didn't care about his sexuality.

"Well, I don't think it's funny," Sarah said. "You need more confidence in who you are. Who cares what other people think."

"True."

"Now, let's get some of those burgers and hot dogs John's cooking up."

Sarah introduced Bernard to the rest of her book club. Edwina, Joan, and Betsy were all pleasant women. None of them hit on him.

Rory came out to greet Bernard. "Sorry, I've been stuck in the kitchen."

"It's okay," Bernard said. "How does the cake look?"

"I think it looks great. It's a cherry-chocolate cake with a cherry buttercream frosting."

"That sounds delicious," Bernard said.

"I hope Sarah likes it."

"I'm sure she will."

"Let's go swimming." Rory took off his shirt and pants. He wore swim trunks underneath.

"I'll change and meet you back here."

They jumped into the pool once Bernard returned.

The cool water was nice with the rising California summer temperature. While they wrestled in the water, Bernard's hand brushed Rory's semi-hard dick.

Is wrestling with me turning Rory on? Or did something else happen?

He couldn't figure out why Rory had a semi, but he enjoyed touching it. It'd been over a year since he touched another man. Any man's cock would have turned him on. This time it was Rory's.

But what if it's more? What if he wants more? Damn it, why can't I find someone who makes me feel the way Rory does?

He shook the thought from his head. Rory might be gay, but he hadn't said it. Bernard wasn't going to pressure him. Rory would come out when he was ready.

I'm going to have to take care of this urge when I get home.

Sarah opened her gifts and gushed at all the books she'd received. She was an avid reader and Bernard bought her the *Chronicles of Narnia* series by C. S. Lewis. He knew she hadn't read them all and wanted her to get the chance.

"I hate to leave this wonderful party," Rory said, "but I do have to get ready for church. Enjoy the cake and I'll see you all later."

John brought out a plastic container with a lid. "We cut a piece for you. No reason you shouldn't enjoy the cake you made."

Rory smiled and took the container. "Thanks, John."

"Oh Bernard," Rory said. "Don't forget the presentation for my final project is at five on Friday the twenty-ninth."

"Thanks for the reminder, I can't wait to see what you and your team built. You've talked about this solar generator, and it sounds exciting," Bernard said.

Bernard made a mental note to leave a little early from work so he could support Rory.

The party wrapped up around six. Most of the guests had left after cake and ice cream.

"Do you need help cleaning up?" Bernard asked.

"No, you go home," John said. "Kelly and I will clean up here."

"Sarah, if you want to go to Rory's project demonstration, we can go together," Bernard said. "If not, we'll have to drive separately since I'll be staying in San Jose to watch."

"I'd love to," she said. "But John and I have a business dinner party planned. His boss is coming over with his wife and we're going all out. I'll probably leave a little early to help set it up, anyway."

"Okay, I'll see you on Monday."

Bernard gave them all hugs and drove home.

On the way, Rory continued to occupy his mind. He'd had a crush on him in high school and during their early twenties, but it was nothing serious. When he came out, if Rory was interested in him, he'd have said something. All he said was he accepted him, and nothing else. So, Bernard gave up hope of being with Rory. It didn't stop him from fantasizing about him.

After a long hot shower, Bernard lay on the bed, naked. His fingers explored his chest and belly. He curled his fingers into his chest hair.

He pinched a nipple. The titillation stiffened his cock. Bernard stroked himself with his left hand while he caressed his balls with his right. His thick seven-inch cut cock throbbed. His moans of pleasure escaped his lips as he rubbed himself.

He reached into his nightstand for lube and his dildo. He squeezed the lube onto his fingers. His finger slid into his hole. Another moan escaped. He pressed against his prostate and bucked his hips. He stretched out his hole before another finger made its way in.

He pumped his fingers in and out as he stroked himself. His ass begged for something larger.

He removed both fingers and lubed up the dildo. He turned to his side, brought the dildo to his hole, and massaged it with the head. The dildo eased into his ass. It expanded his hole.

"Fuck."

He rolled onto his back, lifted his legs, and placed a pillow under him. He continued to fuck himself with the dildo. An image of Rory on top of him popped into his head. Rory leaned over him and fucked him while he jerked off. Bernard wanted it. Rory was big, beefy, and hot. He wanted to feel him inside.

Bernard shot a load that reached his chest. Two more pulses followed, cum hitting his stomach. He pulled the dildo out and lay on the bed. Spent.

As he showered, he contemplated the image of Rory fucking him. He didn't know how to feel. He loved Rory as a friend. Was there something more? Could there be something more? Rory had mentioned if he was gay or bi or anything else, he'd tell Bernard when he was ready. Would Rory be interested in him? He couldn't think about that. Fantasy was one thing. It wasn't the first time he'd jerked off thinking about Rory. It was, however, the first time he imagined Rory inside him. Still, he couldn't act on it. This was just a fantasy.

I need to stop. Rory is my friend, and I shouldn't be having these thoughts about him. It isn't fair to him. If I continue to think this way, I might do something I'll regret. I won't destroy what we have for a dream or a wish.

Chapter Twelve

Rory

Friday, May 29

RORY ARRIVED AT Lyons behind Bernard. Bernard stood by his truck, waiting.

"Hey, Bernard," he said.

"Hi," Bernard said.

"Ready to get something to eat?"

"Let's go."

Rory led the way to his colleagues, who waited outside the entrance. Rory wondered how long it would take to get a table, since he and Bernard disliked booths.

"Hey, Rory," Jeff said.

"Hey, everyone. I want you to meet an old friend of mine, Bernard."

Everyone shook hands and introduced themselves. Nicolas walked over and put his name in with the host. Rory could swear he slipped a twenty to the host.

"They'll have a table for us in about ten minutes," Nicolas said.

"Thanks, Nicolas," Sophia said.

"So, Bernard, what do you do?" Davi asked.

"I'm an actuary for an insurance company here in San Jose," Bernard said.

"Oh, a math guy, nice," Jeff said.

They made small talk until the host called Nicolas's name.

The group sat down and ordered drinks. Bernard ordered a soda.

"Not having a drink?" Nicolas asked.

"Oh, no. I don't drink anymore," Bernard said.

"Why?" Nicolas asked.

"Nicolas, I don't think that's any of our business," Davi said.

"No, it's okay. I had trouble with drinking a while back," Bernard said. "So I don't drink anymore."

Rory helped pick up the pieces the last time Bernard spiraled. His ex, Tracy, cheated on him with some eighteen-year-old guy fresh out of high school. Emilio found Bernard and called nine-one-one. Bernard spent the night in the hospital.

Rory, along with Sarah and John, helped get Bernard sober and back on track. Bernard swore off drinking after that. Rory went to grad school the following year. He hadn't seen Bernard since. A pang of guilt hit his gut. He wanted to tell Bernard the real reason he cut ties but couldn't face him.

"Oh, my mom was like that," Jeff said. "She doesn't drink at all. If she does, she has trouble controlling it. Good for you for recognizing it and working on it. That's amazing."

Rory had to give it to Jeff. The man could make anyone feel comfortable around him.

The server brought their drinks, and they ordered food and the work talk started.

"I thought our generator wasn't going to start," Jeff admitted.

"What?" Sophia pointed her straw at him. "You, the man who reassured us it would work even if it caught fire, thought it wouldn't work?"

"Well, we all have doubts sometimes," Davi said.

"The good news is, we are all now graduates with our master's degrees in electrical engineering." Rory held up his drink, and they all clinked glasses and cheered.

Their food came, and the conversation died down as they ate. Rory dug into his steak and potatoes. His mother would be furious if she knew he was eating like this. He watched as Bernard ate his burger and fries, his go-to meal. Rory smiled.

He took a drink and caught Sophia's eye. She smiled. Her eyes shifted to Bernard and back to him. He furrowed his brow, unable to decipher her meaning.

Rory turned to Bernard and caught sight of the food in his beard.

"You got something..." He pointed at a spot on Bernard's face.

"Where?" Bernard wiped at areas of his face, missing the crumb.

"I'll get it." Rory grabbed the napkin and wiped it off. "There, it's gone."

"Thank you." Bernard smiled.

"No problem."

They finished up and perused the dessert menu.

"I have to use the restroom and wash up. Can you order me a slice of apple pie with vanilla ice cream?" Bernard asked Rory.

"Sure thing."

Rory watched him walk away. His thick body filled out his polo and jeans well. Bernard deserved to find someone who loved him. He was a kind and generous man. Jason and Tracy had broken him.

"So, I thought you were straight?" Sophia asked.

"I am," Rory said.

"Remember when we talked about flirting?" Sophia asked.

"Yes, and how that Chance guy was not really flirting, just trying to get into bed with me."

Sophia pointed at him, then to the restroom. "That was flirting."

"What was flirting?"

"The interactions between you and Bernard," Jeff said.

"I…wait, what? I wasn't flirting," Rory said, his voice pitching the statement slightly into a question.

"Yes, you were," Sophia laughed. "You like Bernard. You've been eying him all night."

"He's an old friend I reconnected with. I didn't get to see him for six years while I was in grad school. We've known each other since middle school."

"Great. How long have you been in love with him?" Davi asked.

"You too?" Rory said. He wiped his palms on his pants. "I'm not in love with Bernard."

"You laughed at every one of his jokes, no matter how bad. You put your arm on his shoulder at least three times in the last hour. And I swear I saw you put your hand on his knee at least once," Nicolas said.

"No, I didn't," Rory protested.

"Yes, you did," they all said.

"We've been around him for two hours and we noticed," Sophia said.

"I think you two would make a handsome couple. It's so sweet," Jeff said.

"He was flirting with you too," Davi said.

"What?" Rory asked.

"Yeah, when you went to the restroom, he checked out your butt," Sophia said.

"He also blushed when you wiped the food off his face. It was so adorable," Jeff said.

"You should ask him out," Sophia said.

"I…I'm not gay." Rory turned away.

"Fine, you're not gay," Nicolas said. "But you're not straight either. I'd say somewhere in between."

"No, I mean…" Rory sputtered.

"Look, Rory." Jeff put his hand on his shoulder. "We've worked together for three years. I've never seen you talk with someone the way you do with him. You might not be ready, and that's fine, but we see how you look at him. You may not see it, but there's something there."

"Rory, don't let him get away," Sophia said.

"He's the real deal," Davi agreed.

"But I can't." Sweat pooled on his neck. His heart raced. He grabbed napkins to clean off his skin.

"Rory, we're sorry," Jeff said. "We didn't know this was such a touchy subject." He removed his hand.

"Rory, it's okay," Sophia said. "I know it isn't easy for you. We shouldn't have pushed."

"We won't bring it up again," Nicolas said.

Rory sat there, unable to form words. Were they right? Could he have romantic feelings for Bernard? It crossed his mind. He and Bernard were just friends, and Bernard would accept him. Could it work? Could he and Bernard have a future? He needed to know.

Bernard returned to the table as the server brought their desserts. "I hope you weren't talking about me," he joked.

Everyone fell silent and looked at their food.

"I was just kidding," Bernard said. "What did you talk about?"

"We talked about how long you and I have been friends," Rory said.

"I can't believe you've known each other since middle school," Sophia said.

Rory smiled at her uptake. She was clever.

"Yeah, we met in seventh grade," Bernard said.

"Our names were next to each other in the alphabet, and we got paired together," Rory said.

"We had so much in common that we became friends," Bernard said.

"That's so cute." Sophia looked over at Rory. "So much in common."

Rory shifted his gaze away from her.

"I'm so glad we became friends. I wouldn't want to be called after anyone else at graduation."

The group looked at Rory. Their gazes all said the same thing. He had feelings for Bernard.

"You need to look in your heart and find your true self before you implode," Davi said as he hugged Rory goodbye.

"Thank you," Rory said.

His friends left Rory and Bernard alone in the parking lot.

"This was a fun evening. Your colleagues are great," Bernard said.

"I think we've all grown past just being colleagues," Rory said. "I see them as my friends now. They've done so much to pull me out of my shell."

"That's great. I'm so happy to hear it."

"So, it's still early. Do you want to see a movie?" Rory asked.

He wanted to spend time with Bernard.

"Yeah, what did you have in mind?"

"Well, I remember you like romantic movies, and I saw that *Hope Floats* was playing at the theater. I looked at movie times and there's a showing in twenty minutes."

"You're not big on romantic movies though," Bernard said.

"True, but I know you like them. Since you spent the evening with me and my friends, I wanted to do something you'd enjoy," Rory said.

He was flirting with his childhood best friend. Someone who occupied his mind, even when they were apart. Six years didn't change his feelings. Feelings he was discovering were more than he'd once thought. He wanted to know where this could go, but doubt crept in. His family and his church disapproved of these feelings.

"Okay, let's go."

*

THEY GOT POPCORN, soda, and nachos and walked into the theater. Only two couples occupied the seats. They sat in the back for a better view.

As Birdee, played by Sandra Bullock, tried to get her life together back home, Rory noticed how often he touched Bernard's hand on the shared armrest. Each touch sent chills up his arm. The urge to hold his hand overwhelmed him. He placed his hand over Bernard's. Bernard didn't move his hand. Rory's heart thumped against his chest. The warmth of Bernard's hand soothed him. It felt right.

What am I doing? I can't. He moved his hand off to grab a handful of popcorn.

*

THEY WALKED OUT of the theater. "That was pretty good," Rory said.

"Yeah, I enjoyed it."

Rory thought about the warmth of Bernard's hand. Bernard didn't mention it. Did he make a mistake? Should he have left it there? Not put it on the armrest in the first place? He didn't know what he should do. He'd never flirted before and wasn't sure what to do.

They stood next to Rory's car after the movie.

"Thanks for the movie." Bernard smiled.

Rory wanted to kiss him. His soft lips called to him.

"It was nice." Rory moved in for a hug.

He squeezed. He held back the urge to pull away and kiss his friend. His mind raced, conflicted between what the church taught was right and what felt right. His stomach ached at being this close to him and unable to be with him. The church had conditioned him, and he couldn't escape their grasp.

"So, do you want to meet at the park tomorrow?" Rory asked.

"I can't," Bernard said. "I'm going to a ball game with Sean."

"Who's Sean?"

"He's…" Bernard paused. "I'm going to be honest. He's someone I had a date with a year ago. I reconnected with him after I ran into you because I thought I needed more friends."

"That's wonderful." Rory's heart ached. He feared this. Bernard didn't want him. This Sean guy had to be Bernard's type. It wasn't Rory. There was no reason to mention Eddie to him now, he'd found someone.

I should be happy he's found someone. Why does it hurt so much? Why can't I get it together?

"I haven't been to a game in over a year," Bernard said. "Oh, and I wanted to ask a favor. John's cousin Kelly is moving next weekend. Would you be able to help?"

"Sure, I'd love to help," he said. "I have to attend mass and lunch with my parents, but I'm free the rest of the time."

Anything that gets me more time with you.

"Great, stop by my house in the morning and we'll drive together."

They hugged once more, and Rory headed home. Tears filled his eyes. He'd wanted to kiss Bernard only moments ago, but that was a mistake. Bernard wanted someone else. He wiped away the tears.

I can't come out now. The only person I want to be with doesn't want to be with me.

Rory entered his apartment, and Mina made her way to his shoulder.

"Hey, baby girl." He petted her. "I had a wonderful evening that showed me I'm attracted to my best friend. But he wants nothing more than to be friends with me." It felt good to say it out loud even if it was just to his cat.

Rory busied himself with cleaning his apartment. Mina hid from the vacuum cleaner.

"There, all clean," he told her.

He prepared for bed and lay there after he read his Bible.

"Dear Lord, please guide me," he prayed. "Why am I attracted to someone I can't be with? Why can't I find a woman I'm attracted to? I can't give in to these urges. It's a sin in your eyes and in the eyes of my family. I don't want to spend the rest of my life alone."

For the first time in years, Rory cried. He lay in bed, unable to sleep. His body hurt. His heart hurt. Why couldn't he have the same feelings for a woman as he did for Bernard? Every moment with him was bliss. He stared at the ceiling, contemplating what these feelings meant. He wanted nothing more than to talk to Bernard about it. Bernard wouldn't judge him. But if he told him, then it might become awkward.

Rory's mind wandered to a life with Bernard. His hugs were a sanctuary. He felt vulnerable and open. That must be what love is. But that's not what Bernard wanted. He had to face the fact Bernard didn't want him.

Chapter Thirteen

Bernard

Saturday, May 30

BERNARD RUMMAGED THROUGH his closet for something to wear. He'd only been to a few games and never bought any merchandise, so he settled on a polo shirt and shorts.

"Okay, Ginger. You're staying with Sarah while I'm at the ball game with Sean."

Ginger barked.

"It'll be fine. Chester will be there. You can play with him."

Bernard knocked on Sarah's door. Kelly opened it.

"Hey, Kelly."

"Oh, is this Ginger?" Kelly bent down and petted the dog. "She's so cute."

"Yes, this is Ginger."

"Well, she'll have a great time with Chester."

"Is Sarah here?"

"No, she and John went to the store to get some supplies or something. She left in a bit of a hurry."

"Well, I'm glad you were here," Bernard said.

"Me too."

"I'll be back tonight to pick her up." They shook hands and Bernard walked back to his car.

Sarah had clearly engineered this interaction. She was so determined that he date someone. He'd have to talk to her again about his lack of interest in pursuing Kelly. He might be ready to find someone, but Kelly wasn't.

Bernard pulled up to Sean's house a few minutes before ten.

Who would have thought I'd find myself back here?

Bernard took a deep breath and knocked on the door. Sean answered, wearing a Giants jersey and shorts. The jersey hid his barrel chest and belly. Bernard remembered them well. Images of Sean on top of him sprung into his head. He pushed them away, reminding himself they were friends.

"Bernard, it's great to see you." Sean shook his hand.

Sean's neighbors appeared interested in their interaction. They watched everything that happened.

"We're heading to a ball game, Mr. Parker. If my package arrives, can you get it for me, please?" he asked his next-door neighbor, a man in his fifties.

"Of course, Sean."

"You have some neighbors interested in what you do," Bernard said.

"A few of my students live in the area," Sean said. "I need to keep a low profile so they and their parents don't get suspicious."

"I get it," Bernard said. He understood discretion. Being a gay teacher couldn't be easy. "Where are we heading for lunch?"

"I was thinking we could hit up Pete's Deli. It's good, fast, and easy."

"That sounds like a plan to me."

At the deli, Bernard took in the scent of garlic bread, grilled onions, and sliced steak. The aroma made him smile.

The hostess found them a table and sat them. "Your server will be with you shortly."

"How have I never been to Pete's before?" Bernard asked himself.

"Wait. You've never been?"

"Nope."

"Man, you're gonna love it," Sean said.

When the waitress arrived, Sean ordered a burger, fries, soda, and milkshake. Bernard settled on a cheesesteak sandwich, chips, soda, and a milkshake.

"I haven't had a good milkshake in a while," Bernard said.

"You'll love theirs."

"I can't wait."

"I'm glad you reached out," Sean said. "I've thought about how we left things."

"You have?" Bernard asked.

"I know things didn't end as planned. I didn't want to rush you into a friendship after that. I wanted to be friends, but when you didn't answer my calls, I thought it best to let you contact me when you were ready."

"Thanks for that. I'm fine with it all now. I took the time I needed."

"I'm happy to hear that."

"When I reconnected with Rory, I realized how important friend-ships are."

"I'm guessing that's a friend of yours."

"Yes. Rory and I were close when we were younger." Bernard glanced upward and thought of their conversation at the barbecue. "I'm glad he came back into my life. He was my best friend."

"Is there something more?" Sean's eyebrows raised.

"What? No, we're just friends. Why?"

"Oh, because you just lit up when you talked about him."

"What are you talking about?"

"Nothing, maybe I'm seeing things."

Bernard watched him, but he didn't say anything else.

Their food came. Bernard bit into his cheesesteak. "This is amazing," he gushed.

The cheese wrapped the meat and onions together. The flavors eclipsed any cheesesteak he remembered having.

"Told you," Sean said with a grin.

They finished up and got their milkshakes. Bernard savored the choc-olate shake. He held it in his mouth to drink the flavor in before he swal-lowed.

"I wanted to ask you something." Sean stirred his milkshake. He re-fused to make eye contact.

Bernard's heart sank at the sight.

"Sure." Bernard tried to catch his eye, but Sean's eyes stayed on his shake.

"Do you think sleeping together was a mistake?"

"Honestly, I thought it was at first." Bernard reached over to put a hand on Sean's hand. "But as I thought about it, I can't live that way. I can't think something like that was a mistake. It happened, and I am okay with it."

He rubbed Sean's hand and waited for a response.

"I'm glad you don't think it was a mistake. I'd feel even worse if you did." His smile didn't reach his eyes. Did Sean want more, but was afraid to connect with someone?

"It was an amazing evening. We had great conversations and got to know each other." Bernard lowered his voice. "We had great sex."

"You thought it was great?" Sean perked up and his smile widened.

"Yes. I even told Sarah it was. I only told Rory yesterday we had a date. Nothing more."

"Why not?"

"I…" Bernard paused. "I don't know. I guess I just got him back, and that's not something he wants to hear about."

Why didn't he tell Rory? He had told him about men he'd slept with, even if not the details.

If I told Rory, would he be jealous?

Bernard dismissed the thought. There wasn't a reason for someone he wasn't dating to be jealous.

"Or you like him and don't want him thinking about you in bed with other men," Sean joked.

"Stop." Bernard punched him lightly. "I'm not in love with Rory."

"Yes, you've mentioned that."

"I stand by that, and—"

Sean cut him off. "I know there's something more there. You light up this place when you talk about him, the connection you have with him."

"Okay, maybe once upon a time I hoped."

"Have you ever told him?"

Rory would run the other way. The reason they were friends was because Bernard didn't hit on Rory.

"Oh no, I'm not doing that. We're friends, he's straight, and I won't do anything to ruin things."

"I can understand that."

"I need friends. He's a great friend, and even if he was gay, I couldn't ask him out." Bernard took another sip from his shake.

"So, if you found out that Rory was gay, you still wouldn't ask him out?" Sean asked.

"No, I couldn't do that." Bernard felt his face flush.

"Why not?"

"He was my best friend, and I have him back after six years. I want that friendship back."

"The best partner is someone who is your best friend,"

"How can you tell what I'm thinking?"

"I'm a high school teacher. I've learned to see the signs. It's not much different with adults. Do you want some advice?"

"What could it hurt?"

"See how your friendship goes. If you see any signs that he might be interested in you romantically, then ask him out," he said.

"That's sound advice."

"Great, now let's get going so we don't have to struggle to find parking."

They reached the parking lot and found a spot in the rear.

"Why are you parking here?" Bernard asked.

"Because they usher people out from the rear first then the front to prevent a traffic jam inside the lot and the outside street."

"That's brilliant," Bernard said.

"I've been to enough games to know."

They followed the crowd through the ticket booths and into the stadium. A crescendo of sound echoed as they walked through the tunnel to the stands. Excited voices surrounded them. A sea of black and maroon came into view as they entered the stadium. The scent of hot dogs, popcorn, and nachos swirled around them.

Sean led Bernard to their seats behind home plate.

"How did you get these seats?" Bernard's eyes widened.

Sean smiled. "From the coach. We went to college here together, so sometimes I get perks."

"This is fantastic."

Sean got him a root beer and a hot dog. Sean got a beer with his. Bernard smiled. Sean remembered he didn't drink. Sean was treating him like they were on a date. Did he want something to happen?

They settled in to watch the game. There wasn't a run until the fourth inning by the Diamondbacks. The Giants came back in the sixth inning with two runs. The Diamondbacks didn't have a chance after that.

After the game, they shuffled out with the crowd. "I can't believe that—4-1. That was amazing," Sean said.

"Yeah. That was a great game," Bernard agreed.

"Hey, Sean." A voice came from behind them.

They turned around to see a man dressed from head to toe in San Francisco Giants gear. His round glasses matched his build. His goatee was dyed a bright orange and his hair a jet black.

"Hello, Hugo," Sean said. Bernard noted his stiffened posture and polite greeting. Sean refused to meet Hugo's gaze.

Hugo had a smile that reached his eyes. He looked over at Bernard. "Hugo Janssen." He held out a hand.

"Bernard Silva," Bernard said. "Nice to meet you."

"You too," he said. "How do you know Sean?"

"I work with his brother-in-law at an insurance company," he replied without skipping a beat. *No reason for him to know we went on a date.*

"Sounds fun," Hugo said.

"Well, it's a lot of paperwork."

"I see."

"How do you know Sean?"

"I teach music at Gilroy High School," Hugo said.

"Oh, so you work with Sean," Bernard said.

"Yes, we don't get to work together much, but my band plays all home games." Hugo changed the subject. "So, are you on a date?" He frowned, looking at each of them in turn.

"No," Sean blurted. "We're just hanging out."

Bernard made eye contact with Sean. Beads of sweat formed on his forehead. His eyes widened as he stared at Bernard. Fear covered his face.

"Sean had tickets and his brother-in-law, Mark, asked if I was free so the ticket didn't go to waste," Bernard said. "I thought it'd be fun to get out of the house and to a game."

"That's great." Hugo didn't smile. "Did you enjoy it?"

"Yes, I haven't been to a game in a while. It was fun."

"I'll see you at the staff meeting on Monday, Sean. Have a good night."

They watched him walk away.

"What's going on?" Bernard looked at Sean. "When he asked if we were on a date, the tension intensified."

"Let's get to the car, I'll tell you there."

Bernard struggled to keep pace with Sean. While Sean was chubby, he was in much better shape than him.

They rushed to Sean's car and jumped in.

"He seemed like a pleasant man," Bernard said. "What is going on between you two?"

"He's my ex."

"Wait, he's what?"

"He and I dated in college," Sean said. "I broke it off before graduation. We both ended up at the same high school and he asked me what happened." Sweat dripped down Sean's face.

"So, what did you say?"

"I told him I wasn't gay, and that I was just experimenting."

"Why would you say that?"

"He got hired at Gilroy High School a few years after me," Sean said. "I didn't want him to out me." He turned on the car and blasted the air conditioning.

"That's rough."

"He doesn't hide being gay like I do," he said. "He doesn't flaunt it, but most of the staff knows and his students have probably figured it out."

"Have you tried talking to him about what happened?"

"Well, not really," he said. "We don't run in the same circles, and he'd shun me anyway."

"He clearly knows you're interested in men, or he wouldn't have asked if we were on a date."

"I know, and it's hard. I liked him, but being out in my career isn't easy."

"Remember the advice you gave me about Rory?"

"Yes."

"Same applies. Talk to him. Let him know you made a mistake and that you want him to know you're gay, but not out."

"But I'd have to admit I lied back then."

"We all make mistakes." Bernard looked at him. "I know from experience."

"Thanks." Sean smiled.

"Just giving you your own advice."

They drove back to Sean's house. He parked in his driveway and glanced over at Bernard.

"So, wanna come in?" Sean waggled his eyebrows and laughed.

"Funny."

"I like my sense of humor," Sean said.

"It was nice getting to hang out and have fun. It's been a long time."

"I'm glad we could spend time together and be friends."

"Me too."

*

ONCE HOME, BERNARD dressed in night clothes and sat on the couch. He put on *My Best Friend's Wedding* and ate some cookies with milk.

Bernard thought about Jules's love for Michael as their relationship played out in the movie, and how it reminded him of his own life. He loved Rory, but deep down his love could only be a friendship. He couldn't lose Rory again because of what he hoped might happen. Could he?

What if Rory is gay? He seemed like he was hinting at it at the barbecue. He placed his hand in mine at the movies and left it there for a few minutes. I want to ask him out so badly.

Chapter Fourteen

Rory

Sunday, May 31

THE SERVICE ENDED, and Rory's family shuffled out of their pews.

"What a lovely service," his mother said.

"It was very nice," his father agreed.

"Okay, let's get home," his mother said.

"Mother, Father, I need to talk to the priest. I'll meet you at home for lunch," Rory said.

"Is something wrong?" his mother asked.

"No, nothing wrong. I'll see you at home." Rory kissed his mother on the cheek and shook his father's hand before heading back into the church.

"Don't be too long. I've invited the Jenkinses for lunch," his mother said.

"Yes, ma'am."

Rory moved through the side aisles to avoid the crowd of people leaving the church. He went to sit on the bench next to the door for confessionals. The priest opened the door and walked inside. No one else seemed to want to confess this morning, so Rory went in.

The large room held a desk and chair, two small wooden-backed chairs, a basin with holy water, statues of various saints, and a large cabinet against the back wall.

One side was for those proclaiming their sins while the priest sat on the other side. Rory slipped in. The booth was tight around his girth, and he knelt toward the dark screen. It was claustrophobic in the room, the air dry and musky.

"Good evening, my child. Our Lord is watching over you and will bless you on this day. How may I assist in helping you redeem yourself?"

Rory placed his fingers in the holy water next to him and signed the cross. He spoke the words engraved in his mind.

"Bless me, Father, for I have sinned. It has been twenty days since my last confession."

"I see, my child. What sins do you wish to confess today?"

"I am guilty of the sin of lust in my heart and my mind."

"Have you acted upon this lust?"

The touch of Bernard in the pool at Sarah's party gave him a partial erection. He couldn't control it, but he didn't fight against it.

"No, Father, it's just thoughts."

"Well, we cannot always control our thoughts. It is good that you have realized this is happening and have restrained yourself from acting upon these desires. Please, tell me more."

"The lust I have felt…" Rory hesitated. Speaking the words out loud made them true. He would have to admit to what he desired. His stomach tightened.

"The road to healing begins with confessing our sins. So please, tell me the lust of your heart and mind so that you may begin the healing process."

"I have lust for one of my close friends," Rory said.

"Does she not desire you?"

"It is not a she, Father."

"Oh, I see. Tell me all that you remember."

"I met back up with an old friend, one from school. We met up at his father's barbecue in April. We spent time together at the park and last weekend we went to a movie together. Hanging out and reconnecting has been such a wonderful experience, especially after our estrangement the last six years."

"Okay, seems most innocent. But I feel there is more to this."

"Yes, Father," Rory said. "I feel like my love for him might be more than that of a friendship. It's that of…" Sweat covered Rory's palms. His breathing was shallow, and he gasped for air. "Father, I don't want to go to hell for the feelings I have. But I've had these feelings for more than the last few days. I care about my friend in a deeper way than I should. I placed my hand on his hand at the movie and it felt right. I wanted to kiss him. I don't know what to do."

"It will be okay, my son. Do you have these thoughts when he's not near you?"

Rory hesitated. The confessional was a safe place, and the priest wouldn't share what he said. He needed to be honest.

"Yes, they're not as strong, but they are there. I've had similar thoughts about other men, but it's stronger with my friend. I've never had these thoughts about women. Why would God give me these feelings if they were wrong?"

"We cannot question the decisions of God, my son. It is a way of testing you, as we all face our own tests."

This was a big test. God gave him no desire to be with women, which he should have. Why would God give him such a difficult test? One that would destroy friendships and his life, no matter which choice he made.

"Thank you, Father. I am sorry for all my sins."

"That is good, my son. Now, ask God for forgiveness."

"My God, I am sorry for my sins with all my heart. In choosing to do wrong and failing to do good, I have sinned against you whom I should love above all things. I firmly intend, with your help, to do penance, to sin no more, and to avoid whatever leads me to sin. Our Savior Jesus Christ suffered and died for us. In his name, my God, have mercy."

"Good. Now for your penance. The only way to rid yourself of these thoughts and feelings is to distance yourself from the source of the sins. You shall remove yourself from the company of your friend until a time comes when you can sit with him without lust in your heart."

Rory gaped at the screen. "But Father–"

The priest interrupted him. "This is the will of God. If you are truly remorseful for your sins, you will do what is required in order to heal."

"Yes, Father." With those last words, Rory made the sign of the cross again and left the confessional.

*

RORY TOOK A seat at his parents' elaborate dinner table. Mr. and Mrs. Jenkins sat at one end, while his parents sat at the other. Duncan, Catherine, and Penelope sat across from Rory and Missy.

Rory's mother served lamb chops with spiced potatoes, green beans, and wine.

"Rory just finished his master's degree in electrical engineering this year," his mother announced. "We're so proud of what he has accomplished."

"That's wonderful," Mrs. Jenkins said.

"That is quite the accomplishment," Mr. Jenkins said.

"Thank you," Rory said.

"And what do you do with that sort of degree?" Missy asked, batting her eyes at him.

"Dr. Sanchez offered me a position at San Jose State in the engineering department," Rory said. "He wants me to teach lower division courses for undergraduates in electrical engineering."

"How fascinating," Missy said.

"That's amazing, son, I'm proud of you," his father said.

"Thank you, Father."

"So, now that you have your degree out of the way and a career on the horizon, you should start thinking about settling down," his mother said.

"Maeve, please leave him alone about dating," his father said.

"I just want him to be happy," she retorted.

"We have company. I don't think this is the time or place to discuss our son's dating habits," his father snapped.

Rory was taken aback. His father, who always stayed calm and collected, just raised his voice to his mother.

"I think it's time he finds someone," she said.

"Missy is also of an age at which she should be married," Mrs. Jenkins interjected. "I have to agree with Mrs. Sinclair. Our children need our guidance to be happy."

"You see, Ronan. Rory has a nice young lady here. There is no reason—"

Rory cut her off. "Mother, I don't want to talk about it."

His parents, brother, and sister-in-law looked at him. Rory's hands flew to his mouth. He had disobeyed her. The ultimate sin in their house. This would not go well.

"You watch your tone, young man. I'm still your mother."

"Yes, ma'am. I'm sorry," Rory said, his face focused on his plate.

He looked up to see Mr. Jenkins and his father share a glance.

"Maeve, it's Sunday lunch. We should talk about joyous things," his father said.

"I'm trying to make it happy. I don't see why discussing our son's future is unhappy. At thirty-five years old, he should be married with children by now."

"He's not a child. He can make his own decisions," his father said.

Mr. Jenkins and Duncan shifted in their seats. The tension in the room grew thick. Rory sat there listening to them talk as if he wasn't there. His family often discussed what he should do with his life, who he should marry, and what career he should have. No one ever asked Rory what he wanted.

His mother perked up. "I have banana cream pie."

"Oh, that sounds delicious," Mrs. Jenkins said.

"That was a great lunch. Why don't the men head out for a stroll and let the ladies have some pie and talk? We'll come back for pie," his father said.

"That sounds good, Father," Duncan said.

"Yes, sir," Rory said.

"Okay, we'll save you each a slice." Mrs. Jenkins smiled.

Rory, his father, Duncan, and Mr. Jenkins headed to the park where Rory and his father had had a heart-to-heart. The spring sun warmed his face.

"I'm sorry for the way my wife is acting," his father said.

"It's not your fault," Mr. Jenkins said. "Mary is just as bad. She is trying to push Missy into marriage with every bachelor she can find."

"Dad, can I talk to Rory alone?" Duncan asked.

"Of course."

Duncan led Rory to a bench and turned to him.

"You don't want to date girls." Duncan didn't phrase it as a question.

Sweat broke out on Rory's forehead. "What do you mean?"

"We're brothers. I've known you my whole life. You're not going to sit there and tell me you don't know what I'm talking about. You know how you feel."

What did he feel? He had lust in his heart for someone he could never be with. No matter how much it hurt to be apart from Bernard, he couldn't pursue him.

"It doesn't matter what I feel. It's better to be alone than to be in an unhappy relationship with someone I don't love. That's it."

"So, you'd rather be alone and sad than be with someone you love?"

"That's how it has to be," Rory said. "There is no other choice."

"There's always a choice. You make the choice."

"No, God makes the choice. I would rather live a life of solitude than live in sin and destroy my relationship with God." Rory found his conviction. His feelings for Bernard could never flourish. He had to fight the unnatural urges that boiled inside him.

"You have to look within yourself and ask yourself what God truly wants of you, not what you're told he wants," Duncan said. "I saw how you looked at Eddie at Penelope's party. It was the same look I had when I saw an attractive woman."

"What?"

"You two were getting along so well. I just thought…"

"I thought you meant for me to set him up with Bernard." Rory was mystified.

"No."

Rory's head swam. Duncan was trying to set him up with Eddie. That wasn't possible. Why would he think something like that?

"I can't…I can't be…you know. I can't disappoint Mother and Father."

"You can't live your life just for them," Duncan said.

"You couldn't possibly understand." Rory stood, panic filling his lungs with lead. "Mother and Father don't question you. You have a wife and daughter and a career, and I'm treated like every choice I make is wrong."

"That's not my fault." Duncan stood to match him.

"I'm not saying it's your fault," Rory said. "But you don't know what it's like to hear 'you're too fat,' 'why is college taking you so long,' 'why aren't you dating that sweet girl we set you up with?'" He mocked his mother's voice. "I have to hear that from Mother every other day. There's always something wrong. What do you think will happen if she finds out…"

"If she finds out what?" Duncan asked. "It's okay to say it."

"I'm afraid of being disowned." Rory broke. The sentence drove a stake through his heart. Tears formed in his eyes. He wobbled on his feet, unable to find the bench.

Duncan rushed to him and placed an arm around him to steady him.

"I'm sorry, Rory. I didn't mean to push this much."

"I can't be…I can't be." Rory's throat closed up.

"Just breathe. It's going to be okay."

Rory's breaths were shallow as he searched for the words. The park blurred as tears clouded his vision. He could make out his father and Mr. Jenkins talking. They were getting closer. They reached him and Duncan at the bench.

"What's wrong?" His father and Duncan helped Rory up on the bench.

"I'm. Okay." Rory got out between panicked breaths.

"What happened?" Mr. Jenkins stood next to his father.

"Rory wasn't feeling well. I think he was just overwhelmed by everything going on. It was probably the pressure of the new job. I think it passed," Duncan said.

Rory gave his brother a weak smile. He'd keep this conversation between them.

"Son, is everything okay?" his father asked.

"I just need to lie down," Rory said.

They helped Rory back to the house.

"Oh dear, what happened to Rory?" his mother asked as they shuffled into the house.

"He had a dizzy spell. He'll be okay," his father said. "We'll set him up in the guest room to have a lie-down until he feels better."

"Oh, the poor dear," Mrs. Jenkins said.

"You have a lie-down and I'll bring you some tea and pie," his mother said.

His mother decorated the guest bedroom in the same fashion as the rest of the house. Teal-blue walls with pictures of saints on every surface. Rory undressed and got under the covers. The cool sheets eased the tension in his body.

"Rory, dear, I brought your tea and pie." His mother's voice turned sugary sweet when he was ill.

"Thank you, Mother." Rory sat up and took the tray.

"You take a nap here. You can head home when you wake up."

"Thank you," he said. "I'm sorry I ruined lunch."

"Don't be silly," she said. "You weren't feeling well. That explains your behavior."

He didn't tell her he felt fine until he talked with Duncan. It was better this way.

"If you need to stay the night, I'm sure we have some of your old clothes. They might still fit." She eyed him up and down.

"Thank you. I'm sure I'll be okay after a nap." There was no chance he would subject himself to a night in this house.

"Of course." She kissed his forehead. "You let us know if you need anything."

"I will."

She opened the window. A soft breeze wafted through the room. She shut off the light and closed the door behind her.

Rory ate the pie and sipped the tea in silence. It was two in the afternoon. He placed the tray on the bedside table and stared at the ceiling.

Duncan knows. The thought echoed in his mind.

He'd developed feelings for Bernard. His friends saw it, his brother saw it, and he was sure his father saw it when he pushed him to meet Bernard at the park. Did everyone know something he didn't? Could he act on these feelings? Bernard might feel the same way. He told Bernard he was straight. Would he act differently if he told him the truth? Bernard needed to know, but he didn't know how to tell him.

Chapter Fifteen

Bernard

Saturday, June 6 / Sunday, June 7

RORY ARRIVED RIGHT on time to help Kelly move. Bernard opened the door, excitement jumping in his stomach at the thought of seeing Rory.

"Ready?" Rory asked.

"Yep," Bernard said, stepping to meet Rory on the front porch.

They got in his truck and headed to meet Sarah, John, and Kelly at the storage facility.

Kelly and John were already loading boxes into a moving truck while Sarah and a woman Bernard didn't recognize hauled boxes out of the unit.

"Well, it looks like you have plenty of help. We'll just head out and have fun at the park," Bernard joked.

"Ha-ha." Sarah stuck her tongue out at him. "Just get in here and grab some boxes."

"We saved plenty of fun for you," John said.

Sarah introduced them to Mai Ishii, another real estate agent and friend of John's. She'd traded for a higher commission property with John so he could sell it to Kelly. In exchange for the sale, she agreed to help Kelly move.

They worked through the morning and got most of Kelly's belongings into the moving truck. Bernard and Rory packed the breakables in his truck.

Bernard tripped on a crack on his way to the unit, and Rory caught him from behind. Rory's hand grazed his crotch.

"Are you okay?" Rory asked.

"Yeah, thanks." Bernard smiled. He shivered as goosebumps ran up his arm. Heat flooded his body.

Rory's eyes shifted down and back up.

"You look okay," Rory said. "Doesn't seem to be anything broken."

"Thanks for the catch."

"Anytime."

Rory smiled at him. The smile warmed him inside. Why couldn't he find a guy who was interested in him and made him feel like Rory did? Rory was the best friend he could ask for. No man would ever live up to his standards. Rory's genuine kindness would make sure of that.

They arrived at Kelly's new house around eleven.

"I've ordered pizza for lunch," Kelly said. "It's the least I could do for everyone helping me."

"Thanks," Bernard said.

"Yeah, that was nice of you," Rory said.

Bernard and Sarah carried a dresser upstairs. She closed the door behind him and rounded on him.

"Okay, when are you going to ask Rory out?"

"What?"

"Seriously, you don't see it?"

"See what?"

"I am one hundred percent certain I saw Rory check out your package and your ass at least three times today."

"He did not," Bernard protested.

Did Rory check me out? Rory was aroused in the pool.

If Sarah was right, and Rory was checking him out, maybe what he was saying at the barbecue was him trying to come out to him. Rory was not straight. He had suspected. Rory gave off some signs, but he was more religious than Bernard ever was. It'd be hard for him to come out. Bernard was lucky with a father and family who supported him. Rory didn't have that support.

"Yes, he did. I saw him."

"It doesn't matter," Bernard said. "Even if Rory was gay, he wouldn't be interested in me. Just like Kelly isn't interested in me."

"Why do you think Kelly isn't interested?"

"He said he wasn't ready to date anyone. He didn't give details, but I think it has to do with his ex."

"Oh."

"So, I'm not pursuing either of them. If I'm meant to be with someone, it'll happen. Right now, I've gained a lot of close friends, and I don't want to compromise that with a slight chance of dating someone that might not work out."

"Okay," Sarah said, "but I'm telling you. I saw Rory check you out."

"I'd want nothing more than to be with him," Bernard said. "I've loved him since high school. I kept my distance because he insisted he was straight. I think I chose Jason and Tracy because I wanted someone who reminded me of him."

He said it out loud. He loved Rory, and now Sarah knew. She deserved to know. She'd done so much to help him find love, and wanted what was best for him. Knowing he loved Rory would help her understand why he rejected all other men.

"They were both horrible people. You know Rory is nothing like them. He's a kind, caring man. He is just struggling right now."

"I know." Tears formed in his eyes. "That's why I've been pushing everyone away. I can't find someone like him. I want him."

Sarah wrapped her arms around him.

"I know you love him. I can see it. Just be patient. I know one day he'll realize his love for you and tell you."

"I hope you're right."

"Dry your tears and let's get some lunch."

Bernard was grateful Kelly brought toilet paper. He blew his nose, washed his face, and headed into the living room.

They sat around the table John and Kelly assembled to eat pizza and drink soda. Mai turned out to be a talented woman. She played the cello, had written a book about how to succeed in a male-dominated world, and studied ballet.

"That's an impressive list of talents," Bernard said.

"Thank you," she said.

"I have her book," Sarah said. "It's helped a lot in the workforce. Men don't try to hit on me anymore in the breakroom."

"Was that an issue?" Bernard asked.

"Oh yeah, constantly."

"You never said anything to me."

"Because I know you'd confront them, and I didn't want to deal with that."

She was right. Bernard wouldn't let rude behavior go by without saying something. No one had the right to make others feel inferior.

"So, Kelly." Bernard turned to him. "I'm only three blocks away. We should plan some doggie play dates or walks. It'd be nice to walk with someone."

"That sounds great," Kelly said. "Chester and I could use the exercise. What time do you usually go out?"

"I get home around six after dropping Sarah off. So, I go out around six-thirty. Then head home for dinner."

"Sounds great. I tend to finish around six. So, that'd be perfect timing."

They made plans to meet Monday at the nearby dog park.

Bernard caught Rory's eye while they talked. He didn't say much during lunch.

Does he think I'm interested in Kelly and that's why I want to go for a walk with him? Is this going to make him jealous? They'd still have their afternoons in the park on Saturday. They were still friends. This wouldn't change anything. Or would it?

They finished unpacking the trucks and moved everything to the rooms designated on the boxes.

"I have to get ready for church." Rory looked at his watch. "Do you need help tomorrow?"

"I'll be unpacking tomorrow," Kelly said. "I'd be happy to have you all over again."

"Count me in," Bernard said. "I'm going to get Rory back to his car and then take care of a few things. What time would you like us here?"

"Noon should be fine."

"I can get here around two after lunch with my family," Rory said.

"That works," Kelly said.

Bernard hugged everyone, except Kelly who insisted on handshakes, and followed Rory out to his truck.

They made it to his house and Bernard went in for a hug. Rory didn't squeeze back with his usual vigor.

"What's wrong?" Bernard asked.

"Kelly seems really nice," Rory said.

"Yeah, he seems like a great guy."

"So," Rory looked at him. "Are you going to ask him out?"

Bernard couldn't tell where this was coming from. It wasn't like Rory to be upset when Bernard dated. He'd had two boyfriends that Rory knew of. He'd helped him through both breakups. Did he think Kelly would hurt him?

"No," Bernard said. "We're not interested in dating."

"Oh," Rory said. "He doesn't want to date you?"

"He doesn't want to date anyone."

"If he was interested, would you date him?"

This was an odd line of questioning. Kelly was attractive, burly, and a sweet man. Bernard didn't know if dating was the right move for him. He couldn't say he'd say no if Kelly asked him out. Bernard was someone Kelly found attractive, according to Sarah. He didn't know what to do. He wanted Rory but had to settle for someone who wasn't him.

"I'm not sure," Bernard said. "He seems like a sweet guy. I might go on a date."

"So, if you and he were both ready, would you date him?"

"Rory," Bernard said. "What's going on?"

"I just don't want to see you get hurt like you did with Jason and Tracy."

Bernard pulled Rory into a hug. Rory cared about him, and this proved it. He wanted the best for him. Bernard couldn't ask for a better friend.

"Rory, I know you won't let that happen. I won't make the mistakes I did with Jason and Tracy. Thank you for being my friend."

"I just want you to be happy."

"I know."

Bernard held the embrace for a few moments longer than he normally would. He didn't want to let go. He never wanted to let Rory go again.

"I have to go change for church," Rory said. "I'll be here tomorrow to help finish up with Kelly's move."

Bernard watched him go.

*

WHEN HE ARRIVED at Kelly's house the next day, Kelly already had pizza and soda ready for everyone.

"Thought we could eat before we unpack."

"I won't say no to pizza and soda," Bernard said.

After they finished eating Kelly gave them directions on what to unpack and everyone moved to their respective rooms. Mai couldn't make it, so it was just the four of them until Rory arrived.

Bernard found box after box of books, which he wasn't sure what to do with, so he stacked them to the side.

Bernard was putting together a desk when Rory arrived. Rory helped finish the desk and walked over to the boxes of books stacked in the corner.

"What do we do with these?" Rory pointed at the boxes.

"I haven't found a bookshelf yet, so I'm not sure what he wants us to do with them."

"He has to have at least three hundred books in these boxes. He may have more somewhere."

"I'll go find him and ask where his bookshelves are."

Bernard headed upstairs to the largest bedroom to find Kelly.

The door was open, and he saw a light coming from the bathroom.

"Hey, Kelly…" Bernard stopped.

Kelly stood in front of the mirror. Small circular scars peppered through his chest and belly hair. Long scars ran down his back. They looked old, but still visible. Bernard looked in the mirror. Kelly was applying a cream to his front. His eyes met Bernard's in the mirror.

He whirled around.

"Kelly, I'm sorry. The door was open and I just–"

"Why did you come up here?" he snapped.

Bernard shrank back. Kelly's face turned a beet red. The veins in his neck protruded.

"We wanted to know where to put your books."

"I'm sorry," Kelly said. "I shouldn't have yelled."

"I had no right to come in here without saying something."

"It's okay, I just…" Kelly took a deep breath. "No one has seen me without a shirt in years. You just surprised me."

Kelly moved to put his shirt back on. He walked out of the bathroom and faced Bernard.

"Please don't tell anyone."

"I would never," Bernard said. "Do you want to talk about it?"

Kelly shook his head. "It's a long story, and I'm not sure I'm ready to talk about it."

"I understand."

"It's just…I had a hard time back home. I lived in a small town, and they didn't take kindly to our kind."

Kelly rubbed the back of his neck. His eyes fixated on the floor. Bernard stood there, not wanting to press him.

"I…I'm doing better." He looked up and smiled. "I'm just not ready to go into detail."

"Kelly." Bernard moved forward. "You don't have to tell me anything you don't want."

Kelly leaned in for a hug. He gripped Bernard with a firm embrace. Kelly had never hugged him. He didn't wear cologne. His musk filled Bernard's nose. It was intoxicating and excited him.

"You're the greatest friend someone could ask for," Kelly said.

Kelly sobbed into his shoulder. His body shook with each shuttered breath.

"I'm glad I can be here for you," Bernard said. "Everything is going to be much better for you here. And if you need anything, call me."

They stood there for a few moments. Bernard rubbed his back. It was comforting to stand here with a friend and share a moment of weakness.

"Sorry to interrupt."

They both turned to face Rory in the doorway.

"Rory," Bernard said.

"Just come get me when you're done. I'll be unpacking other boxes."

Shit, what does he think happened?

"I'm sorry, I didn't mean to cause a problem with you and Rory. It seems like he likes you," Kelly said.

"What?" Bernard said. "No, it's not like that. Rory's straight."

Kelly raised an eyebrow. "I don't think he's as straight as he claims."

"Huh?"

"I just noticed things, but I won't say anything to him. Please don't tell him I said anything."

"I won't." Bernard walked out of the bedroom. "I better go talk to him."

Bernard found Rory in the room he'd left him in. He had unpacked a box with parts of a desk and was assembling them when Bernard walked in.

"Hey, Rory," Bernard said. "You didn't interrupt anything."

"It looked like you two were having a moment," Rory said. "I didn't want to bother you."

"Rory." Bernard sat next to him. Tears streaked his face. "Kelly was telling me something about his past. He's had a rough time, and I was consoling him. That's all."

"What happened?" Rory wiped away the tears.

"He asked me not to share," Bernard said. It sounded absurd. He told Rory that Kelly was upset but couldn't tell him why.

"I see."

"I wish I could tell you more," Bernard said. "But Kelly asked me not to say anything about what we talked about."

"I understand."

*

RORY DIDN'T SPEAK to Bernard for the rest of the day.

They finished unpacking and said good night to everyone.

Rory waited on the porch for Bernard.

"Rory, is everything okay?"

"Yeah, why?"

"You haven't spoken to me since our conversation about Kelly."

"I just needed time to think."

Bernard watched his friend. His mannerisms had changed. He was somber and cold toward him.

"Is there something you want to talk about?"

"Can we talk at your place?"

"Of course."

*

THEY SAT ON the couch at Bernard's house, facing each other. Rory wrapped his arms around himself, shaking.

"Rory, you can talk to me."

"I want you to know, if you decide to date Kelly, I'd support it. He seems like a genuine guy, and you deserve to be happy."

This was not the reaction Bernard expected. Rory was upset when he thought something had happened, and now he was approving a relationship between him and Kelly.

"What's the real reason you're upset?"

"I'm just feeling a little lonely," Rory said. "I think it's because I'm seeing so many happy couples and I feel left out."

Bernard reached over and hugged him. The only couple they'd interacted with was Sarah and John. Rory was hiding something but didn't want to talk about it. It wasn't his place to force anything.

"If you ever want to talk, know I'll be here for you," Bernard said.

"Thank you."

They held the hug until Rory said he should head out.

*

BERNARD COLLAPSED ON his bed after he showered and changed. It had been a busy day. He couldn't get the look on Rory's face out of his mind. Something bothered him. His friends were right. Sarah said Rory was checking him out and Kelly thought Rory was interested in him. Maybe he should ask Rory out. What if Rory rejected him? He didn't know what to do. His feelings for Rory had grown strong over the last few months. They were even stronger than when he was twenty-five and wished Rory was gay. He needed to move forward; he just didn't know how.

Chapter Sixteen

Bernard

Saturday, July 4 / Sunday, July 5

IT WAS THE Fourth of July, and Bernard dressed for a day at the lake. He, Sarah, and John had a tradition of going to Coyote Lake on the Fourth of July every year. This year, Kelly and Rory would join them. He looked forward to a day of great food and fun.

Bernard arrived early to get a good parking place and a great spot for the perfect view of the fireworks that night.

He looked out over the water. A few people drove their boats next to the docks. He breathed in the warm lake air.

Bernard was setting up the barbecue and blankets when John, Sarah, and Kelly arrived. John and Kelly carried a giant cooler between them.

"I take it you brought all the food we'll need to cook for the next week." Bernard pointed at the cooler and laughed.

"Well, I never know how much anyone's going to eat, so we brought extra," John said.

"There's another one in my truck," Kelly said.

"I'll help." Bernard followed John and Kelly to the truck.

Bernard helped them carry the cooler, a folding table, folding chairs, and camp chairs from Kelly's truck to their site. Sarah brought a navy-blue cloth to cover the table. Bernard helped her put out chips, potato salad, coleslaw, and plates on the table while John and Kelly prepared the grill.

Rory arrived at half past ten. Bernard and Rory joined John and Kelly at the grill. John was the best griller of the group, so he took the reins while they watched.

Crowds of people filled in the space around their site as the group prepared lunch.

"John, should we tell them?" Sarah asked as they sat around the table to eat.

"I think we can," John said.

"The agency approved our application to adopt," Sarah said, squealing with joy.

"That's amazing," Bernard said.

"Congratulations," Rory said.

"You've been on that list for over three years," Kelly said. "I'm so glad they approved you."

"We received the letter a few months ago," John said. "But we didn't want to say anything until they completed it. We'll get to meet our new child soon."

"That's great," Bernard said. "You two are going to make wonderful parents."

A pang of jealousy hit him. He was happy for them, but he had wanted a child for years. He wouldn't get the chance. Adoption was nearly impossible for a gay couple, and a single gay man wouldn't get a second look. He hated the sting of resentment. It wasn't their fault the government passed biased laws. He hoped one day to have a child. He'd thought about in vitro and finding a surrogate. But in vitro was expensive, and he'd have to save for years.

He resolved to be supportive. Sarah and John found out five years ago they couldn't have children. They never said why, and Bernard never pushed the issue. Sarah had taken a week off work when they found out. She wasn't herself for months after. He gave her the space she needed and was there when she wanted to talk. She wanted children, but never mentioned adoption.

John and Sarah talked about everything from how old the child would be to what they'd like to do for fun. They didn't care if they got a boy or girl, just that they would give a loving home to a child.

They played poker after lunch and Bernard was astonished by how good Rory was.

"How'd you get so good at this?" Bernard asked.

"Oh, we played a lot of poker games when we were waiting on codes to process during grad school. I grabbed a book on how to play and studied it."

"Impressive," Kelly said.

They played as the sun descended. Sweat beat down Bernard's face.

"I'm sorry, it's too hot. I'm taking this polo off," Bernard said.

He pulled the polo shirt over his head to reveal his tank top.

"Good idea." John removed his shirt, revealing his bare skin.

"Sure." Rory took off his shirt. He didn't wear an undershirt either.

Bernard stared at his hairy body. The hair covered him like a light sweater. Bernard had the urge to run his fingers through it. To feel the soft fur. Rory was everything he looked for in a man. He was considerate and honest, but straight. That's what he had to tell himself. Rory was straight. He couldn't have these feelings.

Kelly didn't take off his shirt, but Bernard was the only one to notice. His heart ached for Kelly. He hid his scars, and he hadn't mentioned it since Bernard walked in on him.

Bernard stole glances at Rory as they continued playing.

"Oh, I forgot to mention," Rory said. "I took the job at the college. I start in August."

"That's wonderful," Bernard said.

"That's great, Rory," Sarah said.

John and Kelly both congratulated him and toasted him with their beers.

"I'm heading to the bathroom. I'll be right back," Rory said.

Once Rory was out of earshot, the others turned on Bernard.

"What's wrong with you?" Sarah asked.

"What?" Bernard said.

"Are you and Rory the only ones who don't see it?" John said.

"See what?"

"Dear God, man," Kelly said. "You and Rory keep eyeing each other like you want to rip the rest of each other's clothes off."

"No, we don't."

"Yes, you do," they all said.

"I can't help that I find him attractive." Bernard shrugged.

Sarah huffed, clearly frustrated with Bernard. "But it's happening on both ends. How can you not see that? You need to say something to him, or I will."

"You wouldn't," Bernard said.

"Try me."

She would. Sarah was brazen. If she thought it would help someone, she did it. She'd tried to set him up with Kelly, despite denying it.

"Don't," Bernard said. "If he's gay or bi or whatever, I'm not forcing him out. That's not my place. I get you all are trying to help, and you see things I don't. But I don't want to lose him again. I'll be there for him, and I'll support him, but I won't force him out."

"His reaction when you helped me move tells me everything I needed to know," Kelly said.

"What reaction?" Sarah asked.

"Rory saw us hug and had a look like someone shot his dog," Kelly said.

"Wow, that's intense," John said.

"I just know what it's like for him," Bernard said. "Remember, I came from a similar upbringing. I was lucky with my family. I don't know if he'll be as lucky. It's best to let him discover himself in his own time."

Sarah agreed not to say anything and let Bernard move forward at his pace. She warned him not to let Rory go. If another man approached him at the right time, Bernard would lose his chance. They all agreed Rory wasn't straight and the way he looked at Bernard proved it. There was something more. Bernard needed to let Rory come out when he was ready, not when it suited him.

Rory returned, and their game continued. It was silent and ominous. The tension in the group grew thick, and Rory had to sense it. Bernard looked everywhere except at Rory. He didn't want the emotions that flooded him when Rory was near. He didn't know how their alone time would change. They spent almost every Saturday morning and early afternoon together. It was hard to resist saying something.

"Well, I better head home and get ready for church," Rory said. "Thanks for having me."

"Anytime," John said. "Have a safe trip home."

"I'll see you tomorrow afternoon?" Bernard asked.

"Yes, I'll be at the park around one."

"Great, see you then."

They exchanged hugs. Rory's hands slid up and down his back. He resisted getting aroused. He willed himself to stay soft.

Rory waved at them as he walked to his car.

"That hug lasted a little long," Kelly said.

"He didn't rub my back when we hugged," John joked.

"Stop it. I said I'd let him come out when he was ready. He is taking his sweet time about it."

Rory gave hints he was interested and might expect Bernard to make the first move. He couldn't do it. Rory needed to say something, not drop hints. He didn't want to play the what-if game.

"I hope he comes to his senses soon," Sarah said. "He's a catch and you'll be upset if some other hot bear gets him first."

"I know if Rory asked you out, and you said no, you'd be a fool," Kelly said.

Kelly was right. Rory had everything going for him. He was smart, funny, sweet, and handsome. Rory wouldn't hurt him. Bernard would say yes.

They cooked up some hamburgers for dinner. There were still plenty of chips, potato salad, and coleslaw left.

They watched the fireworks from the lakeside while they ate. It was a sky of every color.

They cleaned up and packed everything away. Bernard said his good-byes and headed home.

He unpacked the leftovers Sarah and John gave him in the fridge after letting Ginger back in. She seemed unphased by the fireworks.

He sat and played *Final Fantasy VII*. The conversation with the group occupied his mind, distracting him from thoughts of Rory.

He defeated Sephiroth, the final boss, and watched the end credits. Ginger sat next to him on the couch.

"Another one down," he said. "I have to figure out what game I'll play next."

Bernard rummaged through his closet and found *Tomb Raider*.

He played for a few hours. He looked at his watch and saw it was past ten.

"Let's go to bed, Ginger."

He saved the game and changed. Rory might be interested in him. They noticed Rory looking at him the way he looked at Rory. He wasn't sure what to make of it.

*

THE NEXT MORNING, Bernard took Ginger for a walk. He made it to the dog park at nine to see Kelly there with Chester.

"Hey, Kelly," Bernard said.

"Hi, Bernard. Good to see you here."

"Nice to see you too. I'm glad there's a dog Ginger knows, so she has someone to play with."

"Same. Chester loves other people but is skittish around strange dogs sometimes."

They watched the dogs run around and play.

"I'm sorry about yesterday," Kelly said. "With you and Rory."

"It's fine."

"It's not fine." Kelly looked at him. "It's obviously something that bothers you and that you're struggling with. I should know. It isn't easy to have feelings for someone who may never return them."

"Thank you."

"I'm here for you, you know. If you ever want to talk. I'll be a willing ear."

"That means a lot. Thanks."

He knew he needed to figure this out. The urge to tell Rory boiled up inside him. Even if Rory wouldn't return the feelings, he'd know how Bernard felt. He'd know what torment it was to have feelings for someone and never be able to be with that person. Rory had to know the feeling. He'd never dated in his life, as far as Bernard knew. If Rory had feelings for him, and he suspected he did, Bernard would have to tread carefully. Rory's connection to the church was stronger than his own. He went with his family, but after his excommunication, he kept his prayers slim. The church destroyed his faith when they removed him. He didn't want Rory to face the same fate.

Chapter Seventeen

Bernard

Sunday, July 5 / Monday, July 6

BERNARD LOADED LEAVES, broken pots, and old soil into a garbage bin. He started cleaning out the greenhouse in his yard. He needed to make sure it was fit for plants. It would take a while to get it ready, and summer was as good a time as any.

His watch alarm went off at noon. He put the bin inside the greenhouse and went inside to shower and change.

He packed up some snacks, leashed Ginger, and headed to the park to meet Rory.

The park was filled with families. Summer brought locals outdoors to get some sun and allow their children to play. The hot air was muggy, but he loved it. Living his whole life in Gilroy, he got used to the weather. It was funny when the Garlic Festival hit. Tourists came from far and wide to taste the garlic ice cream. The festival was a few weeks away. He'd decided years ago not to attend anymore. It was hot, crowded, and expensive, and he didn't have his mother to go with.

Bernard waited in his truck with Ginger and the AC.

Rory arrived around one. He walked over to Bernard's truck carrying a basket.

"Hi there," Rory said, smiling.

"Hey, Rory." Bernard hugged him. "What have you got there?"

"Look, you're great and all, but I couldn't eat more of those snacks you bring. I made some cupcakes." Rory punched him lightly.

Chills ran up his spine. He wanted this to last. He wanted Rory's touch.

Damn it, Rory. Tell me you want me already.

"I'll take those over these store-bought snacks any day."

They walked into the park, Ginger right beside Bernard in her harness.

"It's pretty packed today," Bernard said. "I hope we can find a spot."

They moved through the park. A light breeze eased the heat of the blazing sun. July was always hot.

They searched for thirty minutes before they found a shaded area to set up.

"I still brought milk." Bernard pulled out a bottle. "I can't have snacks without milk."

"That sounds fine to me."

They ate cupcakes and watched the surrounding families enjoy the lake. Children ran to the playground while their parents sat on benches nearby.

Bernard noticed couples everywhere. They held hands, kissed, and made eyes at each other. The memory of the man who confronted them when they walked the trail a few months ago assaulted his mind. Did these people prevent him from dating again? Did the fear of always defending his relationships hold him hostage? He couldn't let them hold him back.

"What's on your mind?" Rory asked.

Bernard shook his head. "Oh, nothing."

"That was not a 'nothing' look," Rory said. "That was a deep in thought look."

"I'm just…" He searched for the right words. "I'm upset that I'm sabotaging my own happiness."

"What do you mean?"

"See all the couples nearby." Bernard pointed out each couple along the path and on the benches.

"Yeah, so?"

"I keep thinking about that man who thought we were a couple and how he reacted," Bernard said. "We're not even a couple. I hate how he treated us. That wasn't the first time and I know it won't be the last. I think I give up on dates because I don't want to face that."

"I'm sorry you have to go through that." Rory put his arm around him. "I know it can't be easy. What if you found someone you had a strong connection with? Someone who you could face that with and know nothing would break you apart?"

Bernard met his gaze. Did Rory mean him? He could face any

obstacle with Rory, but he didn't have the guts to say anything to him. He couldn't tell Rory his feelings. It hurt, but it's what he had to do.

"I think I could," Bernard said. "One day, I hope to find that person. I'd cherish every moment if I could be with someone who was like a best friend, confidant, and partner all in one."

What was he saying? He just told Rory he wanted him. His face heated. What would Rory say? He couldn't be rejected by him now. He'd spent this time keeping him at arm's length.

"I'm sure you'll find that man one day," Rory said. "You might have met him and the two of you just haven't realized it."

Rory's green eyes dug into his own. Rory meant himself. Bernard's insides squirmed. This was his chance to tell him.

"Maybe one day," Bernard said. "For now, we should walk off these cupcakes."

I'm a coward. He gave me an opening, and I blew it.

"Let's go."

They walked around the lake. The sun shimmered on the water's surface. The soft breeze ran through his hair. He stole glances at Rory. Three months ago, he didn't think he'd have Rory back. Now, almost every Saturday belonged to them.

"Yesterday was fun," Rory said. "I wish I could've stayed for the fireworks."

"They were great. So much fun."

"Maybe next year."

"That would be nice."

Bernard couldn't help noticing every couple who passed. They held hands, some kissed, and they did it in the open. No one confronted them or harassed them. They existed without harassment. Why couldn't he exist? Why couldn't those who disagreed just leave them alone?

"Would you like to come over for a movie and some takeout?" Bernard asked as they packed up the supplies.

"That sounds nice. What were you thinking?"

"I was thinking Fook Xing, they have amazing General Zao's chicken."

"Sounds good."

"What would you like?"

Rory wanted hot and sour soup, orange chicken with rice, and steamed vegetables.

"Got it."

"I'm going to head home, feed Mina, and I'll be over around six?"

"See you at six."

Bernard placed an order to be delivered at six-thirty. They'd have time to choose a movie and get settled in before the food arrived.

He dashed to clean his living room as best he could. It was already five.

Rory arrived with a stack of movies in hand.

"I didn't know what movies you had, so I thought I'd bring some of my favorites to give us options."

Bernard shuffled through them, and they decided on *The Devil's Advocate*.

They ate takeout and watched the movie. Bernard sat on the edge of the couch, as far from Rory as he could. He didn't want to give the wrong impression.

When the movie finished, Rory got up to leave. "I should get home and get some sleep."

"I have to get to bed soon too."

"Thanks for inviting me over."

"Thanks for coming over," Bernard said. "It was fun."

"Yeah, I had a good time."

They hugged. Bernard squeezed him.

They parted, and Bernard leaned in to kiss Rory.

Bernard backed away. Did Rory notice? How close had he gotten? His stomach churned. Rory's eyes widened.

"Rory, I'm…" he choked.

"It's nothing," Rory said. "It was an accident."

Rory walked out, and Bernard collapsed on the couch. What was wrong with him? He'd resisted this for years, and now he almost kissed Rory.

He picked up the phone and called Sarah.

"Hello?" Sarah asked.

"I tried to kiss Rory."

"You did what?"

"We had dinner and watched a movie. We hugged as he was leaving and when we broke the hug, I leaned in to kiss him. I stopped before anything happened."

"What did he do?"

"He backed away and said accidents happen. Then he left."

"You didn't talk about it?"

He didn't want to talk about it. It all happened so fast. Would Rory never speak to him again? He broke Rory's trust. He never hit on Rory, never. Now, he'd tried to kiss him. He couldn't blame it on alcohol. He needed to fix this.

"No, it all happened so fast."

"What are you going to do?"

"I'm going to give him time," Bernard said. "I'm going to let him make the next move. If I do anything it might look like I'm trying to coerce him into something. I don't want to do that."

"Okay, we can talk about it more tomorrow. I want you to tell me everything that happened today."

"Okay, I'll grab you tomorrow."

*

THE NEXT MORNING Bernard told her everything that happened. Every detail of their conversation and how Rory responded.

"You want my honest opinion?"

"You know I always do."

"I think he's falling for you but isn't sure how to proceed," Sarah said. "He's testing the waters. Seeing if you're interested. I think what happened last night confirmed his thoughts. He may want to be with you."

"I always figured he was straight."

He turned to see Sarah with a raised eyebrow.

"What?" Bernard said.

"You and I both know he isn't totally straight. I knew you weren't when we were in high school."

"I guess I take people at their word," Bernard said. "If he thinks he's straight, then he's straight. But you're right. He has feelings for men, but I'm not sure about women."

"He's thirty-five and has never had a girlfriend. I think he'd have found someone."

"What if he doesn't have sexual attraction at all?"

"That's possible," Sarah said. "John's sister Emily is like that. I believe she used the term asexual. She says she's not sexually attracted to most people. She's married, but I don't know if they have sex." Sarah shrugged. "That's obviously too personal for me to know."

"She was a bridesmaid, right? The tall brunette?"

"Yes, and she met her husband at our wedding. She married Chris."

"Chris North, one of John's groomsmen?"

"Yeah, they hit it off and started dating."

"I think I got an invitation to their wedding. I couldn't go because…"

The memory flooded back. In the hospital. He'd drunk too much and was rushed to the hospital. He was there overnight and spent the next few days recovering. Tracy did that to him. The hurt he endured always came back to Jason or Tracy. He allowed them to control his life.

"You don't have to say it."

"That's amazing. Why couldn't I meet someone at your wedding?"

"Well, you would have met Kelly, but he wasn't able to make it."

Bernard suspected the scars on his body were the reason. Those scars came from someone he was dating, but he didn't push Kelly for information. That was Kelly's story to tell when he was ready, not his to pry into.

*

AFTER A LONG day at work, Bernard dropped Sarah off and made it home.

He grabbed Ginger and met Kelly for their evening playdate.

"Hey, Bernard," Kelly said. "Why the long face?"

"I think I screwed up."

"What happened?"

Bernard retold the story of the previous day. Every time he replayed it, he noticed Rory's responses to what he said. There were clues. Rory might have feelings for him, but he didn't know how to find out.

"Well." Kelly tapped a finger on his lips. "I think it's what we've been talking about. You and Rory have feelings for each other, but neither of you knows how to proceed."

"That's what Sarah said too."

"He's been told his whole life that being gay is a sin, and that he's supposed to be with a woman. Now that he has feelings for you, he isn't sure if those feelings are real or just lust."

"I'm going to give him space and let him reach out to me when he's ready to talk again."

Bernard hoped Rory would reach out. Even if nothing romantic happened, he didn't want to lose his friend again. He enjoyed the time they spent together. He needed that friendship.

"I'm sure he'll come around."

They watched the dogs play as the sun set over the buildings. Pollen spread through his nostrils. Bernard inhaled the scent of fresh-cut grass.

Kelly placed a hand on Bernard's.

"I'm going to tell you what I see as an outsider," Kelly said. "Be patient with him. If he has feelings for you beyond lust, let them blossom naturally."

"Thanks, Kelly."

They parted ways, and Bernard walked Ginger home.

He sat on the couch watching reruns of *I Love Lucy*. Kelly's words echoed in his mind. Rory flirted with Bernard in his own special way. His reaction when he thought something was going on between him and Kelly. His response when he told him he wondered if there was someone out there for him. Kelly, Sarah, and John noticed. He understood his own feelings, but what were Rory's? Rory could be the one, but how long would he have to wait? Months? Years? If he dated someone else, that might push Rory away. He didn't want anyone else. He wanted Rory. Now that he saw what others did, he yearned for him. He had to decide what he needed.

Chapter Eighteen

Rory

Monday, July 6

RORY WOKE UP with a hard-on. He'd dreamed of Bernard. They held each other on the couch. Bernard kissed him. His soft lips moved down his neck. His touch eased the pain in his heart. Bernard whispered he loved him. His warm embrace gave Rory hope for the future.

Rory and Bernard had spent the last three months hanging out almost every Saturday, and his urges grew stronger.

Bernard almost kissed him. He wanted to feel those lips against his.

I should have gone in for the kiss. He wanted to kiss me, and I wanted to kiss him.

"I need to figure out what I want."

Rory showered. Bernard mentioned Castro Street in San Francisco, a place for people to explore their sexuality. He'd try to figure things out there.

*

RORY PARKED AND walked the streets of Castro. It was a hot morning. The sun beamed on him. Rainbow flags flew throughout the street. He noticed other flags that he did not recognize. One even had a paw on it. People walked up and down the street, dressed in clothes that would not go over well in his church. His eyes wandered around until someone stopped him outside their shop.

"You look lost," a large man wearing leather said. He was in his fifties, with graying hair, a long thick beard, and toned abs.

"I've never been here before," Rory admitted.

"What are you looking for?" he asked.

Rory didn't know. He'd been walking down the street in an aimless fashion. "I…I'm not sure," he said.

"Well, come in, look around, and see if something strikes your fancy."

Rory entered the shop. The store stocked DVDs and VHS, all with half-naked men on the covers. There were dildos, oils, lubrication, and some leather clothes that matched those of the man outside the store.

"What is this?" He placed his hand on a leather hammock.

"That, my friend, is a sex swing," the man said.

"A what?"

"Watch." The man got into the swing. His legs hooked onto the ropes and he lay there, spread eagle. "So, the bottom lies here," he said. Then he pointed in front of him. "And then the top stands right there. Go ahead, I won't bite."

Rory shuffled forward to stand between the man's legs. He shifted his eyes around. Sweat beaded on his body.

"Oh, wow, umm…" Rory said.

"I see this is not what you're looking for." The man got out of the swing. "So, do you have a boyfriend?"

"I…no, but I'm not sure if I want a boyfriend."

"Ah, you're questioning your sexuality." He looked Rory over. "Is there someone you'd like to be your boyfriend?"

I want Bernard.

"I have a friend who is gay," Rory said. "And I think I like him more than a friend. I'm trying to figure out if it's just lust, or if it's more."

"Are you looking for a gift for your friend?"

"No. I want something for myself."

"So, you want to experiment by yourself before you decide whether you want more with this friend of yours," the man said. "It's smart to try it on your own first. You're not sure if you're gay, bi, straight, or something else?"

This man was good. He pinned Rory within minutes of meeting him.

"Well," Rory said. "I don't think I'm straight. I find men attractive but can't remember ever finding a woman attractive."

He'd always referred to himself as straight. He just confessed to a stranger that he didn't think he was straight. This guy wouldn't say anything or judge him.

"Well, do you find your friend attractive?"

"I think he's handsome, yes."

"Okay, fair answer," he said. "So, what does he look like?"

Rory described Bernard in intricate detail. His soft wavy black hair. His close-cropped beard. He even described how one corner of his mouth went higher than the other when he smiled.

"Well, that is very specific," the man said. "Either you like him, or you're just good with descriptions."

"I'm not sure."

"Here." He handed him a DVD titled *Bear With Me* and a bottle of lube.

"Why do I need this?" Rory asked.

"Well, this video has men built like your friend, so if it turns you on, then you might have deeper feelings for your friend," the man said.

He looked at the cover. Two half-naked husky men held each other in a tight embrace. On the corner was a flag he saw earlier but didn't know what it was. Even stripes of dark brown, orange, yellow, tan, white, gray, and black. In the top left corner of the flag was a black paw.

"What's this?" He pointed at the flag.

"That's the bear pride flag," the man said. "It represents larger men. Those who don't quite fit in the norm of the gay community."

"Ah, so like me and my friend."

"Exactly."

"Okay, and the lube."

The man raised an eyebrow. "Have you ever, you know, jacked off?"

Rory's face warmed. "I…once in a while, I've never used lube though. I just jack off in the shower and I'm done."

"Here." The man handed him a magazine. "This will give some descriptions of self-pleasure. It goes beyond just jacking off. There are some great diagrams and explanations."

Rory's eyes opened wide with shock.

The man's voice softened. "It has details on how to pleasure yourself, areas you can explore. I'll throw it in for free."

"Thank you."

Rory paid and took his items in a plain bag. People passed by as he walked down the street. He entered a few more shops, but nothing grabbed his attention. He thought porn, a bottle of lube, and a self-pleasure instruction manual were enough for his first trip.

He ate lunch at a little cafe. A few men whispered how attractive he was. Two men caught his eye and winked. He blushed when the server called him handsome. He'd never been told he was handsome by strangers.

After lunch, Rory headed home. The drive home was quiet. The radio played hits from the eighties. It took him back to the bars with Bernard. They laughed, joked, and had a great time. The memory brought a smile to his face. He hadn't smiled this much in years.

He entered his apartment. After petting Mina, he walked to his bedroom, shut the door, and pulled out the magazine. It had detailed diagrams of the male body. He read how to tease the outer rim of his ass and how to massage the prostate.

Rory definitely wanted to try it out.

He got into the shower and made sure every inch of him was clean. He rubbed the outside of his hole. Moans escaped his lips as he rubbed harder. He slipped his finger inside. The sensation caused a jolt of pleasure in his cock. He closed his eyes and moaned as he massaged his prostate.

Is this how it feels to be fucked? Would a dick fit in my ass?

Rory dried off without finishing himself off in the shower. He grabbed a dry towel and laid it on the bed. He rummaged through the bag and pulled out the bottle of lube and the video. He put the movie on and propped himself up on pillows, still naked, to watch.

The movie opened on two men, similar in size to him and Bernard. The first scene was them meeting in a bar. They went up to a hotel room, kissing along the way. The passion on the screen enticed Rory.

What would it be like to kiss a man? What would it be like to kiss Bernard?

Rory's cock came to life as the men undressed. They kissed and caressed each other. They had hairy bodies and large cocks. He looked down at his now hard cock. His dick didn't match theirs in size. He was only six inches. He measured it once in his twenties. The cocks on the screen were at least eight inches. He wondered if Bernard would want one of his size. Did Bernard have a dick as big as theirs? He couldn't remember what it looked like. How big were his balls? Were they tight or did they hang low like his? His cock stiffened. He'd seen Bernard in the showers and wished he'd paid more attention.

The men on the screen ran their fingers through each other's body hair. The larger one got on his knees to suck the other one's cock. Rory wanted to feel Bernard's lips around his cock. What would it feel like to suck Bernard's cock? What would it taste like? He wanted to know the pleasures of another man. He lubed up a finger and massaged his hole with it. Groans of pleasure escaped, echoing through his room as he entered his hole.

"Mmm." He slipped his finger deeper inside his ass. He hit his prostate and let out a gasp.

He continued, pressing against his prostate a few more times. His body convulsed with each thrust.

Rory pulled back his foreskin and poured lube onto his cock. He stroked with a slow, even movement.

His strokes quickened as he fingered his ass. His balls jiggled with the combined effort of his finger and his hand.

The men on screen took turns eating each other's asses. Running their tongues in and around. He wanted to try that so badly. He wanted to taste Bernard. He wanted all these pleasures he'd never experienced.

He jerked faster as one man fucked the other on the screen. He imagined himself fucking Bernard. Bernard was smaller than him, although not by much. That was the image on the screen. The bigger guy was fucking the smaller one. He wanted to do it with Bernard. He wanted to hear Bernard's moans of pleasure as he pounded into him. As he stared into his eyes. As Bernard begged him to fuck him hard. Bernard's cock smacking against his belly as Rory pumped. His hands pressing against Bernard's chest.

Rory shot a load onto his chest and belly. His body spasmed as multiple shots came out of the tip. He'd never come this much. He slid his finger out. His breath was shallow from the effort of it all. His body collapsed onto the bed.

"I can't believe I did that," he panted. "That was amazing."

His mother's voice appeared in his head. *How could you do something so disgusting? Watch two men fornicate and please yourself. You should be ashamed of yourself.*

Panic set in. He realized he'd committed a mortal sin. He ran to the bathroom and threw up.

"Oh my God, what did I do?" he cried.

He jumped into the shower and washed his body. He scrubbed every inch of himself.

He'd just masturbated to gay porn. What was wrong with him?

Once he'd cleaned up, he dried off, put on fresh pajamas, and threw the towel into the laundry basket.

Rory pulled the tape out, slipped it in its case, and put it with the lube into the bottom drawer of the nightstand.

This feels right though. I need to call Bernard. I need to be with him. I want to feel the passion and love that everyone else gets to feel. My mother is wrong. Being with another man isn't a sin. It can't be.

Rory didn't know how to tell Bernard how he felt. He dreamed of him at night and jerked off to him. He wanted to be close to Bernard. He wanted to be with Bernard.

Chapter Nineteen

Rory

Friday, July 10

RORY WAS EATING breakfast when his phone rang.

"Hello?"

"Hey, Rory, it's Jeff."

"Hey, Jeff. What's up?"

"We all have great news to celebrate, so we're hoping you could come out tonight for drinks."

"That sounds great, what time?"

"The usual, six-thirty."

"I'll see you all there." Rory hung up.

It was nice to be spending time with his friends. After graduation, they still called him to hang out. He hadn't had friends like this since the high school group with Bernard and Sarah.

Rory spent the day cleaning his apartment. He had neglected it for a few days and now needed to catch up.

Once he finished and had eaten lunch, he put on *Jerry Maguire*. He half-paid attention while he pulled out the new yarn and began knitting.

On Wednesday, he'd taken a quick trip back to Castro Street to grab something with the pattern he wanted to make for the sweater. He found a shop that carried a variety of bear merchandise. The bear community was diverse with muscular men, chubby men, or men in between. The bear culture was secure in who they were. He'd grabbed a sticker with the pattern, and perused the bear porn section, but didn't think it would be appropriate to buy another video. Masturbating and porn were sins, and he'd sinned enough.

After the movie, Rory got up, showered, and prepared to meet his friends.

"Bye, Mina." He petted her on his way out. "I'll be home soon."

Rory sat at a table with his friends in Shaffers. Nicolas had ordered appetizers for the table, and everyone had a drink. They laughed, talked, and shared their successes.

Davi had received a job offer with a company that meant he could extend his student visa to a work visa and stay in the United States. He was excited to work for a company that limited waste.

Sophia got a job at her mother's clinic, where she oversaw the operations of all generators. She made sure they were up to code, maintained, and ready in case of emergencies.

Nicolas took over his father's business developing portable battery jumpers. It was the reason he studied engineering. He oversaw the development of batteries and used his knowledge to improve on the designs he claimed were outdated.

Jeff got a position with a nonprofit to eliminate unnecessary power usage in low-income areas. He assisted the development team and ran a small section of his own.

"You guys are doing great," Rory said. "I'm so happy to have been part of such a brilliant team."

"You are too. Didn't you take the position at the university?" Jeff asked.

"Yes, I did," Rory said.

They all cheered for their successes. Each of them followed their passion and made a difference in their own way.

Rory ordered more appetizers for the table. They munched on potato wedges and discussed their futures. If he worked hard at the college, he could earn a permanent position as an adjunct professor.

"I have some more exciting news," Sophia said.

"What is it?" Jeff asked.

"A radiologic technician at the clinic asked me out on a date."

"Oh, tell us about them," Nicolas said.

"Well, he runs the X-ray machines at work, his name is Victor Masters, and he is so cute."

Rory couldn't help but giggle. Sophia always played the prim and proper grad student in public. She went out for drinks, but always kept it light. It was great to see another side of her. A side she could let loose and be herself, not what the world expected of her.

"That's great," Rory said. "When's your date?"

"We're going out tomorrow night. I can't wait."

"That's so exciting," Davi said. "I'm sure you'll have a fun time."

"Did he say where he's taking you?" Nicolas asked.

"No," Sophia said. "It's a surprise."

"Well, I hope you have a wonderful time," Nicolas said.

Rory glanced at Nicolas. He wasn't his usual confident, suave self. There was something different. If he wasn't mistaken, Rory could swear Nicolas had feelings for Sophia. Was Nicolas upset that Sophia had a date? He'd never asked Sophia out, as far as he knew. So, what might have changed?

"So, what about your love life?" Sophia asked Rory.

"What love life?"

"You're telling me you still haven't asked Bernard out on a date?"

"No, we're friends."

"Friends who are in love," Jeff said.

"We're not in love."

"Why can't you admit it?" Nicolas said.

Why couldn't he admit he was in love with his best friend? They'd been friends for over twenty years, and still he couldn't confess his feelings for him.

"I'm going to tell you guys the truth. Please don't judge me."

"Rory, we're your friends. We wouldn't do anything to hurt you." Sophia placed a hand on his shoulder. "You can tell us."

Rory took a deep breath. It was now or never; he needed to be truthful with his friends.

"Because if I act on my desires for Bernard, I'm going to go to hell."

They stared at him, open-mouthed.

"What?" Davi asked.

"I'm a devout Catholic. If I do anything with Bernard, then I'll go to hell. I'd rather live a life alone than face my mother and the church."

Rory gazed into his drink. The bubbles drifted to the top and popped. They were having a great time, and now he'd ruined it. He brought everyone down.

"I don't think that's true," Jeff said.

"It's what the Catholic Church taught."

"Why would God make you this way, to love a man, if He was going to punish you for it?" Nicolas said.

"It's just His way of testing me, and I have to resist the temptation."

"Well," Davi said. "That's a horrible thing to do to yourself. I'm Catholic as well and I have a gay cousin at home. No one in the family judges him for it. We say it's his life to live, and that is between him and God."

"You don't think I'll go to hell for it?" Rory locked eyes with Davi, a kindred spirit in their religion. He'd known Davi was Catholic, but they never discussed it.

"No, I don't," Davi said. "You are a good person. Kind and generous. I don't think God would punish you for your love."

"Thank you, Davi," Rory said. "That means the world to me."

His friends gathered around him and wrapped him in a hug. He had friends. He still couldn't wrap his head around it. People outside his church who wanted to spend time with him. Encourage him. They didn't care how he turned out. They liked him for who he was and didn't expect anything else.

"So," Sophia said. "Are you going to go ask him out on a date?"

"What if he says no?" Rory said.

His heart ached. Bernard's rejection of his love would crush him.

"You'll never know unless you try," Nicolas said.

"You got this, big guy," Jeff said.

"Okay." Rory stood. "I'm going to go ask him right now."

"We'll be rooting for you, Rory," Nicolas said.

"You have to let us know how it goes," Jeff said.

"You'll do great," Sophia assured him.

Rory left the bar and headed to Gilroy. He needed to ask now, while he had the courage. A thousand thoughts ran through his mind. What would he say? If they went on a date, where would they go? What would it be like to kiss him? What would it be like to…? He stopped. He had thought about sex with Bernard. What it would feel like. Would he be able to? He had to stop thinking about the negative. Right now, his goal was to get to Bernard's and ask him out.

Rory took a breath and knocked on Bernard's door. A pool of sweat covered his face. His heart jumped into his throat when Bernard answered the door.

"Oh, hey, Rory," Bernard said. "Is everything okay?"

"I…can I come in?"

"Of course," he said, scrunching together his eyebrows in concern. "It's ten at night. What happened?"

"I just need to talk to you."

Rory followed Bernard in. Bernard's house was nice but not as clean as his apartment. He wanted to grab a broom, mop, vacuum, and duster, and tidy the place. He needed to help Bernard.

Rory's mind jumped to cleaning when he was stressed. He could clean a mansion right now.

"Do you want something to drink?" Bernard asked.

"A soda would be great."

Rory sat on the couch, hands between his knees.

Bernard returned with two glasses of soda. Rory held it in both hands and stared at the bubbles as they fizzed. Bernard sat next to him.

"What's going on?" Bernard asked.

"I…I have to… I need…"

"What's going on? Are you okay?"

Rory looked up at Bernard. His eyes fixated on him.

"I…I'm sorry, I'm sorry. I just need to…I don't know. Damn it, I'm sorry."

"Sorry for what? What's going on?"

Bernard placed his hands on Rory's shoulders and steadied him.

His hands feel nice. I love his touch.

"I'm like you. I mean, I'm gay like you. I've had feelings for you for so long, I don't even remember when it started. I'm sorry I didn't say anything before. I want to be with you, but I'm afraid I'm too late. Please, for the love of God tell me I'm not too late. Tell me I have a chance with you, that we have a chance. I'm sorry I waited so long. My heart aches for you. It has for so long. I don't know what to do now. Please, help me."

Bernard wrapped his arms around him and squeezed. He cried into Bernard's shoulder, releasing the anguish that had built up inside him over the last twenty years. He'd finally admitted everything out loud.

"I…I can't live the lie anymore. I let the church dictate who I should and shouldn't love," Rory said. "But my brother, my friends, and even my father know I have feelings for you."

His father didn't come out and say it, but he pushed him to go to the park with Bernard back in April.

"I'm here for you, Rory. I've had feelings for you for years too. I never thought this day would come. I'm here though. Whatever you need, I'm here for you."

"I want to kiss you," Rory said.

"You want to kiss me?"

"Yes, I've thought about it before, and I want to know what it's like to kiss you."

"I'd love nothing more than to kiss you."

Rory pressed his lips against Bernard's, heat surging through his body as they connected. He pushed his tongue into Bernard's mouth, searching for his tongue. His body exploded into a hundred emotions. He explored Bernard's body as they embraced, touching every inch of the man he'd dreamed of being with. Bernard's kiss was better than he'd ever imagined, and he wanted more of him. He wanted all of Bernard's body against his.

"That felt right," Rory said as he released the kiss.

"You feel right," Bernard said.

"I want to go on a proper date with you. I want to take you out."

"I'd love that."

"Does next Saturday work?" Rory said.

"Yes, next Saturday will be great." Bernard's beautiful brown eyes gazed into his. "What did you want to do?"

"I'll plan something. It'll be a surprise. I want to spend the whole day with you."

"I look forward to it."

"Can I stay here a little and just have you hold me?"

"Of course."

Bernard held him against his chest. The sound of their breathing filled the silence as they drifted off to sleep.

Rory woke to hear Bernard gasping for breath. He watched for a moment, and Bernard would stop breathing, then gasp.

"Bernard, wake up." He shook him.

"What—what happened?"

"You stopped breathing," Rory said.

"Oh, yeah. That happens if I don't use my CPAP."

"You use a CPAP? I'm sorry, I didn't know."

"It's okay, I don't talk about it much."

"I'm sorry, you fell asleep because of me. You should have been able to go to bed."

Rory closed his eyes, fighting back tears. He'd prevented Bernard from going to bed and using his machine to make sure he breathed.

Bernard pulled him in tight. "You don't have to be sorry. Holding you was worth it."

"Still, you shouldn't do that again."

"I promise I won't do it again."

"I should head home. I have to make the preparations for our date. I'll pick you up at ten next Saturday."

"I can't wait." Bernard leaned in to kiss him. Their lips met and Rory felt sparks shoot through him, stronger than the last kiss.

I'll never get enough of his kisses.

"You are an amazing kisser," Rory said.

"You have such a sweet kiss. I like it."

Rory's face warmed. This was his first kiss, and Bernard had enjoyed it as much as him.

*

AS HE DROVE home, adrenaline rushed through his body. He was disobeying the church and his mother. Bernard was in his heart. He'd had feelings for him since high school. He'd get the chance to fulfill his dreams of being happy. Of being with someone who cared about him.

Rory slept better that night than he had in months. A day with Bernard would be magical. He would give Bernard the date he deserved, one that ended with a kiss and a promise to do it again. They could be happy together.

Chapter Twenty

Rory

Saturday, July 18

RORY PULLED INTO Bernard's driveway at a quarter to ten on Saturday. It was their first official date, and excitement filled every part of him. A date with his best friend, the man he should have asked out years ago.

He had a spring in his step as he made his way to the door. He took a breath and knocked.

"Good morning," Bernard said.

His warm smile eased the knot in Rory's stomach.

"Good morning, are you ready for our...our date?" Rory's cheeks warmed at the words.

"I'm ready. What do you have planned?"

"Well, I thought we could start with mini golf at that little place in San Jose, then we could grab lunch."

"I think this is going to be the best date I've ever been on."

"That's not all," Rory said. "I have tickets to a show, then we can complete the evening with dinner, and then I'll bring you home."

"Are you expecting a goodnight kiss?" Bernard giggled.

"Let's see how the evening goes, and then we can decide."

He yearned to kiss Bernard and feel his warm, soft lips pressed against his own.

They headed to Casey's Mini Golf Extravaganza. Neither of them was good at mini golf. They kept hitting the side of objects or past the hole.

Rory stumbled along the path, and Bernard caught him, laughing.

"Hey, move along and make out somewhere else." A husky voice came from behind them.

They both looked over to see a man with two children by his side.

Rory turned to Bernard. He had the same look he had when the guy told them to stop hugging in the park back in April.

"Bernard," he whispered. "Leave it. He didn't say anything offensive. He has children with him."

"You're right, I'm sorry."

Bernard didn't confront the man, which Rory appreciated. He'd only ever seen Bernard angry a few times, and each time it was because someone directed hate toward him. He kept Bernard calm, which brought a smile to his face. Bernard respected him enough to not cause a scene, and it was endearing.

Rory won the game by two points.

"That last shot was lucky," Bernard said as they sat down for lunch.

"Maybe I'm just really good," Rory laughed.

Rory chose a cozy diner for lunch. He got a club sandwich with chips and soda, and Bernard ordered a burger, fries, and a root beer.

"I'm having a wonderful time," Bernard said.

"I'm so happy to hear that. I was pretty nervous."

Rory bowed his head. He couldn't look Bernard in the eyes.

Bernard reached across the table and placed his hand over his. Bernard's touch warmed his heart.

"It's okay to be nervous," Bernard said. "I'm still nervous. It's been so long since I've had a date."

"I've never had an actual date."

"I know, and I know you're scared of what might happen. That's okay. I'm here with you. I like being with you."

Rory smiled. "I like being with you too."

They ate and discussed what they wanted for their futures. While they'd been friends for years, they never discussed what the other looked for in someone they wanted to date.

"I looked for someone like you," Bernard said. "I think I always wanted to be with someone who cared about me as much as you do."

"You did?"

"Yes. You've always been sweet, caring, compassionate, and a wonderful friend. What more could I ask for in a partner?"

The answer took him aback. Bernard wanted someone like him as a partner. He'd never imagined he'd be someone's type, and here his best friend told him he was worthy of being his partner.

"I never truly understood my feelings," Rory said. "The church made

202 - Jole Cannon

me reject my feelings. Now that I'm here with you, I don't feel that it's wrong. You are the one I've wanted to be with, always."

"We are here now, and I'll never let you go again."

Rory searched Bernard's eyes as they held hands. He was honest, protective, and a kind and patient man. This was what he'd waited for.

They finished lunch and headed to the theater. They shuffled in for the two o'clock matinee.

It was a large theater, and he'd got tickets in the third row.

"How did you get tickets so close to the front?"

"Jeff's uncle owns the theater. He holds on to tickets in the first few rows. I asked about them right after you said yes and got tickets for the show."

"That was so sweet of you."

They watched *Who's Afraid of Virginia Woolf?*

The performance captivated Rory. He was never interested in theater, but Bernard liked stage plays in high school, and hoped he still enjoyed them.

"That was a wonderful play," Bernard said as they moved with the crowd.

"I'm glad you enjoyed it."

"Didn't you like it?"

"I was never interested in stage plays, but this performance was amazing. I need to go to the theater with you more often," Rory said.

"If you didn't think you'd enjoy it, why did you get tickets?"

"Because you like them."

Bernard wrapped his arms around Rory. The pressure took the air out of his lungs.

"That is the sweetest thing anyone has done for me."

Bernard pulled away and looked at Rory. Tears formed in Bernard's eyes.

"I'm glad I could make you smile."

"You are the most wonderful person in the world."

"Thank you."

*

RORY DROVE THEM to a little restaurant, Café Des Amis. It was in downtown San Jose, and parking was a nightmare.

"This looks fancy," Bernard said.

"I made reservations."

"I'm going to guess one of your grad friends has an in?"

"Yes. Nicolas's mom runs it."

"Look at you, using connections to impress me. How sweet."

"I wanted tonight to be special, so I called in a few favors."

"That makes me feel special."

They sat down to eat. They both ordered the special, chicken cordon bleu. Rory ordered a glass of wine, while Bernard selected iced tea.

"Hello, gentlemen." A tall woman approached the table. She'd tied her blonde hair in a bun on the back of her head.

Rory had met Nicolas's mom a few times. She was a wonderful woman.

"Hello, Mrs. Dubois," Rory said.

"Hello, Rory." She held out her hand. "It is nice to see you again." She had a thick French accent.

Nicolas's parents moved to the States in the seventies, just before

Nicolas was born. They both came from wealthy families, which allowed them comfort in their new homeland. Despite their wealth, they were kind and giving people. They donated to multiple charities.

"Who is this handsome friend of yours?"

"This is my date, Bernard," he said. "Bernard, this is Nicolas's mom, Mrs. Dubois."

"Enough formalities," she said. "Call me Marie."

Bernard took her hand. "It's a pleasure to meet you, Marie."

"Are you gentlemen enjoying your meal?"

"Yes, it's amazing," Rory said.

"It's fantastic," Bernard said.

"That is wonderful to hear."

"I have a question about the restaurant's name," Bernard said.

"You want to know why I chose it."

Bernard nodded.

"Me and a friend opened this restaurant twenty years ago. The name translates to friends' cafe. She has since passed, but I held on to the name."

"That is so sweet of you," Bernard said.

"Merci. Well, if you need anything, please let your server know and I will make it happen."

"Thank you," they both said.

They finished their dinner, leaving nothing on their plate.

"Want to get dessert?" Rory asked.

"Let's see what they have."

Rory decided on cherry clafoutis, and Bernard ordered a chocolate mousse.

Rory savored the decadent dessert. He wanted the recipe and would ask Nicolas if Marie would share it. It could be a guarded secret, but there was no harm in asking.

"I need to tell you something, Bernard," Rory said. His hands shook. He forced himself to calm his breathing.

"What is it?"

"I want to tell you the real reason I didn't talk to you for six years."

"You were in grad school. I understand."

"No, it's more than that."

Rory's vision blurred as he took in Bernard's features. He was so handsome. His smile, his dimple, and his brown eyes behind those blue-rimmed glasses.

"What is it?" Bernard placed a hand on Rory's shaking one. "You can tell me anything."

"I…my feelings for you were growing stronger," he said, "and I didn't know how to deal with them. After what Jason did to you, I knew you deserved better. I was so angry that the men you dated treated you so horribly, that you deserved better. I thought I could be better for you. That scared me, and I was afraid if I stayed, I'd do something that I'd regret. So, I broke contact hoping those feelings would go away."

"Since we're here, I'm guessing the feelings didn't go away."

"No." Rory shook his head. "When I saw you at your dad's house, the feelings came flooding back. I thought I could suppress them and be friends, but I wanted more. It took my friends to convince me to ask you out."

"I'm glad they did," Bernard said. "I'd thought about you for a long time."

"I still can't believe you thought of me so much." Rory smiled.

Rory stared into Bernard's eyes. So many wasted years. If he'd asked him out when he realized his feelings, Bernard wouldn't have gone through those horrible relationships. Rory hated Jason and Tracy for what they did to him. They were heartless, and if he ever saw either of them again, he didn't know if he could hold back.

"We're here now, and that's what matters," Bernard said, squeezing his hand where it rested on the table.

Once they'd finished dessert, Rory paid, and they headed back to Gilroy.

"I hope you've enjoyed the day with me," Rory said, getting out of the car.

He walked over and opened Bernard's door for him.

"Thank you." Bernard got out of the car.

Bernard placed his hand in Rory's as they walked up to the porch. Anxiety filled his heart. He was going to kiss Bernard.

"I had a wonderful time," Bernard said.

"I don't want this night to end."

Rory looked into Bernard's eyes. His glasses magnified the golden specks in his brown eyes.

"Well, it's the first night of many, I hope."

"I know it will be the first night of so many nights together. I don't want to be apart from you again."

"I want you in my life. Closer than a friend," Bernard said.

They stood on Bernard's porch. The light illuminated their faces. Rory looked into Bernard's eyes. He was handsome. He reached out to take both of Bernard's hands in his.

"I'm so glad you said yes when I asked you out," Rory said. "I was afraid you'd say no. Because I didn't know if I'd be the right guy for you."

"I am so glad you asked me out," Bernard said. "You are the perfect guy for me."

Rory leaned in, Bernard's warm breath on his face.

"What in God's name are you doing?" A shrill voice echoed in the cul-de-sac.

Rory jolted away from Bernard and turned to the street. Standing there in her church clothes stood his mother. Her face twisted in disgust at the sight of them.

"Mother, why are you here?" There was no reason for her to show up at Bernard's. He didn't even know if she knew where he lived.

"When you didn't come to service, I got worried," she said. "So, I checked at your place and you weren't there."

She stormed up the steps to face Rory.

"I figured you must have come to his house." She pointed at Bernard. "Mr. Silva told me where he lived."

"Mother, I…"

"I don't want to hear it. You get home right now and we're going to have a talk."

"With all due respect, Mrs. Sinclair," Bernard said. "Rory is a grown man and can make his own decisions."

"Like you did, you faggot!" she yelled.

Rory winced at the word.

"You have filled his head with indecent ideas and thoughts of perversion," she said.

"Mother, please," Rory begged, tears of humiliation filling his eyes. "He didn't do anything wrong."

"I want this piece of garbage to know what he's done to you," she spat. "He's corrupted you into thinking you're a queer like him."

"Excuse me?" Bernard stood at his full height. "Rory asked me out."

"My son would never do something like this on his own!"

"I asked him out, Mother," Rory said.

"He must have tricked you." She grabbed his hand. "Now, let's go before he tricks you into something more sinister than a kiss."

"You have no right, you controlling bitch," Bernard said.

Rory and his mother looked at him. Bernard's hands covered his mouth and his eyes went wide.

"You can't talk to my mother that way." Heat rose through Rory's body. He balled his hands into fists. "Despite what she does, she's my mother and I won't allow anyone to talk to her that way."

"I...I..." Bernard sputtered.

"Maybe I was wrong," Rory said. "Maybe you're not the man I thought you were."

Rory allowed his mother to lead him down the stairs. He turned to see tears streaming down Bernard's face.

"Rory, I'm sorry," Bernard choked. "I shouldn't have...I want to be with you."

"It doesn't matter what a pervert like you wants," his mother said. "Your kind is an abomination who preys on the weak. My son is better off not knowing you."

Rory turned and walked to his car in silence.

He made it home before his mother, and he sat on his couch.

His mother entered, a soft expression on her face.

"Oh, poor dear," she said. "I can't believe he said those awful things about me."

There was no sign of his father. Did his father know what his mother did? He encouraged him to be himself. Did he not approve of him being gay? Did Rory misunderstand?

"I've never heard him talk like that before," Rory said.

"Well, that's what sinful people do." She sat down next to him. "They trick you, and their true colors show when you confront them."

Rory leaned against his mother. "I thought I loved him."

"I know you did, dear." She rubbed his hair. "That's what he wanted you to think."

Rory cried in his mother's arms.

"You get some sleep, and we'll see you at service in the morning."

She kissed him on the head and stood. She walked to one of his surfaces and ran a finger across it, then rubbed her index and thumb together.

"Maybe you should do some cleaning," she said. "That might take your mind off of everything." She closed the door behind her. Rory was alone.

He lay on the couch. Tears streamed down his face. Conflict battled in his mind. His mother had called Bernard a faggot. A horrible thing to call someone. Would she call him one too? Bernard called her a bitch, but it was in retaliation to what she'd said.

He curled up tighter. Mina jumped to his face and licked his tears.

"Thank you, baby girl."

She curled up on his side as he cried himself to sleep, unsure of what to do.

Chapter Twenty-One

Bernard

Sunday, July 19

BERNARD STUMBLED THROUGH the house, eyes burning from a restless night. He fed and watered Ginger, then sat at the kitchen table, unable to make food or coffee.

"What am I going to do? I've ruined everything."

Fresh tears filled his eyes.

"I don't deserve love because I ruin everything and push away everyone who tries to love me."

He grabbed the bag from the liquor store. He'd bought five bottles of whiskey after Rory left. They remained unopened.

Bernard opened a bottle. He grabbed a glass, filled it with ice, and poured himself a whiskey. Ginger lay at his feet and watched as he drank his pain away.

He drank glass after glass. His vision blurred, and the pain intensified. The more he drank, the more he realized how he had ruined his relationship with Rory. Rory deserved better.

He wasn't sure how much time had passed, or what time it was when there was a knock at the door.

Bernard stumbled to the door and opened it to see Sean. He squinted his eyes. He'd dressed in his Giants' gear.

"Hey…" Sean stopped. "What happened?"

"Huh?"

"Did you drink all that?" He pointed to the whiskey.

Bernard looked down. A quarter of the bottle was gone.

"Yes."

He tried to focus on Sean. Sean was sexy. A short, stocky, beefy bear of a man. He remembered that night and how great it felt to have Sean inside him. Would Sean ravage him again?

"It's nine in the morning. Let's get you inside."

Sean led Bernard back to the table. Bernard sat down and stared at the whisky bottle. He was about to pour another glass when Sean took it.

"I think you've had enough of that."

"Sean, I want you naked again," Bernard said.

"Sit here. I'm going to make some coffee."

Bernard registered Sean in his kitchen, and the smell of coffee warmed his senses.

"Did you hear me?"

"I heard you," Sean said, "and I know it's the whisky talking."

"No, that was one of the best nights of my life. I want to do it again."

"You don't," Sean said. "You want Rory naked in bed with you, not me."

Tears formed at the mention of Rory. It would never happen now. He'd made sure of it. Rory wouldn't talk to him again, let alone get naked with him.

Sean brought over a hot cup of coffee and placed it in front of him.

"I thought you stopped drinking years ago," Sean said.

Bernard picked up the coffee in front of him and drank. The bitter liquid slid down his throat.

"I did until I ruined everything with Rory. I don't deserve to be happy." Bernard put his face against the table. "I screwed up, Sean. He's gone because of me."

"Tell me what happened." Sean sat across from him with his cup of coffee.

Bernard told him everything that happened.

"So, I did it. I pushed away the one man who wanted to date me, just like I always do."

He'd never verbalized it. Every date he had after Tracy ended because he wasn't ready. He told them as much. He didn't even have a second date with any of the men Sarah set him up with. Sean was the first guy he slept with after Tracy, and that was the first time he thought about continuing a relationship. Then Sean told him he wasn't interested in a relationship. That's when he gave up on finding love.

"She called you what?" Sean asked.

"A faggot."

"She is a bitch."

"Sean!"

"What?"

"That's Rory's mom."

"I don't give a shit who she is. That's a disgusting thing to call some-one."

Bernard lowered his head. She had used a vile term, but he shouldn't have retaliated. He needed to stay calm for Rory, but he didn't.

The phone rang as Bernard continued to sip his coffee.

"I'll get it. Stay here." Sean got up and walked to Bernard's kitchen phone.

"Hello?" Sean stood silent. "This is Sean, I'm a friend of Bernard's. I came to get him for a ball game."

Sean stood as the voice on the other end spoke.

"Nice to meet you, Kelly. So, if you have no plans, maybe you can come over to Bernard's. He might need another friend."

After saying thanks and goodbye, Sean hung up.

"You're going to miss the game," Bernard said. "I'm sorry I've ruined your day."

"It's just one game." Sean put his arm around him. "There will be more. What's important right now is to help you."

*

TIME SLIPPED BY and there was a knock at the door.

"I'll get it," Sean said.

Voices drifted into the kitchen. Bernard strained to hear but couldn't make out any words.

He picked up his head to see Kelly and Sean sitting across the table.

"Sean told me what happened," Kelly said.

"We want to help," Sean said.

"There's nothing you can do. I've destroyed my one chance at happiness."

It was true. After the way he treated Rory and his mother, Rory would never come back.

"That's not true," Kelly said. "If it were, then we'd all give up."

"What am I supposed to do?" Bernard stood. He grabbed the table to balance himself. "I called his mom a bitch. He won't talk to me after that."

"I don't agree with calling her a bitch, but she pushed you. Calling someone a faggot is much worse. She sounds like a horrible, controlling person," Kelly said.

"I apologized, but it was too late. Now I'll probably never see him again."

Bernard broke down in tears. Sean and Kelly got on either side of him and consoled him.

"John's off today too," Kelly said. "Why don't we grab him and have a boys' day out?"

"I don't think I'll be much fun," Bernard said.

"It'll be great. We'll head over to Santa Cruz and hit up the boardwalk. We'll have fun."

Kelly picked up the phone and dialed.

"Hey John, it's Kelly. Are you busy today?" Silence. "Perfect. Sean, a friend of Bernard's, and I are taking him to Santa Cruz and wondered if you'd like to join us?"

Sean and Kelly helped Bernard dress after forcing him to shower, then dragged him out to Sean's SUV. Kelly brought Ginger and Chester with him.

"We can leave Ginger and Chester with Sarah," Kelly said.

They stopped at John and Sarah's house, unloaded the dogs, and loaded up John.

"So, what's the issue?" John looked at Bernard. "Man, what happened?"

Bernard had to listen to the story of how he screwed up his relationship with Rory again as Sean and Kelly retold it.

"Man, that's harsh," John said. "I'm sure it'll work out. You just need to give him time."

"What would you have done if Sarah called your mom a bitch with you standing right there?" Bernard asked.

"Well, she has," John said. "When we were first dating. Didn't she tell you?"

Bernard thought hard. He didn't remember Sarah ever mentioning it. If she called John's mom any names, he was unaware of it.

"She never told me."

"Well," John said. "I won't go into details. But she called my mom a bitch once. It hurt. But we got through it."

Bernard cocked an eyebrow.

"I got past it because I knew she didn't mean it and it was out of anger," John said.

"Are you close with your mom?" Bernard said.

"Yeah, but I know we're not as close as Rory and his mother. It might take time."

"He'll come around," Sean said. "You've known him for a long time. I'm sure he'll forgive you."

"The fact he's in love with you helps too," Kelly said.

"What?" Bernard asked.

"We know he's in love with you," John said.

"We just had one date," Bernard said.

"Yeah, but I've seen how he looks at you," John said. "I'm surprised it took this long for you two to go on a date."

Rory told him he wanted someone he could talk to and be honest with, like him. He'd said being in the cafe with him was what he wanted. The question remained, was he in love with Rory? He didn't see why he couldn't be. Rory had always been on his mind. Someone he thought about more than anyone. He thought about Rory more than Jason or Tracy when he dated them. Rory had also been there to pick him up when both of them hurt him. He'd also masturbated to thoughts of Rory with him.

"We're here," Sean said.

They got out and entered the park. Bernard had sobered up after the car ride. They'd stopped to get food in his stomach.

Kelly bought wristbands for everyone, John said he'd pay for drinks, and Sean would buy lunch. They all refused to allow Bernard to pay for anything. This day was for him. Bernard couldn't imagine having a better group of friends.

The four of them went on every ride they could, from the Big Dipper to the Ferris Wheel. John, Kelly, and Sean all took time out of their lives to spend it with him. They wanted to make sure he had a fun day out instead of wallowing at home with a bottle of booze. He regretted drinking again.

It never ended well.

John and Kelly whispered a few feet away while Sean bought corn dogs for everyone.

"Hey Bernard, want to join me on the Gondola?" Kelly said.

"Sure, sounds fun."

"We'll meet you guys back here," John said.

"All right," Kelly said.

They got in line to get on the Gondola. It took guests from one side of the park to the other. Kelly insisted they ride to the other side and back.

As they rode across the park, Kelly asked if he was doing okay.

"I don't know. Thank you for being here for me."

"Well, you helped me move on your time. So, it's only fair."

"I think this is a little different, but I appreciate what you're all doing for me. I couldn't ask for a better group of friends."

"Thank you."

Bernard had a small group of friends in high school. Their number dwindled to two when he came out. Now, he had a group of friends he fit in with.

"So, I wanted to tell you something," Kelly said.

"What is it?"

"Remember when you saw me in the bathroom, and the scars on my chest and back?"

"Yes, I remember."

"Well, I thought now would be a good time to tell you what happened."

"Kelly, you don't have to."

"I know," he said. "But I think it's important. I don't have many friends and you've been a wonderful friend. I wanted you to know."

Bernard looked at him. Kelly smiled. He'd come out of his shell with Bernard. He seemed reserved before, but now he was talking about a horrible part of his past.

"Well, my ex left those scars."

Bernard stayed quiet. He didn't know how to respond to this. He'd known men whose partners abused them, but none of them talked about it.

"He and I started dating when I was twenty. He was ten years older than me. It started out great. But two years into the relationship he... changed."

Tears formed in Kelly's eyes as he spoke. Bernard could only imagine how hard it was to go through the abuse and now to talk about it.

"It was little things at first. Just disregarding my feelings, or telling me I didn't do the dishes right, or dinner wasn't ready on time."

Bernard sat in silence.

"He started putting cigars out on my chest and stomach," Kelly choked. "During sex, he cut deep into my back with his nails."

"Kelly, I don't know what to say."

"You listening is all I need." Kelly took a deep breath and continued. "He berated me daily. He physically and emotionally abused me. You'd think a guy my size wouldn't have put up with that. But I was twenty-two, and smaller. He was big, I mean huge. He scared me." Kelly was crying now.

Bernard reached an arm around to comfort him. He watched this mountain of a man cry. Kelly made himself vulnerable. Bernard stayed silent, letting Kelly lead the conversation.

"For eight years I stayed. For eight years he abused me. I gained weight. I became depressed, and I let it continue."

"Kelly, you can't blame yourself. That man sounds evil."

"I don't blame myself anymore, but I did for a long time. I went to the police, but they laughed at me. Four years ago, I left him. I couldn't bear to stay in the same town, so I moved here. John and Sarah helped."

Bernard now had both arms wrapped around Kelly. His body jerked with each sob.

"So, I'm here and I'm healing. I have friends like you to help me."

"Thank you for trusting me, it means a lot."

"I wanted you to know, so you knew why I didn't want to date. I think you're a great guy, but what I've gone through still haunts me."

"Rory asked if I would have dated you if we'd both been ready," Bernard said. "I said I didn't know."

"Who knows. If things had been different, I might have considered a date. What I know now is you've become a wonderful friend, and that's what I needed. I'm still not ready to date, but I know one day I'll be ready. One day I'll find someone special."

"You will."

"But you're ready now," Kelly said. "You told me you weren't ready when we talked. But I know you were. You just needed the right man. That man is Rory. You belong together. You can't let him go."

"I—"

"No excuses," Kelly said. "I lived a lie for years. I know what it's like. You've been single for so many years, and you deserve happiness. You deserve love."

Bernard tightened his grip around Kelly. Tears filled his eyes. Kelly was right. If this man, who'd been through hell and back with his ex, could see there was still hope for himself, then Bernard could do the same. He wanted nothing more than to be with Rory. He loved Rory but didn't know how to get him back.

"So, I just have to figure out what to do. He's probably still mad at me."

"The best thing to do is let him know how sorry you are. Let him know you made a mistake and that you'll be here when he's ready. He will come around. He loves you."

"Thanks, Kelly."

They finished the Gondola ride and met back up with Sean and John.

*

THE SUN WAS SETTING when they left the park. Sean dropped off John, picked up Chester and Ginger, and took Kelly and Bernard to Bernard's house.

"I wanted to thank you both for a wonderful day," Bernard said. "It was eye-opening. I'm ready to move forward."

Bernard hugged them both and waved as they left.

He filled Ginger's food and water bowls. Bernard showered and got ready for bed. It was a long day. He'd had a great time. He still thought about what Kelly said. Kelly had opened up to him about his past, but still made it about Bernard. He wanted Bernard to be happy. He didn't hit on him, flirt with him, he was a genuine friend. Kelly advised reaching out to Rory.

He put on *When Harry Met Sally…*. Harry and Sally, after bickering for years, fell in love with each other. He was in love with Rory. He wanted to be with him. The phone called to him. He yearned to call Rory and hear his voice. Time ticked by and he hadn't decided. He needed to decide what to do. One call couldn't hurt. One call could fix everything. One call could ruin everything. Everything rode on what he did next.

Chapter Twenty-Two

Bernard

Monday, July 20–Friday, July 24

BERNARD MADE HIS way through another week of work without contact with Rory. He checked his answering machine every morning when he woke up. Nothing. He came home every day and checked it. Nothing. He took Ginger for a walk and checked it when he got home. Nothing.

On Wednesday evening Bernard met up with Kelly at the dog park. They met every Monday and Wednesday for their dogs' play date. Time spent with his friend eased the tension in his stomach. The tension caused by his actions that had led to Rory's absence in his life.

"How are you doing?" Kelly asked.

"Honestly?"

"Of course. I want to know how you've been."

They sat down on the bench. Bernard took a breath. Kelly knew the situation and wouldn't judge him. He was a wonderful man. He'd opened up to Bernard about his past. Nothing he could say would scare Kelly away.

"Not so good," Bernard said. "I miss him so much."

"I know you do."

"I've been waiting to hear from him, but he hasn't called yet."

"He may need more time," Kelly said. "There's no telling how long it'll take for his scars to heal. He's close to his mother from what I've heard, so that had to be hard for him to hear."

"I know. I just hope he can forgive me."

Bernard would take any punishment imaginable as long as Rory forgave him. His heart pounded with every thought. Dogs barked in the park, happy to play with one another. He thought back to when he reunited with Rory. They'd watched Bonnie and Ginger play. So innocent and free. They had wanted that.

"You have to remember who raised him," Kelly said. "That woman is horrible. I'm sure it's hard for Rory to know what to think."

"I wasn't as patient with him as I could have been. I know what it's like in the church, and I lashed out. I wish he could see what his mother is."

"I'm sure with enough love and patience from you, he will. You need to let him know how you feel."

"I will, I promise."

"I trust you'll do the right thing."

"So, how are you doing?"

Bernard wanted to show support for Kelly. He was in a strange new place and needed a friend to reassure him he was in a safe place.

"I'm really good," Kelly said. "I'm going to turn one of my spare rooms into a little library."

"That sounds amazing."

"I'm sure you've noticed all my books. I had more, but..."

"I know." Bernard placed a hand on his shoulder. "You had some horrible years. You were strong enough to get away though. Now you're here, and we won't let anything happen to you. I promise."

"Thank you," Kelly said. "That means a lot."

They walked home together. Kelly's house was closer, so they stopped by his place first.

"Hey, I haven't eaten yet," Kelly said. "I'm going to order a pizza if you want to join me."

Bernard was quick to agree. Since his fight with Rory, he hadn't had the energy to cook and was going to order takeout anyway. And this way, he wouldn't be eating alone.

"Sure, I'm in."

When the pizza arrived covered in pepperoni, sausage, bell pepper, and extra cheese, they dug right in.

"This is great," Bernard said.

"I only order Round Table Pizza," he said.

"I haven't had it in years. It's wonderful."

They finished the pizza and talked for a bit about life and work.

Bernard checked his watch. "It's getting late, I better head home."

"It was great having you," Kelly said. "Thanks for having dinner with me."

"Thanks for cheering me up."

They hugged, and Bernard headed home with Ginger.

There were no messages when he got home, so he went to bed.

*

THURSDAY WAS THE same as the rest of the week. No calls from Rory.

"You need to reach out to him," Sarah said during lunch on Friday afternoon.

They'd decided on Carl's Burger Hut for lunch today. It was a bit of a drive, but well worth it.

Carl's only had outdoor seating. Bernard and Sarah grabbed a table outside and placed their orders.

He decided on a Philly cheesesteak with onion rings and iced tea. Sarah ordered a burger with fries and diet soda.

"I know," he said. "That's what Kelly said."

"That's right, you guys have dog play dates. How's that going?"

"It's going great. We meet on Mondays and Wednesdays, and we had dinner at his place Wednesday."

"I'm so glad you guys are getting along. It's good to see you spending time with friends."

"It's nice." He smiled. "Now, I need to figure out what to say to Rory. I miss him."

"I know you miss him. You will find the words. Just speak from your heart."

"I know. It's just really hard," he said. "So, how's the adoption going?" He changed the subject. He wanted to talk about Rory, but it felt repetitive. Everyone gave their advice and nothing more would come of just rehashing it.

"It's going great." Sarah's face lit up. "We didn't want to say anything yet, but we are supposed to pick him up at the end of this month. His name is Michael, but he goes by Mikey, he's four, and he is the most adorable kid."

She pulled out a picture. A small blond boy with large round blue eyes stared back at the camera. His clothes hung on his thin frame.

"He's so cute," Bernard said.

"We're setting up his room now. He'll have a bed, toys, and everything he needs. I'm so excited."

"That's amazing," Bernard said. "I'm so happy for you two. You're going to make wonderful parents."

"Thank you." She beamed.

"So, what are you going to do about work?"

"I've put in for a leave of absence for a year. I'll stay home with him and take care of him. Once he starts school next year, I can go back part time."

"I'm gonna miss my carpool buddy, but I understand."

"You'll be fine."

Bernard bit into his food. The juice slid down his throat. Rich salty beef mixed with the warm cheese and onions. The combination produced a perfect cheesesteak.

"This is fantastic," Bernard said. "I'm glad we came here."

"It is superb."

They finished up their meal and headed back to the office. In three weeks, Bernard would make the trip alone. He and Sarah had been making this trip together for over five years. They'd missed a few trips here and there. Now, he'd have to do it alone for a year. Talking to her was therapeutic.

"Hey, Bernard?" A voice at his door woke him from his dreamlike state.

"Hey, Rich," Bernard said. "What can I do for you?"

Rich stood in a well-fitted tan suit. It emphasized his muscular build. Rich was a strict boss. He valued hard work and dedication. He was genuine and kind to all his employees and everyone liked him.

"I'm just coming to check on you," he said.

"Oh. Did someone say something?"

Sweat permeated Bernard's pits. He was out to four of his coworkers. Rich was not one of them. If anyone asked, he wouldn't lie, but he'd rather keep his personal life under wraps.

"Not at all," he said. "May I sit down?"

Bernard indicated an empty chair. His mouth dried out. He tried to swallow, but nothing came. He grabbed his coffee and took a sip.

Rich shut the door. He sat across from Bernard with his infectious smile.

"So, to what do I owe the pleasure?" Bernard managed.

"I've just noticed you acting differently, and I wanted to check on you."

"I'm fine."

Rich raised an eyebrow. "I don't think you are. Do you need some time off?"

"No, I'm saving my time for a nice vacation next summer."

"Okay, but if you need time off, let us know. I'm sure we can find someone to cover your caseload while you're out."

"Thank you," Bernard said. "Is there something that drew your attention to me?"

"You just seem stressed, and that can have a negative effect on your work."

Bernard looked into Rich's eyes. He couldn't tell what his boss was getting at. His body tensed. Goose bumps ran up his arm. Bernard concentrated on his breathing.

"Everything is fine." Bernard took another sip of coffee.

"If you're stressed, just let me know. I'd rather you take some time and come back fresh than to underperform."

Bernard had a clean work record. He'd always performed above standards. If his performance drew the attention of Rich, he needed to fix it.

"I'll let you know," Bernard said.

"Okay." Rich stood. "I'll see you on Monday."

Rich closed the door on his way out.

*

BERNARD TOLD SARAH what happened on the way home.

"What?" she said.

"I need to get it together. This thing with Rory is affecting my work."

"Call him," Sarah said.

"Sarah. I—"

"You obviously miss him. I'm sure he misses you. He's going through a lot right now, and it is compounded by the fact that his overbearing mother and the man he's in love with are at odds with each other. You need to reach out to him."

"Okay, I'll call this weekend."

"Good, now get home and work out what you're going to say."

*

BERNARD ARRIVED HOME and checked the messages. There was one from his brother, checking in on him. He called back and they talked for a few minutes about life, work, and how their dad was doing.

Bernard went for his evening walk with Ginger. The warm air filled his lungs. The scent of grilled meats and vegetables wafted from backyards as he passed. His mouth watered and his stomach growled.

His walk took him to the local park. Children played with their parents on the swings and slides. A few dads watched their children. Would he have children one day?

He walked home, filled Ginger's bowls, and grabbed leftovers for dinner.

He tried watching TV, but nothing interested him.

He looked over at the phone. Rory hadn't called. He wanted to hear his voice. Hear his laugh. Hold him. Kiss him. He wanted to be with him. He'd never felt this way before and may never feel it again. Rory might be out of his life forever, and it was his fault.

They hadn't spoken in a week. He couldn't resist anymore. He had to call. It was Friday evening and Rory would be home.

The phone rang, and he heard Rory's voice.

"You've reached Rory Sinclair. I can't answer the phone right now. Please leave a message and I'll call you back."

"Rory, I wanted to say I'm sorry. I'm sorry I lashed out. Your mother said some nasty things, and they weren't just directed at me, they were directed at you. I didn't want you to face that kind of hatred from your own family. I miss you and I want you back in my life. I want to talk and work this out. Please call me."

Bernard breathed a sigh of relief. He'd reached out and let Rory know how he felt. He prayed Rory would return his call.

Bernard went to bed crying. He hugged his pillow.

"Lord, if you can hear me, please bring Rory back to me. I miss him and need him back in my life."

He'd hurt Rory. He didn't care how Mrs. Sinclair felt. She was a selfish, spiteful woman. Rory deserved to be happy, and he'd be damned if he let that woman ruin his happiness.

Chapter Twenty-Three

Rory

Friday, July 24–Sunday, July 26

IT WAS FRIDAY afternoon. A week had gone by since Rory and Bernard's date. Rory had little to occupy his time now that he'd started summer break. He needed to prepare for the classes he'd be teaching, but that wouldn't take long. He'd use the same curriculum he'd used for the last three years, with minor alterations.

His mother continued to try to convince him to take Missy out on a date. That would never happen, but his mother refused to give up. She was determined to find him a wife. He was sure Missy's mother was doing the same thing. They didn't know he and Missy had talked and didn't want to date.

Rory was finishing up lunch when the phone rang.

"Hello?" he said.

"Hey, Rory. It's Jeff. We're going out tonight and want you to join us."

"I'm not sure. I'm not feeling so good."

"Oh, are you sick?"

"No, it's just… Things have happened."

"Well, you need to come out and talk about it. We're here for you."

"I don't know."

"Drinks are on me?"

"Well, when you put it that way." Rory laughed. "Okay. You've convinced me and I hope you're ready for some sad stories."

"We wouldn't miss it for the world."

"Okay, see you at Shaffers at six-thirty, as usual?"

"We'll see you there."

Rory spent the afternoon cleaning his apartment, which relaxed him. When he was done, it was five. He showered and dressed.

He was heading out the door when the phone rang. He looked at his watch. It was almost six.

I don't want to be late. I'll check it later.

He shut the door and headed to Shaffers.

His friends sat at a table in the back when he arrived at six-thirty. He moved through the thick crowd to meet them. They each had a drink in front of them and a gin and tonic for him.

"Aww, you remembered what I drink," Rory said.

"Of course," Davi said.

"Okay, now what's going on?" Jeff said.

"Not much," Rory said.

"How's it going with Bernard?" Sophia asked.

"It's not going anywhere now."

"What happened?" they all said in unison.

"Well, it was our date last Saturday…"

Rory went into detail about their date and how much fun they'd had. Mini golf, the stage play, and dinner. He thanked each of them for helping him with the setup. He came to the end of the date. They almost kissed. His heart fluttered as his lips approached Bernard's. Then his mom arrived.

"Then he called her a controlling bitch," Rory said.

"He said what?" Sophia put her hand to her mouth.

"Yeah," Rory said, "so I left, and I haven't talked to him since."

"Has he tried contacting you?" Nicolas asked.

"No," Rory said. "He's probably never going to. I stormed away."

They all sat there in silence. He met each of their gazes. They'd convinced him to ask Bernard out. He could blame them for this, but he wouldn't. He'd had feelings for Bernard before they said anything to him. It was the push he needed, but it was a mistake. It was a bad idea from the start. The whole thing was absurd. He couldn't be in a relationship with a man. Rory had to live alone. His mother would hound him about finding a nice young lady. So long as he wasn't with a man, the church wouldn't consider him an abomination and excommunicate him. What else could he do?

"Are you going to call him?" Jeff asked.

"I can't call him," Rory said. "He insulted my mother."

"Bernard didn't seem like a horrible person to me," Davi said. "He seemed like a nice guy who cares about you."

"He called my mother a bitch though. Who does that?"

"Someone who's hurt," Sophia said.

"Or someone who sees something wrong happening and is angry about it," Nicolas said.

"She..." He stopped. She'd called him a faggot and accused Bernard of tricking him into going on a date.

"She pulled you away from him. You also said she told you never to see him and that he would corrupt you," Jeff said.

"She also called him a horrific word. Who calls someone that?" Davi said.

"Remember that man in the park? The one who confronted you and Bernard for hugging?" Sophia asked.

"What about him?"

"What he said to you and Bernard? Your mother sounds like she was doing the same thing."

"He made me question my faith."

Why was Rory defending his mother? She'd done horrible things.

Am I defending her because she's manipulated me into believing everything she says? My mother is in the wrong, not Bernard. What am I going to do?

"Oh please," Nicolas said. "You were friends with him for years before that date. Did he ever hit on you?"

"No."

"Did he ever try to get you into bed with him?" Jeff asked.

"No."

"Did he ever ask you out?" Sophia asked.

"No."

"Then he never tried to manipulate you," Nicolas said. "Your mother's telling you what to do, not Bernard. If he hasn't called, then he's giving you space. He's not trying to force something on you."

They had a point. Bernard always gave him space. He never asked him out or tried to get him naked. Bernard wasn't like the gays his mother warned him about. Bernard was a great man who he cared about.

They all finished up their drinks and said their goodbyes.

"Don't be too hard on Bernard," Sophia said. "He's a great guy. You need to give him another chance."

"I'll see how I feel after a few days."

"Don't wait too long," Jeff said. "Or you'll miss your chance."

*

THE CONVERSATION REPEATED in his mind on the drive home. They had valid points. His mother hurt and upset Bernard. He needed to talk to him, but he didn't know what to say.

He walked past his phone and ignored the blinking light. It could wait. He needed sleep now.

*

SATURDAY WENT BY in a blur of grocery shopping, errands, and cleaning.

Rory sat in the pew with his family on Saturday evening. His mother opted to sit next to him. She wrapped her arm around his shoulder and squeezed tight. He recoiled at her touch.

"I hope you're doing better, dear," she whispered in his ear. "You're better off without that Silva boy. He hurt you and you don't deserve to be hurt."

The thing was, he didn't feel Bernard hurt him. He did nothing to hurt him until his mother attempted to intervene. That's when Bernard became upset. He could see why. His mother was controlling. She forced him to live the life she wanted, rather than the one he wanted. She'd called Bernard a fag. He still didn't know how to approach Bernard. He needed to apologize for what he'd done, but also expected Bernard to apologize too. Bernard had insulted his mother. For all her faults, she was still his mother.

His mother met with the priest after church.

"Oh Father, that was a lovely service," she said.

"Thank you, Maeve, I'm glad it touched you," the Father said.

"It's so good to feel the Lord's spirit when you speak."

"I'm so blessed that the words moved you, my child."

"We must have you over for Sunday lunch one day."

Rory cocked an eyebrow. Father Joseph was not married and had no children. She didn't invite people who had no daughter to palm off on him over for Sunday lunch.

"That would be lovely," Father Joseph said.

"You have a niece, right?"

Here it was. She'd found out he and Missy had no connection and didn't want to date. Missy must have said something to her parents, and they didn't want to come over again. There was no other explanation.

"Yes, my niece Harriet."

"Oh, what a lovely name," his mother gushed. "How old is she now?"

"She's twenty-five now."

"Oh, what a wonderful age," she said. "Would she like to join us?"

Father Joseph raised his eyebrows. This man knew what Rory's mother was doing.

"I'm sure she would love to," he said. "As long as she could bring her fiancé."

"Oh, of course, he's welcome to join." His mother deflated. She'd wanted to set Rory up again, and it failed.

"Let us know when and we'll be happy to join you," Father Joseph said. "Now, I must be going. Have a blessed day."

The family moved to the exit to leave. Rory's parents whispered angrily back and forth as they made their way to the car. This was another argument about him. His father had insisted his mother stop trying to set him up, but she refused to give up. If only she knew. He only had eyes for one person. Bernard.

His parents invited him to dinner, and he reluctantly agreed. He didn't want to be alone.

*

RORY PICKED AT his food. He wasn't hungry. He'd barely eaten the past week.

"Mother, Father, I think I'm going to take a walk."

"Okay, dear," his mother said. "Take a sweater. It's a little chilly."

Rory grabbed his sweater from the hook and headed outside. He walked down the street. His mother was wrong. It wasn't cold. The warm August wind blew through his hair.

He walked with no purpose. His feet took him to the park. The same park where his father talked to him. The same park where his brother pushed him to accept who he was.

Rory sat on the bench and watched the wildlife. The birds sang to one another. It reminded him of being in the park with Bernard. He wanted to hold his hand. He wanted to kiss him. Now, he'd never see him again.

"May I join you?" His dad walked up to the bench.

"Yeah." Rory didn't look up.

"How are you feeling?"

"I don't know."

"Rory, I'm sorry about what happened between you and Bernard. I know you care about him."

"It's fine," Rory said. "Mother's right. It's disgusting and I should be ashamed of what I was doing. It's not normal."

"Your mother is wrong."

Rory stared at his dad. Crow's feet decorated the corners of his eyes. He'd turned sixty back in February. Rory's own green eyes looked back at him. Rory saw his future self in his dad.

"What?"

"Loving another man isn't disgusting, and there's nothing wrong with you."

"But the Bible–"

"The Bible doesn't determine who you can love."

"It says my love is a sin."

"I don't believe that at all," his dad said. "I loved a man once."

Rory gaped at his dad. He had never mentioned this. His dad was straight. He was married to his mother. How could he have been in love with a man?

"You?"

"His name was Angus. We went to school together. He and I kept it a secret for years. We were in love, but it was not acceptable."

Rory couldn't believe his ears. His father just admitted he loved a man.

"But you're with Mom?"

"Yes, I fell in love with your mom."

"You've loved both a man and a woman?"

"That's right. I'm attracted to men and women."

"Then, you're bisexual."

"Yes."

"What happened to Angus?"

"After we left school, we went our separate ways."

Tears formed in his father's eyes. The pain of the memory reflected on his face.

"We were from a small village. Someone was bound to find out. So, we separated. I haven't heard from him since."

The tears pooled around his cheeks. He wiped them away.

"You're still in love with him?"

"Yes, I've never forgotten him."

"I'm so sorry, Dad."

"It's okay. I love your mother dearly. I wouldn't trade our time together for anything."

"Why are you telling me this?"

"Because I know you have the same feelings for Bernard that I had for Angus." He placed a hand on Rory's shoulder. "The difference is you have shown no interest in women. I don't want you to live a life that makes you unhappy."

"But what do I do?"

"Do you still love him?"

"Yes, with all my heart."

"Then you need to decide if you want to be with him, wait for someone else to come along, or live alone."

"But...will I honor God?"

"I don't believe God will punish you for loving another man. You're both consenting adults, and what you do, so long as it doesn't harm others, is no one else's business."

Rory wrapped his arms around his father. "Thank you, Dad."

His dad held him tight.

"I want you to be happy," he said, "and don't worry about your mother. I'll help you when the time comes."

*

RORY STOPPED FOR fast food on his way home. He didn't want to cook; even reheating leftovers seemed daunting.

He said hello to Mina after she leaped onto his shoulder. She followed him into the bedroom. He changed into his pajamas and headed to the living room to watch television while he ate.

His father had given him a lot to think about. Bernard wasn't a mean person. He'd been protecting Rory in his own way. Rory had to make amends.

He walked into the kitchen to throw away his bag and the light on the answering machine still blinked.

I never checked that message.

He pushed play. Bernard's voice played. He apologized for what he'd said and had defended Rory.

Tears welled up in Rory's eyes as he dialed Bernard's number.

Please pick up. Please pick up.

"Hello?"

"Hi, Bernard."

Rory's heart ached. *He picked up.* Rory took three deep breaths. He didn't know what to say.

"Rory, are you there?" Bernard asked.

"I'm here, Bernard," he said. "I got your message. I'm sorry for not talking to you. I've realized what my mother has been doing. I want to see you."

"I want to see you too."

"Let's meet at the park tomorrow after church."

"Can you come over now?"

Could he see him now? He wanted to be with Bernard. He needed to be with Bernard.

"Yes, I'll be right over."

Rory's heart sang. He and Bernard were going to make this right. They were going to be together, like they'd both wanted. Nothing was going to stand in their way.

Chapter Twenty-Four

Rory

Saturday, July 25 / Sunday, July 26

BERNARD OPENED THE door and Rory leaped into his arms and hugged him.

"I'm sorry. I should have talked to you instead of walking away. I'm so sorry, Bernard. I hope you'll forgive me." The words tumbled out of him. His grip on Bernard loosened.

"You have nothing to be sorry about. I hurt you. I shouldn't have called your mom a bitch. I hope you can forgive me."

"Yes, I forgive you. I do." Rory squeezed him.

He allowed Bernard to hold him tight in his arms. The warmth of his body enveloped him like a blanket. He was safe.

"Come in."

Bernard brought in soda and a bowl of chips.

"Rory, I should have kept my calm when your mother called me a faggot, but it was too much. It felt like she was calling you one too, and I didn't want you to face that. I've been through it, and I should protect you."

"Thank you for thinking of me. You called her out on what she'd said. It might not have been the nicest way, but she hurt and upset you. I understand."

Bernard pulled Rory to him and wrapped his arms around him. Rory laid his head against Bernard's chest and let out a breath.

"I want to be with you," Bernard said.

"I want to be with you too."

Bernard began snoring as Rory drifted off.

He shook Bernard awake. "You should probably go to bed and use your machine."

"But I like holding you right here," Bernard said.

"I like it too, but I don't want you to stop breathing. It scared me."

"Okay. What if you stayed the night?"

"I'd like that. Let me run home and grab a few things, then I'll be right back."

*

RORY PACKED THE supplies he needed for the night, fed and watered Mina, and cleaned out her litter box.

"I'll be back tomorrow," he told her as he walked out the door.

*

BERNARD LET HIM shower first. He was going to spend the night with Bernard in his bed.

Will he expect something? I don't want to disappoint him. Will he want sex? I don't know how. I'll just disappoint him.

"I normally sleep in just my underwear," Bernard said, "but I'll put on a T-shirt and gym shorts if it makes you more comfortable."

"Just sleep how you normally do," Rory said. "I'll be fine."

"Underwear it is," Bernard said. "I can't say I won't get hard while sleeping next to you, and you might feel it."

Rory's heart warmed at the consideration. He'd always slept in pajamas. He didn't know why he still did, but he did.

They got into bed. Rory couldn't help but notice the bulge in Bernard's underwear. He didn't appear hard. Was Bernard turned on by him? Just looking at Bernard half-naked caused his cock to stir. He concentrated on keeping it soft.

Bernard curled up behind him and wrapped his right arm over him. He tucked away his left arm under the pillow.

"While I enjoy holding you, I need to face the other direction so that my CPAP works properly," Bernard said after twenty minutes of cuddling.

"Okay."

Bernard filled and started his machine.

"You can hold me if you want. I'll just sound weird when I talk."

"That sounds nice."

Bernard faced the edge of the bed, his back facing Rory. The hum of his machine echoed in Rory's ears.

Rory positioned himself behind Bernard. He wrapped his arm around his big body. Bernard grabbed and squeezed it against his chest.

They were together after twenty years of friendship.

I'm in a relationship for the first time in my life. How long have I yearned to hold someone? How long have I yearned to hold Bernard? We have a lifetime ahead of us.

*

RORY LOOKED AT his watch when the alarm went off. It was six. "Oh, I better get home and get ready for church."

"Okay, do you want to meet at the park this afternoon?" Bernard asked, his voice robotic from his CPAP mask.

"Yes, I do." Rory smiled. "Does two sound good?"

"Two is perfect."

Bernard removed his mask so they could kiss before Rory headed out.

*

RORY SAT BETWEEN his parents at church. He missed everything being said. His thoughts remained with Bernard, and the evening they spent together. Comfortable in Bernard's arms and his bed. This was love.

"It's good you have decided church is the place to be," his mother said, "not gallivanting around."

Rory nodded but didn't respond. He didn't care what she thought right now. What did she know about his feelings? She didn't know what his heart wanted; all she knew was what tradition told her. He wouldn't live his life that way anymore.

The priest approached him after service. "Rory, I would like to talk to you."

"Yes, Father Joseph." He looked back to his parents. "I'll see you at lunch."

"Come with me," Father Joseph said.

Rory followed him. Had it been too long since his last confession?

They entered a small office, not the confessionals.

"Is there something wrong, Father?"

"No, your mother has brought up some concerns to me and asked that I intervene."

Had his mother talked to Father Joseph about his personal life? That was unacceptable. She had no right to talk to anyone about what he did. What had she told him? Did she tell him about Bernard? Did she tell him she thought he was gay? He feared they would try to send him to a conversion camp. While they designed those places for teenagers, adult conversion camps existed. They could hold his standing in the church as ransom until he completed a course.

"What did she say?" His throat dried out as he said the words.

"She's concerned that you're still unmarried."

"I haven't found the right person yet."

He'd said person and not the right woman. Father Joseph seemed to notice as well. He raised an eyebrow.

"The right woman is probably in front of you, but you are too blind to see." He emphasized the word woman.

"I'm sure I'll know when it's right." Rory wasn't going to give Father Joseph any more ammunition.

"Well, I'm sure you could learn to love the woman you marry. You're getting older and at some point, you'll have to choose. Missy is a lovely girl.

You might give her a chance."

His mother had told him more than he'd ever want anyone to know. He and Missy had this discussion. They were not interested in each other.

"Yes, Father. I will do as you ask."

Years in the church taught him to agree with his elders and do as they say. You don't back-talk, argue, or disagree. You do what you're told and move on. He had no intention of courting Missy, but Father Joseph didn't need to know that.

"On another subject. It's been a while since your last confession. You may want to stop by soon."

"Yes, Father."

*

RORY WAITED IN the parking lot of the park after lunch. He checked his watch; it was ten minutes to two. Bernard would be here soon. He wondered if he'd got cold feet or decided that he wasn't ready. Rory wiped the sweat from his brow with his sleeve.

Bernard pulled up five minutes later. Rory walked over and helped pull out the basket for lunch.

"You didn't have to make anything," Rory said.

"Well, if we're going to spend the day at the park, we have to have something to eat."

They walked down the path, Ginger on her leash, until they came to the clearing near the lake.

"I like this spot," Rory said.

"Then we'll eat here."

They unpacked everything and sat for lunch. Bernard let Ginger explore the surrounding grass.

"Did you make peanut butter and jelly sandwiches?" Rory asked.

"Look," he said, smiling. "You didn't give me a lot of notice. I threw together what I had."

They both laughed while they ate their sandwiches and chips.

"Thank you for making lunch," Rory said.

"It's my pleasure. I don't care what we eat, so long as I get to eat with you."

"You're so sweet."

When they finished, they lay down on the blanket. Ginger curled up between them. Rory stretched out his hand and ran his fingers through the grass. It was soft and lush.

He looked over at Bernard. Bernard lay there, eyes closed. Rory just listened to him breathe. He wanted to kiss him. He wanted to press his lips against Bernard's and never stop.

We're in public. How would he feel if I kissed him in the park? What would other people think?

The image of the man yelling at them flashed through his head and he resisted kissing Bernard.

Bernard sat up. "It's such a beautiful day."

"It really is."

"Do you want to go for a walk?" Bernard asked.

"I'd love to walk with you."

The scent of the lake drifted outward. Rory wrinkled his nose as a hint of muck hit him. When was the last time they cleaned the water? It was a man-made lake, and the few ducks and fish were not enough to keep it clean.

As they walked around the lake Rory resisted the urge to reach out and grab Bernard's hand. He yearned to feel his touch. The movie theater was the last time he touched his hand.

"I love the warm summer air," Bernard said. "It's so nice."

"Yes," Rory said.

Bernard stopped and moved off the trail. Rory followed. Bernard collapsed against a tree and held himself. Tears filled his eyes as his breathing staggered. He was hyperventilating.

"What's wrong?" Rory knelt beside him.

"It's…down the trail… I saw…I saw Jason and Tracy."

"What?"

"They were kissing and hugging on the side of the trail. It was them, I know it. God, I can't see them."

"We don't have to see them," Rory said. "Let's go back the other way."

"I can't move. I'm…I'm not strong enough."

Bernard was paralyzed from his past. Rory remembered when Jason and Tracy had each cheated on him. How they broke him. Those men were heartless and vile. Bernard deserved to forget what they did, but here they were, reminding him of his past. Rory's heart ached for him.

"Come on." Rory helped him to his feet.

"I thought that was you," a voice came from the trail.

Tracy stood there, a smug look on his face, Jason behind him.

"Still the same man," Tracy said, "so emotional."

"What's your problem?" Rory asked.

"Is this your boyfriend?" Jason stepped forward.

"Yes, and I'm a much better boyfriend than either of you could ever be."

"He'll leave you too," Tracy said. "He's a sad, pathetic man who doesn't know what he wants. He acts like he does, but really doesn't."

Rory looked around. Bernard had fallen back to a sitting position. He was shaking, crying, and wasn't defending himself.

Bernard always stands up to bullies. What's wrong?

"You both cheated on him." Rory rounded on them, trying to control his anger. "You betrayed your relationships and now you're together. I guess you wanted an open relationship but didn't have the guts to voice it to Bernard because you know he wouldn't go for it. He knows what he wants, and it's neither of you. So, why don't you move along. You obviously deserve each other."

"Fuck you," Jason said.

"No, fuck you!" Rory said. "Get lost. You had no reason to come talk to us except to be assholes. So, just go."

The pair turned around. "They deserve each other," Tracy said as they walked away.

"He's as sad and pathetic as Bernie," Jason said.

Rory knelt next to Bernard. Tears still soaked his beard.

"They're right, I'm pathetic," he said.

"No, you're not. They're assholes. I know it hurts, but you have me. I'm here for you, no matter what. I'll never treat you the way they did."

Bernard smiled up at him. "How did I find someone so wonderful as you?"

"Because you're a sweet and wonderful man who deserves to be happy. I'm glad I could give you that happiness."

They made it back to the blanket and Bernard dried up his tears.

"So, do you have snack cakes for dessert again?" Rory stifled a giggle.

"Actually," Bernard said, "I brought Hostess apple and cherry pies."

They both laughed. It was nice to hear Bernard laugh. He needed to forget about Jason and Tracy.

Rory grabbed an apple pie while Bernard ate a cherry. They talked about how the last few weeks went, skirting around the obvious discussion of how they left things the last time they saw each other.

"So, when do you start the position at the college?"

"Classes start in a week," Rory said. "I'm teaching three classes this semester."

"That's amazing," Bernard said. "I'm so happy for you."

"It's really exciting. I'll be doing the same thing as before, but a little more pay."

Bernard leaned over and embraced him in a hug. It was cozy. Rory hugged him back. He missed this. Bernard's touch. His compassion. His genuine interest in him. These were the things that mattered. Bernard was the man he hoped to spend the rest of his life with.

"Sorry." Bernard pulled away. "I didn't know if I should hug you in public."

"It's nice," Rory said. "I like your hugs."

"I like your hugs too."

They packed up and headed to the parking lot.

"I'll meet you at your house," Rory said.

He needed to spend time with Bernard.

He is one of the few people who doesn't tell me what or how to feel. He lets me decide. My friends are right, Bernard never tried to coerce me.

"That sounds nice."

Rory's heart raced as he followed Bernard home. He didn't know what would happen, but he knew they needed to complete their day. Running into Tracy and Jason had to be difficult for him. Rory needed to be there for him.

Rory stood on Bernard's porch. They locked eyes. He looked deep into Bernard's eyes. He took in Bernard's warm smile. His soft beard. The small crook of one side of his mouth was higher than the other. Bernard had thick lips. He wanted to run his fingers through his wavy hair. Hold the strands between his fingers. Bernard had let it grow out. He'd never wanted to do this with anyone else. He'd never had feelings this strong for anyone.

Rory grabbed both of Bernard's hands. He smiled at him. He slowed his breathing as they held hands.

"I'm so glad we could talk," Rory said. "It hurt being away from you."

"It hurt me too." Bernard put his hand on Rory's cheek.

"We all make mistakes."

"I'm sorry about what I said. I know it was heart-wrenching for you and I felt like the worst person in the world for doing it."

The mix of emotions running through Rory over the past week had been overwhelming. Anger at his mom for spying and interfering, then calling Bernard a slur. Anger at Bernard for calling his mother a name. He was angry, sad, hurt, and disappointed. He cried himself to sleep so many nights. His friends and father brought him to his senses. Bernard wouldn't do anything to hurt him, not on purpose.

"I understand you were upset. I know you didn't mean it the way it sounded. You were worried about me."

"I promise never to hurt you like that again."

"I know you won't."

Rory placed his hand over Bernard's. Bernard had a gentle touch. He pressed his face against Bernard's hand. He closed his eyes and took a deep breath. Heat filled him. A burning desire he couldn't explain.

"I would like to kiss you," Bernard said.

Rory opened his eyes to see want in Bernard's. The words he'd longed to hear.

"I want to kiss you too."

Rory closed his eyes. Their lips met. Soft and warm. He was kissing Bernard for the second time. This time was different. It was gentle and soft.

Rory wrapped his arms around Bernard and pulled him in. He opened his mouth and their tongues met. His body tensed at the flavors in Bernard's mouth. Sweet strawberry jam and peanut butter with a hint of cherry. His cock perked up. Bernard's arms rubbed his back. Rory wanted to reach down to see if Bernard was hard as well. He wanted to feel what he did to him.

Rory pushed his body against Bernard's. He held him tight as they kissed. Bernard returned the pressure. Bernard's arms tightened around him. They fit together.

Rory was kissing a man in broad daylight. In public. He didn't care who saw. His heart burned for Bernard. He didn't want this to end.

They broke the kiss. Rory stared into Bernard's eyes. He cared about this man. Bernard was the first man he'd ever kissed, and Rory wanted him to be the last. No one could compare to the passion he felt for him.

"Kissing you has been the best experience of my life." Rory kissed him again. "I want to kiss you for the rest of my life."

"I'll be here for you to kiss, for the rest of my life."

They embraced again and kissed. Bernard didn't judge him for being inexperienced. He treated it like it was normal to be thirty-five and kissing someone for the first time. It made him want Bernard more. Did Bernard enjoy kissing him? He had two exes and had probably kissed other men too. Were they better kissers? Did Bernard want someone with more experience? He didn't want to think about it. Bernard was an honest man and if he didn't want to be with Rory, he'd tell him. He needed to let this be what it was. A wonderful day, with a wonderful man, that ended in the best kiss he could imagine.

I want to spend every night with him. Would that be too much, too fast? I don't know how to do this.

"I had such a wonderful day," Rory said. "I should get home and take care of Mina. Can we go out next Friday?"

"We can go out any night or day you want to."

Bernard kissed him again. He escaped into the kiss. If this was what it was to be in love, then he'd been missing out for so many years. They had a lot of catching up to do.

Rory said goodbye and headed home.

He went to the phone and called Sarah.

"Hello?"

"Hi, Sarah. It's Rory. I need to talk to you."

"What's going on?"

He told her about the day they had. Mentioned the apology, him running back to Bernard, and about the run-in with Jason and Tracy.

"What were those assholes doing at the park?" she asked.

"I don't know," Rory said. "But they are together. I got his mind off it, but I think it's best to not mention them. He was bad, I mean real bad. I don't want to see him like that again. If anyone brings up Jason or Tracy again, he might relapse."

"Don't worry, I'll let everyone know."

Rory called Davi, Sophia, Nicolas, and Jeff to let them know what happened. Everyone needed to be aware. While he'd said he was fine, today proved otherwise. Rory wanted to protect Bernard.

After getting the calls out of the way, he had a few hours before bed, so he worked on the sweater for Bernard, a tribute to his bear.

He put on *Seven* as something to watch while he knitted. He'd seen it a dozen times, so it worked as background stimulation.

"What if this doesn't last?" he asked Mina. She'd curled up on the back of the couch behind his head. "What if what I'm feeling is just momentary and Bernard and I drift apart?"

I need to stop thinking that way. I need to take it one day at a time. Just let things progress.

He had to let it play out and accept if it ended. When it ended.

Chapter Twenty-Five

Rory

Friday, September 11

RORY AND BERNARD kept their relationship a secret from his mother. His father and brother knew but kept his secret. They'd been back together for over a month and Rory couldn't be happier. He'd spent every Friday cuddled up with Bernard on the couch after dinner.

A month together, and they'd only kissed. The fear of hell prevented Rory from going further. He wanted to be intimate with Bernard, but years of conditioning held him hostage. Bernard never pressured him, and if he said no, Bernard respected him. Their shirts came off a few times, but nothing else. It couldn't continue this way. Rory knew if he didn't do something more with Bernard soon, Bernard would leave him.

Bernard held Rory in his arms as they watched *The Rocky Horror Picture Show.*

Bernard had bought snacks, soda, and popcorn for them to enjoy. He popped Milk Duds into his mouth and let them melt. The chocolate coated his tongue before it slid down his throat.

"Have you met Mikey yet?" Bernard asked.

"Who's Mikey?"

"Sarah and John's son. He's so adorable."

"Aww, I hope I get to meet him soon."

"Sarah took a leave of absence for a year to take care of him. I'm not sure if she's going to return or not since they can survive on John's income. She'll probably want to be a stay-at-home mom."

"I think it's amazing they could adopt a child."

"Do you ever want to have children?"

Rory glanced up at him. He loved spending time with his niece and had a blast playing with Bernard's nephews. He wanted kids but didn't know how that would be possible.

"I'd like kids one day," Rory said. "But I'm not sure if it'll ever happen."

"I'd like kids too, and it's hard for a gay man or a gay couple to adopt. Maybe one day we'll be able to."

Rory smiled. Bernard said "we," including him in his future. He could see himself raising a child with Bernard. A child would receive so much love from them.

"I hope we can someday."

Rory lay in Bernard's arms, taking in the moment.

"Being with you is nice." Bernard leaned down and kissed Rory.

He wrapped his arms around Bernard's and pulled him tighter. He never wanted to let him go.

Rory sat up and leaned in to kiss Bernard. Bernard's hands explored his stomach, chest, and back. Rory ran his fingers through Bernard's hair. The soft waves wrapped around his fingers. Bernard's mouth moved down to Rory's neck. Rory leaned back and moaned.

"That feels nice," Rory said.

"You like that?"

"Yes."

Bernard lay on top of him. His hands moved inside his shirt and fingers tickled his chest hair. His warm, soft hands caressed his nipple. A pinch sent shivers down his spine.

"Yes," Rory moaned.

Bernard's tongue explored his neck and ear. His gentle nibble aroused his cock. He unbuttoned his shirt and threw it off. Bernard's tongue found his nipple and took it between his teeth. His cock pressed against his jeans as Bernard flicked his nipple.

Rory reached over to unbutton Bernard's shirt. Bernard sat up to help him take his shirt and undershirt off. He ran his fingers through Bernard's chest hair. He took a nipple between his thumb and index finger and gave it a pinch.

"You can do that a little harder," Bernard said.

Rory obliged. He squeezed and twisted Bernard's erect nipple.

"Yes," Bernard moaned.

Rory took his other nipple between his fingers and tweaked it.

"Damn, that feels good."

He leaned in and nibbled one of Bernard's nipples. He didn't know how rough Bernard wanted it, so he kept it light.

"Harder," Bernard said.

Rory nibbled with more pressure.

"Yes."

Rory kissed Bernard's chest. He moved his hands over his body. He curled the hair between his fingers.

"This feels amazing," Rory said.

He moved Bernard to a lying position and got on top. He pressed his lips against Bernard's full, soft lips. Their tongues explored each other's mouths with vigor. Rory pressed his stiff cock against Bernard. Bernard was hard. His hand explored the bulge. Bernard was thick. Was he thicker than him? He wanted to taste his cock. He wanted to play with it like he did his own. Bernard was circumcised, and he wanted to hold it in his hands. What would it be like to stroke a cut cock?

He reached down and rubbed Bernard's cock through his jeans. Bernard let out a groan of pleasure. He begged for more.

Rory wanted to undo Bernard's pants but wasn't sure what to do.

Bernard's hand rubbed Rory's crotch. His cock strained against his jeans.

"Shall I take these off?" Bernard asked, playing with the buttons on Rory's jeans.

Rory nodded.

Bernard laid Rory back and undid his belt. He unbuttoned his jeans. Rory's dick stretched against his underwear.

"That feels like a very nice cock," Bernard said.

He rubbed his palm against his underwear. His cock jerked. Bernard put his mouth on his cock and sucked the shaft through his underwear. He squirmed.

"Do you like it?" Rory asked.

"Yes."

He'd compared himself a few times to men in the locker room. They were all soft, so it was hard to compare. He grew. Some porn men grew a lot, and he was nowhere near what they had. Did Bernard like his cock or was he saying it in the moment? He wanted to know.

Bernard pulled his underwear down.

"I love an uncut dick."

Rory leaned against the side of the couch, his pants and underwear pulled down around his knees.

Bernard moved his legs apart and stroked his cock. He pulled his foreskin over his tip and down again. His eyes caught Bernard's. They stared as Bernard stroked him.

"I want to suck your cock," Bernard said.

"You do?"

"Yes, I want all of it in my mouth."

"I'd love to feel your lips around it," Rory said.

Rory's cock disappeared into Bernard's mouth. He jerked back at the sensation. Bernard's warm mouth fit around his cock. Bernard took every inch. He watched as Bernard continued to suck. This was new for him. He'd never had sex, even oral sex.

Rory wrapped his fingers in Bernard's hair. He gyrated with Bernard's rhythm. Each push filled his body with ecstasy.

"Keep going," Rory said. "I want to come."

Bernard pulled his cock out of his mouth and licked it. "I can taste your pre-cum. I can't wait to swallow your load."

"You want to swallow?"

"Fuck yeah, I do."

Bernard returned his cock to his mouth. He stroked as he sucked.

Bernard's saliva lubed his cock. The strokes became long and even. Bernard's mouth played with his foreskin. Rory's balls tightened. His load would soon fill Bernard's waiting mouth. The anticipation caused the hairs on his arm to stand up.

You are disgusting, came a voice in his head, *you let some pervert do this to you? Touch you like this. What a disgusting pig you've become. You're a disgrace. Hell has a special place for someone like you.*

"Wait," Rory said.

Bernard lifted his head. "Did I hurt you?"

"No, I just…" Rory's throat closed up. Tears welled in his eyes.

"What's wrong?"

"I…I can't do this right now." Rory pulled up his underwear and pants. "I'm sorry." He stood and fastened his pants.

"You have nothing to be sorry for." Bernard pulled him into an embrace.

He moved away. He couldn't stand to be touched right now. Contradicting thoughts raced through his head.

"Rory, it's okay," Bernard said. "You didn't do anything wrong."

"Yes, I did," he choked. "We were going to finally…then I had to question what I was doing. I'm sorry, I'm so sorry."

Rory hated himself. He'd gotten past his fear, and it overwhelmed him again. The church destroyed him.

"Rory." Bernard pulled him back into a tight embrace. "I know exactly what you're going through. I went through it too. I won't push you into anything you don't want to do."

"But…" Rory coughed. "What if I'm never ready? You don't want to be with someone who can't be intimate with you. Someone who can't please you."

Bernard pulled away and looked him in the eye. Bernard's beautiful brown eyes shone with compassion. This man would do anything to make him happy.

"I don't believe you'll never be ready," Bernard said, "and I don't care how long it takes for you to be ready. I want to be with you, not just for sex. If you never feel comfortable having sex with me, we'll work something out. We'll find a way to be together. Even if that means we watch each other jack off and that's it."

Rory couldn't help but giggle. "You'd be satisfied with just watching me jack off?" he said.

"You're hot. I'd be happy if you lay on the bed naked and let me jack off just looking at you."

"You're so wonderful." Rory leaned in and wrapped his arms around Bernard.

He doubted himself, and Bernard stayed with him. Bernard meant every word. He was happy with Bernard, and one day he'd be able to give him what he deserved.

"I'm not going to push you into anything you're not ready for," Bernard said. "I won't lose you over something silly. You have to go at your own pace and don't let anyone, not even me, push you faster than you're ready to go."

Bernard held him in his arms as they finished the movie. His warm embrace eased the tension in his mind. He was right to trust Bernard. He'd never hurt him or push him.

*

HIS COCK HARDENED as he showered. He jerked off. The memory of Bernard sucking his dick made it easy to come.

"I'm sorry about earlier." Rory lay down with his back to Bernard.

"You have no reason to be sorry." Bernard wrapped his arm around Rory. "My first time was much worse."

"What happened?"

Rory wasn't sure he wanted to know. Bernard had been with guys, but he didn't want to hear the details. He wanted to pretend he was Bernard's first, even though that was impossible.

"I..." Bernard giggled. "I came in my pants as soon as the guy took off his clothes and touched me." He buried his face into Rory's back. He was laughing.

"What?"

"Yes, I was twenty," Bernard said. "I'd just started exploring and it was with someone from High School. No, I won't tell you who. We were at his parents' house. They were out of town, and we were going to experiment. Well, we did little after that."

"I'm sorry that happened," Rory said. "I know it must have been embarrassing."

"I haven't spoken to him since."

They went silent. Rory held Bernard's arm. He stroked the hairs. Bernard's arm hair was soft.

Chapter Twenty-Six

Bernard

Saturday, September 25 / Sunday, September 26

IT WAS A quarter to ten, and Bernard was running late. He still needed to pick up Rory and drive twenty minutes to the park.

Bernard rushed out the door, Ginger in tow, and drove off to Rory's.

He arrived at ten and knocked.

Rory answered in a blue T-shirt, tan shorts, and sunglasses. Bernard lifted Rory's glasses and stared into his beautiful green eyes.

"Don't hide your eyes." Bernard smiled.

"You're sweet." Rory's cheeks reddened.

"Are you ready to go?" Bernard asked.

"Can't we stay in and cuddle?"

Rory wrapped his arms around him and kissed him.

Bernard melted in Rory's embrace. He pulled him closer. The warmth of Rory's lips erased all urgency in leaving.

Bernard pulled away slowly and ran a finger up and down Rory's chest.

"As much as I'd like that, we're already late. We were supposed to be there at ten."

"All right, we'll go then." Rory pouted.

Bernard laughed.

"You said you invited your friends too?" Bernard asked as they walked to his truck.

"Yes, Davi, Nicolas, Sophia, and Jeff have all said they'll join us. It's going to be fun."

*

THEY ARRIVED AT ten-thirty to find everyone had settled around a park bench and were socializing. Davi and Sophia were in an animated conversation with Sarah.

"Well, it looks like we don't have to introduce anyone," Bernard said. "You all seem to have done that."

"Well, we all got here around ten. Where were you two?" Kelly teased.

"That's my fault. I was running late picking up Rory. Then we had a short make-out session."

Everyone whooped.

"Oh my, is that Mikey?" Rory asked, pointing to a blond-haired boy sitting with Chester.

"Yup." Sarah scooped him up and carried him to Rory. "Would you like to hold him?"

"I'd love to."

Rory gently held Mikey in his lap, tickling him until the boy was giggling. It warmed Bernard's heart that Rory had such a way with children—they just loved him at first sight.

"Who you?" Mikey asked. He grabbed on to Rory's beard.

"I'm Rory, but my niece calls me Roro."

"Hi, Roro."

Rory carried Mikey around, telling him a story about a little girl who met magical ponies in a far-off land. Bernard smiled. Rory would be a wonderful father.

"He's fantastic with kids," Sarah said.

"He wants children one day."

A pain shot through his chest at that. He wanted children too. But it wasn't feasible for them. No adoption agency would ever consider them. Single people had a chance, but once they found out he and Rory were gay, the agency would remove them. Surrogacy was an option, but it was beyond his price range. He and Rory wanted children, but it hurt that they may never be fathers.

"I'm sure you'll be able to have children one day."

"I thought about getting a surrogate, but I don't know. It's so expensive and even then, a lot of women won't choose a gay couple."

"Well, give it time. You never know what the future holds. You both would raise wonderful children."

The groups sat around two tables and ate burgers, hot dogs, chips, potato salad, and coleslaw. Mikey insisted on sitting in Rory's lap for lunch.

Conversations rose as the two groups became more acquainted.

"We told Rory to ask Bernard out a long time ago," Nicolas said.

"We told Bernard the same thing," Kelly said.

"Hey," Bernard said. "We ended up together in the end. That's what matters."

Bernard leaned over and kissed Rory. Rory's cheeks pinked with an adorable blush. Bernard couldn't help but smile. He was with someone who wanted him. No matter the struggles they'd face, they would support each other.

"I already said I should have asked you out twenty years ago," Rory said.

"Who knows what would have happened?" Bernard said.

"You'd have been together twenty years is my guess," Nicolas said.

"Seriously," Sophia said. "You two are so sweet together."

Bernard smiled at Rory holding Mikey. Rory was handsome, sweet, caring, and deserved happiness. He wanted to give him everything he needed.

"Oh, I have a story," Sarah said, pulling Bernard out of his thoughts. "We were in our early twenties. We were at the Round-Up Saloon."

"Sarah, no," Bernard and Rory said together.

"Oh, if they don't want us to hear this, then we need to hear this," Nicolas said.

"So, we had a few drinks and were walking to get something to eat when Mitch said we should jump the fences in the neighborhood because it was faster."

"Mitch just wanted to get Sarah in her underwear," Rory said. "He had the biggest crush on you."

"It didn't work," Sarah said.

"He got a nice shot of our butts though," Bernard laughed.

"Wait, how did you end up in your underwear?" Jeff asked.

"We jumped a few fences and my pants got caught, so instead of trying to get them unhooked, I just took off my pants so it wouldn't happen again," Bernard said.

"Then, so he wasn't alone, I did the same," Rory said.

It was a sight he'd burned into his mind. Rory had a nice ass, and Bernard jacked off to the image for years. He wanted to touch it, kiss it, and run his tongue inside it.

"So, we ended up in Mr. Caster's pool in the middle of November," Rory laughed.

Everyone laughed. Looking back, it was a terrible choice, but they had a lot of fun. They'd done so much together before Bernard came out. It pained him to think about all the friends he lost in the months following him coming out. After he pushed Rory away, he only had Sarah and John left. Now Rory was back, and he had Kelly and Sean.

"No one needs to hear these perverted stories." An elderly woman walked up to the group.

"Excuse me?" John said. "What are you talking about?"

"Talking about running around naked in a neighborhood, and with a child."

They all looked over. Mikey was out like a light in Rory's arms.

"We weren't naked," Bernard said. "We had our underwear on. It was just some stupid stunt we did when we were younger. No one got hurt."

"Well, I saw what you did earlier."

"What did we do?" Rory asked.

"You two making out like two horny teenagers," she spat.

"I gave him a kiss. It's not illegal," Rory said.

"Well, it should be." She glared at Rory. "You two should be ashamed of yourselves."

"Should we also be ashamed of ourselves?" John asked, pointing at him and Sarah. "I kissed her just a few minutes ago."

"That's different."

"Why is it always different with you people?" Bernard stood.

He wouldn't take this anymore. People who believed they had a moral high ground telling everyone else how to live their lives.

"Every time someone like you confronts us, it's 'it's different with them' when it's a straight couple," Bernard said.

"It is," she said. "It's the natural order of things."

"We're two consenting adults. There's nothing sinful about our relationship," Rory said.

"I never mentioned sin," she said. "I just think it's wrong. Two men shouldn't be together. You can't procreate that way."

Bernard's breathing intensified. People would come up with every excuse to discriminate, and it had to stop.

"Actually," Davi said. "That's untrue. Many species of animals exhibit homosexual behaviors. So, it isn't unnatural."

They all looked at Davi.

"I minored in biology," he said.

"Well, either way," she said. "I shouldn't have to see it."

"Then don't look," Sophia said. "No one's making you look at them."

The woman glared at Bernard and Rory, her hands balled into fists. She looked as if she was going to say something but thought better of it.

They outnumbered her, and if she continued to harass them, they could file a report.

"You're disgusting," she snapped before turning and walking away.

"What in the world?" Nicolas said. "What got into her?"

"I'm sorry we couldn't do more," Sophia said. "You shouldn't have to deal with bigots like that."

"We face it every day," Bernard said. "At least those who are caught like we were, or those who appear more effeminate. It's horrible stereotyping."

"This happens a lot?" Jeff asked.

"More than you'd think," Kelly said.

"You've dealt with that?" Rory asked Kelly.

"I…" Kelly paused. "I had some trouble getting help from the law. I'll leave it at that."

"Why does anyone care what two adults do if it's not hurting them or anyone else?" Nicolas said.

"It's about control and what they considered normal," Bernard said. "While homosexuality has been around for as long as man has, it's gone through phases. Some places didn't see it as an issue. I think religion had a hand in making it unacceptable. While you have people who are not religious oppose it, it still stems from religious doctrine."

"Well," Nicolas said, "it's messed up. I hope it gets better in time."

"We can only hope," Kelly said.

"Rory, would you like to take a short walk with me?" Bernard asked.

"Okay."

Bernard led him around the lake to a small bench. It was quiet, with few people milling around the lake.

"How are you feeling?" Bernard asked.

"I'm okay, why?"

"I know you haven't faced discrimination in public like this, except for the one guy, and I want to see how you're feeling."

"It hurts to hear those things. I'm not sure what to do." Rory looked down. A few tears fell into his beard.

Bernard's body ached at the sight of Rory. This wonderful man had to face new obstacles now that he was out. Bernard would do anything to protect him.

He wrapped his arms around Rory.

"I'm here with you," he whispered. "I'll always be here for you."

"I hear these things at church, and I'm lost. I don't know what I'm supposed to do."

"You're supposed to be the best person you can be."

"I still believe in God, but I don't know what to believe." Rory shook in his arms. "Do you still believe in God, Bernard?"

"I do. I just do it my way. I don't believe I have to attend church every Sunday or pray all the time. I just try to be a good person and do the best that I can do."

The church removed Bernard's standing when they discovered he was gay. He left religion behind while he discovered himself. He still believed in God, but not the God the Catholic Church taught. His God was one who loved you no matter what and didn't require constant worship.

"Does it get easier?" Rory asked.

"Not much, but we'll get through it together."

When they made it back to the group, Sophia and Nicolas had to head out for work. Kelly and John started cleaning up while Sarah took

Mikey to the play area.

Bernard and Rory joined in to help clean up.

"So, Bernard," Jeff said. "I have a question."

"Yes," Bernard said.

"We asked Rory this, and he never gave us an answer." He grinned at Rory. "How long have you been in love with Rory?"

"You asked Rory how long he'd been in love with me?"

"I did," Davi said. "But he didn't answer."

"I'm right here," Rory said. "I still don't know when I fell for him."

"It was our junior year of high school. We'd finished studying for our history exam. I looked over and saw Rory in a different light. At that moment, I found myself attracted to him. Sitting across from Rory is the first time I truly accepted I was gay."

"That's the sweetest thing I've ever heard," Jeff said.

"I wish I knew then what I know now," Rory said.

"I tried dating, but you know how those relationships ended. I think somewhere deep down I chose the wrong men because I didn't think anyone could compare to you."

Davi and Jeff were now wiping tears from their eyes.

"You two are so handsome together," Davi said. "I hope I can find love like yours one day."

"Davi," Rory said, "you are a wonderful man. I know you'll find someone who makes you happy."

"Thank you."

They finished cleaning, and Bernard got Rory back home in time for church.

"Thank you for a wonderful day," Rory said. "I had a lot of fun."

"I did too." Bernard resisted kissing him. Rory lived in a safe neighborhood, but he didn't know which neighbors went to his church.

"Another afternoon together tomorrow?" Rory asked.

"Would you like to stay the night?"

"I wish I could," Rory said. "But I can't risk it. I'm so sorry."

"I understand. What about tomorrow night after our day in the park?"

"Yes, I'd like that."

*

ONCE HOME, BERNARD let Ginger out back and sat on the couch. Their friends supported their relationship. Bernard had sworn off relationships before, but Rory was different. Special. He'd hide their relationship forever if it meant staying with him. One day, Rory would come out to his family when he was ready. Bernard knew the fallout would be horrible, but he'd be free to be himself. The world may not accept them, but they had friends who did. They didn't need the world.

*

THE NEXT DAY they spent a wonderful afternoon in the park. Rory went home to get his evening supplies and check on Mina. Bernard went home to start dinner.

"Sweetie, I'm home," Rory called from the living room. Bernard smiled. "I hope it's okay that I let myself in."

"Sweetheart, don't be silly. That's why I gave you a key."

He met Rory in the living room and kissed him.

"What's for dinner?"

"I've made baked barbecue chicken, mashed potatoes, and steamed veggies."

"Sounds good."

They ate in the living room and watched a recorded episode of *Three's Company.*

"I can't believe you still have these old shows recorded."

"Oh, yeah, I have this, *Dear John, I Love Lucy, Laverne and Shirley, Gilligan's Island.* All the old classics."

After dinner, they snuggled up in bed. Bernard held on to Rory, keeping him close. He hadn't tried anything since Rory panicked. He didn't want to make Rory uncomfortable. He still wasn't ready, and Bernard didn't want to push him into something he didn't want to do. Rory would know when he was ready.

"I love you," Rory said.

Rory turned over to face Bernard. Bernard looked at him. This was the first time Rory said he loved him.

"I love you too." Bernard kissed him. Deep. Passionate. Their tongues tangled together in their mouths. He wanted his naked body against Rory's. His cock stiffened.

He felt Rory's hand on it.

"Do you want to?" Bernard asked.

"I...I don't know," Rory said.

"That means no, and I'll respect that."

"Why are you so patient with me?" Rory sat up. "You have done nothing but be patient with me, and I can't even be intimate with you."

"Because I love you and I know what it's like to be pushed into something you're not ready for."

Rory looked stricken. "What happened?"

"Jason talked me into a threesome a year into our relationship. I should have said no, but I wanted to hold on to him. It turned out he was interested in a guy and did a threesome with me to get him into bed. A month later, I found them in bed together. We never discussed an open relationship. I was mad and hurt. It took me another year before I left him."

"I'm so sorry, I didn't know."

"No one knew. I kept it a secret. You're the first person I've told. That's why I don't push. I don't want you to regret anything you do with me. Jason cheated because I allowed it. I gave him permission."

"He was going to cheat no matter what." Rory held Bernard's face in his hands. His soft, kind hands. "It was just a way to get there faster. It wasn't your fault, and you shouldn't blame yourself for what he did."

"Thank you." Bernard choked. "That means a lot to me."

They held each other for what seemed like hours and Bernard didn't want to let go.

"We should get some sleep. We have to be up early."

Bernard put on his CPAP and lay there with Rory's arms wrapped around him. He was still hard, but sex was the last thing on his mind. He'd told someone something that was eating him alive for years. Rory understood and didn't blame him. The weight lifted.

Chapter Twenty-Seven

Rory

Friday, October 2

RORY CURLED UP on the couch in Bernard's arms. It was the beginning of October, and he was warm in Bernard's arms. Bernard had been patient with him. They didn't go further than making out, sometimes with their shirts off. Bernard tweaked his nipples once or twice but stopped when Rory wanted to. After leaving a make-out session, Rory would jerk off at home. He wanted to see Bernard jerk off. How big was Bernard's cock? He wanted to play with it.

Bernard had recorded episodes of *Will & Grace*. It was nice to see representation on television. Neither of them identified with Will or Jack, but some young gay men out there did. That's what was important.

Rory leaned up and kissed Bernard. "I love you, sweetheart."

"I love you too, sweetie." Bernard squeezed him. "I'm so happy you're here with me."

"Can I ask you something?"

"You can ask me anything."

"Well, I think I'm ready to be intimate, but…" Rory paused. How could he bring up anal sex without offending Bernard? Bernard had had anal before, hadn't he? He'd been out for years now, he must have. Could Rory compare to the experienced men he'd been with?

"What is it?"

"I…I don't know if I can do anal sex."

"We don't have to."

"We don't?"

"No, we can do whatever you are comfortable with." Bernard kissed him. "Is that what's been bothering you all this time? You thought we would have to have anal, and that scared you?"

"A little." Rory's face burned.

"What gave you the idea that we had to do anal?"

"I watched some porn, and they seemed to enjoy it a lot. I just thought…"

"Did you think that is the only way I'd have sex with you?"

"I don't know. I'm not sure what I expected."

"Well, we'll take everything slow," Bernard said. "I know this is your first time and I'll go at your speed. We'll try things as long as you are comfortable with them."

"I…I'm afraid," Rory said.

"What are you afraid of?"

"That I won't be good enough," Rory said. "That you'll expect what you got from other men, and that I won't live up to your expectations."

"I don't have any specific expectations."

"I just don't want to disappoint you."

"You won't disappoint me. We'll explore and discover what we like. We're in this together."

"I…" Rory's throat closed up. He didn't know how to please another person. He'd explored his own body and discovered his enjoyment of playing with his prostate and his nipples, and how to stroke his cock. He'd never done it with another person.

"Let's go take a shower together." Bernard grinned. "We'll get all clean and then explore each other in bed. We can do what you're comfortable with, and nothing more."

Bernard stood, and Rory took his hand.

Rory faced Bernard in his room. Bernard reached over and unbuttoned his polo. Rory lifted his arms so Bernard could remove it. He looked down at his body. He liked his curves, his body hair, and his belly. Did Bernard like them too?

Rory unbuttoned Bernard's flannel and let it drop to the floor. Bernard lifted his arms and Rory slipped off his T-shirt. He ran his fingers through Bernard's hairy chest, the soft hair tantalizing.

"I don't know why I didn't notice you before," Rory said. "We had two years of gym class. I've seen you naked, but not like this."

"I noticed you." Bernard smiled. "But not like I do now."

"Thank you."

They embraced and kissed. Rory's hands ran through Bernard's chest and back hair. Bernard's soft hands explored his body, caressing every inch of his chest and belly.

"I want you to explore my body, Bernard."

"I will," he said. "And you'll explore mine."

They undressed and walked into the bathroom. Bernard had a separate tub and standing shower. Rory looked at the large shower, big enough to fit both of them.

Rory stood with his back to the running water. Bernard soaped up a rag and moved it around Rory's body. Each gentle stroke sent shivers up his spine. Bernard had a softness he loved. Bernard reached around and stroked his already hard cock.

"That feels so good," Rory said.

He leaned back against Bernard. Bernard's cock pressed against his ass cheeks. Bernard kissed his neck and moved up to his earlobe. Rory let out a gasp as Bernard nibbled.

"Wait until I have you on my bed," Bernard said.

Bernard ran the rag around his ass and inside his thighs.

"Do you want me to clean you inside?" Bernard asked as his fingers traced down his spine and between his cheeks.

"Will you be gentle?" Rory asked.

"If you don't like it, say so and I'll stop."

Rory spread his legs to give Bernard access.

Bernard's finger teased the outside of his hole, circling and teasing until Rory relaxed. His finger slid inside with ease. He moved slower than Rory had the first time he'd done it to himself.

Bernard's finger continued a slow rhythm in and out. Rory moaned with pleasure at each entrance.

Bernard pulled his finger out. "My turn."

Rory stepped fully under the spray to rinse off.

He grabbed the rag and soaped Bernard up, front and back. With Bernard's back to him, he reached around and stroked Bernard's hard cock. It was longer and thicker than his.

"Your cock's bigger than mine," he blurted out.

Bernard turned around, smiling. "You have nothing to be ashamed of. You have a nice cock."

"How big are you?"

"Seven inches."

"I just hope mine is big enough for you. I'm only six inches," Rory said.

He hated how he compared himself to other guys. But he still wished he was as big as Bernard, and as confident and experienced. Bernard didn't care about his cock size, but Rory did. He wanted Bernard to have the man he deserved. Someone with experience, a large dick, and the confidence to be out.

"I had your cock in my mouth, remember?" Bernard asked. "It's amazing. Your body is amazing. You're amazing."

"You think so?"

"Yes, and you need to know it. I'll tell you every day that you're gorgeous until you believe it."

"Thank you. You're gorgeous too." Rory soaped up his finger. "May I?" he asked.

"Yes, please." Bernard turned again and spread his legs.

Rory slid his finger in. He did as he practiced on himself. He found Bernard's prostate and massaged it.

"Yes, that's great." Bernard leaned forward and spread his legs further.

"You like that?"

Bernard nodded. "Yes, keep going."

Rory continued to work Bernard's hole. He moved his finger around inside. He reached around and found Bernard's hard cock and gave it a few strokes.

"Okay, you need to stop before I blow my load," Bernard said.

Rory removed his finger. "It's that good?"

"You have more skill than you give yourself credit for." Bernard grinned.

They dried off and Bernard led Rory into the bedroom. Bernard had Rory lie on his back and laid next to him on his side. Bernard reached over and ran his fingers through his hair, massaging his scalp. Rory looked into his eyes and smiled.

"You are so handsome," Bernard said.

"You are too," Rory said.

Bernard's hand found Rory's cock, soft again after drying off.

"I think I want to wake this guy up."

Bernard stroked Rory's cock with slow, even motions. Rory let his head fall back on the pillow. Bernard nibbled on his nipple.

"That feels good," Rory said.

"I know what will feel better."

Bernard leaned down and took his entire cock in his mouth. Rory moaned as his cock hardened in Bernard's warm mouth. Bernard pulled his cock out and ran his tongue inside his foreskin. He took his foreskin into his mouth and nibbled. Rory groaned. Bernard knew what he was doing.

He only hoped he'd be able to please Bernard in return.

Bernard traced his tongue to Rory's balls. He took each one into his mouth and sucked. He continued to stroke Rory's cock. Rory gripped the bed and his back arched. His eyes closed, and he reveled in Bernard's touch. His mind swam with pleasure he didn't know existed.

"You like that?"

"Yes, keep going," Rory said.

"Gladly."

Bernard stroked Rory's cock as he sucked his balls. His balls ached and tightened. He bit his lip.

"Mind if I go lower?" Bernard asked.

"What do you mean?" Rory asked.

"The area between your ass and balls. I want to lick it."

"Okay," Rory said.

He hadn't explored the area before. Anticipation flooded his body as he waited for Bernard to start.

Rory let out a yelp when Bernard's tongue ran from his ass to his balls. His body stiffened at the sensation. He gasped for air.

"Dear God, that feels good," Rory said.

"I thought you might enjoy that."

"I do."

"That's your taint, and it's sensitive."

Bernard continued to move his tongue around Rory's taint. He moved from cock to balls to taint in slow movements. Rory moaned as Bernard's hands explored his body; his fingers reached up and tweaked his nipple.

Bernard pushed his face into Rory's inner thigh and licked.

"Oh, Bernard."

"May I go a little lower?" Bernard asked.

"Wait, you want to—"

"Yes, I want to rim your ass."

"I...I don't know," Rory said.

"I won't if you're not comfortable with it."

"I want to try," Rory said.

"Are you sure?"

"Yes, please."

Bernard pulled Rory to the edge of the bed. He lifted Rory's legs and put them on his shoulders. His ass cheeks were spread, and a tongue ran across his hole.

"*Oh fuck!*"

Rory bucked his hips against Bernard and pulled a pillow over his mouth to stifle the screams.

"No, I want to hear you."

"But the neighbors?"

"I don't care."

Bernard continued to eat his ass. His moans of pleasure echoed through the room.

"Does that feel good?" Bernard lifted his head to face him.

"Yes," Rory moaned.

The pleasure was indescribable. Bernard was bringing out feelings he didn't know existed.

"Stroke your dick while I eat your ass."

Rory reached down and stroked his cock. He increased his strokes as Bernard's tongue dug deeper into his ass.

"I'm going to come," Rory moaned.

"Come for me." Bernard sat up and watched.

Rory looked into his eyes. "Play with my hole, please."

Bernard grabbed the lube from his drawer and lubed up his finger. He slid it in. Rory gasped at his entrance.

"Yes, keep going, make me come," Rory begged.

Rory stroked in rhythm with Bernard's thrusts. He wanted Bernard to see him come. He needed Bernard to see what he did to him.

"Are you going to come for me?"

"*Yes!*"

Rory shot his load all over his belly. His body convulsed with each pulse. He squeezed out the last of his cum and it dripped down his shaft.

"That was hot," Bernard said.

"What about you?" Rory said.

"Take some lube and finger my ass while I use your cum to jack off."

"You're going to use my cum as lube?"

"Yes."

Bernard got on his knees, and Rory looked at his thick cock. It was so big. The desire to suck Bernard's dick overwhelmed him.

"Wait," Rory said.

"What?"

"I want to suck your cock."

"You do?"

"Yes, I do, please. Can I suck it?"

"Of course you can."

Bernard got on his back. Rory moved between his legs and took Bernard's cock in his mouth. He got about halfway before he stopped. He pulled it out and ran his tongue up his shaft.

"Yes, that feels so good," Bernard moaned.

"You like that?"

"Yes. Your mouth is so warm."

Rory leaned back down and continued to suck. Inch by inch, he took more of Bernard's cock into his mouth. With his right hand, he played with Bernard's balls. Bernard's cock was thick. Rory's saliva dripped down it.

Rory lifted himself up. "I think I need more practice."

"You're amazing."

Bernard wiped some cum off Rory's belly and smeared it on his cock.

"Now, finger me while I use your cum to jack off."

Rory lubed up his finger and slid it into Bernard's ass. Bernard stroked his cock.

"Do you enjoy watching me jerk off?" Bernard asked.

"Yes," Rory said.

"That's what I like to hear," Bernard said. "Do you like my cock?"

"Yes, I love your cock."

"Yeah, I want you to talk dirty to me."

"What do you like to hear?"

Rory didn't know how to talk dirty to someone. The men in porn talked dirty sometimes, but he didn't know how to do it with Bernard.

"That you want me to stroke my massive cock while you finger my ass," Bernard said.

"Oh, you like that?"

"Yes, I do. Now, add another finger."

Rory added another finger, and Bernard's ass tightened around it.

"Stroke that massive cock for me," Rory said.

"Just for you, sexy."

Bernard's strokes increased. His face reddened as Rory played with his balls. He pushed his fingers deeper into Bernard.

"You like this?" Rory massaged Bernard's prostate.

"Yes," he groaned. "Faster," he begged.

"You want me to go faster?"

"Please, I want you to go faster, baby. Finger my ass."

Rory shoved his fingers deep and fast.

"I'm going to come."

"Are you going to come for me?"

"*Yes!*"

Bernard shot his load. The sound of Bernard getting off turned him on. His grunts of pleasure were getting Rory hard again.

"Damn, you know how to work your fingers," Bernard said.

"I'm glad you enjoyed it."

Rory leaned forward and kissed him. Rory savored the flavors of Bernard's sweat and the taste of his cock in his mouth.

"It looks like you're hard again."

Bernard stroked Rory's cock, now fully erect.

"Hearing you moan turned me on."

"Well, let me take care of that."

Bernard took Rory's cock in his mouth and sucked. Rory pumped with Bernard's motion.

It was a few minutes before Rory was ready to blow his next load.

"I'm going to come again," Rory said.

He attempted to pull out, but Bernard grabbed his ass and held him.

"I'm…" Cum shot out of him into Bernard's mouth. Bernard sucked and swallowed every drop.

"Damn, you taste good." Bernard wiped his mouth.

"You swallowed my cum."

"I did, and I liked it."

"That felt amazing."

"Well, I'll do that anytime you want."

"I'll have to take you up on that."

"Let's shower and then we can cuddle."

After another shower, Bernard held Rory in his arms. It was warm, safe, and comfortable. They were both still naked.

"I've never heard you talk like that," Rory said.

"Like what?"

"Well, talk dirty."

"Well." Bernard giggled. "I've never had a reason to talk to you like that."

"I mean." Rory hesitated. "I don't know if I can talk as dirty as you, without being prompted."

"You don't have to. You're fine the way you are. I think it's hot when I say something and you respond in your cute way. Wanting reassurance. I want you to know that I'll always reassure you that you're an amazing lover."

"That turns you on?"

"It does."

Bernard kissed the back of his neck.

"I'm glad me being myself is what turns you on."

"I wouldn't expect you to be anyone else."

"I have another personal question," Rory said.

"I will answer any question you want," Bernard said.

"Well, I've only seen a few gay pornos," he said. "And they all had anal sex in them."

"That's common."

"Well, it's always the larger guy who tops," Rory said. "I'm bigger than you. So, if we do anal, do I have to top?"

"God, I love you," Bernard said. "No, you don't. Top and bottom are preferences and are based on individuals. It doesn't matter who is physically larger."

"Oh," Rory said. "What is your preference?"

"My preference is whatever makes you happy." Bernard kissed him again.

"Okay, that's a cop-out. If it wasn't me, what would be your preference?"

"Okay, I prefer to top, but I also enjoy bottoming. It depends on my mood."

"So, I'll have to learn to top and bottom?"

"You don't have to learn to do anything. What we did tonight is enough for me. If we never do anal, I wouldn't care."

"You wouldn't?"

"No, the most important thing is pleasing you. If you want to try to top or bottom one day, I'm happy to do it. It's not required."

Rory breathed a sigh of relief. Bernard didn't put expectations on him, and that made him smile. He wasn't experienced sexually, and Bernard was willing to compromise and be patient.

"Thank you. I love you so much."

"I love you too."

Rory couldn't imagine this with anyone else. Bernard was the kind of person he'd hoped for his entire life. Someone who loved him for who he was and wouldn't intentionally hurt him.

Chapter Twenty-Eight

Bernard

Saturday, October 31 / Sunday, November 1

BERNARD FINISHED GETTING ready for Sarah and John's annual Halloween party. He'd decided on something simple and dressed as Theodore Roosevelt. He'd even shaved his beard and kept the mustache to fit the costume.

He rubbed his hand over his smooth skin.

"I can't believe I shaved," he laughed. "Luckily, it'll grow back in two weeks."

He looked at his watch. It was four-thirty. He let Ginger out and headed to Sarah and John's house.

The party was warming up when he arrived. Costumes galore. John and Sarah were dressed as Sonny and Cher. Mikey was a bunny.

"Come in," Sarah said. "We have soda, snacks, and *Friday the 13th* playing on the TV in the family room if you want to watch. I think it's almost over. Not sure what's on next. It's a horror film marathon."

"I could go for a scary movie," Bernard said.

"Have at it. You know I hate horror movies. John loves them though."

"I remember."

"So, are you Taft?"

"No, I'm Theodore Roosevelt."

"Ah, I see it now. The hat should've given it away."

"And you're Cher," Bernard said.

"Yes." She licked her lips and tossed her hair back.

They both laughed.

"Well, mingle and have a good time."

He looked around at the guests. He recognized a few people

from Sarah's birthday party and sighed with relief that Jeanine was absent.

Bernard found Kelly at the punch bowl. He'd dressed as a pirate, complete with a hooked hand.

"Nice costume," Bernard said.

"Thank you."

He grabbed a cup of punch and made his way through the small crowd to the snack table. He struck up a conversation with Thomas, one of John's colleagues at the real estate agency. He regretted it immediately. Thomas was boring. All he discussed was the shifting prices of homes in the area. The best time to buy, how to refinance, and the best upgrades you can make to your home to increase its value.

Bernard excused himself and headed back to the living room, where music played and conversations didn't revolve around work.

He ran into Devon and Marsha, who were dressed as Fred and Wilma Flintstone. They'd arrived after him.

Devon worked in marketing at his company, and Marsha was the secretary to the vice president. They were a cheerful couple. They discussed their upcoming Alaskan cruise. He'd wanted to take a cruise for years but didn't want to do it alone.

"Oh, you need to go," Marsha said. "This is our third cruise, and it's so relaxing."

"Maybe one day Rory and I will go."

Bernard thought about a cruise with Rory. They'd be free to hold hands whenever they wanted, no one judging them. They'd need to find a couples' gay cruise. A regular cruise for gays was hook-up central and he and Rory had already discussed the idea of an open relationship, and agreed it wasn't for them. It was common in the gay community, and that was fine for some, but they weren't interested.

"Oh, you'll love it," Devon said. "I have a cousin who's an agent. I'm sure he can find a cruise for you two."

"Thanks, I'll let you know when we're ready."

"Sounds good."

Six-thirty rolled around, and Rory walked in dressed as William Howard Taft. Bernard grinned.

He moved to meet him at the door.

"I'm glad you made it." Bernard kissed him.

Rory had shaved as well, leaving his mustache. Bernard ran his hand along the smooth skin. It was soft. The leftover stubble tickled his palm.

"Do you like it?" Rory asked.

"I prefer the beard, but I wouldn't kick you out of bed."

"You're such a charmer." Rory kissed him.

They spent the evening watching horror movies playing in the family room. Having each other around other couples warmed Bernard's insides. They were like everyone else.

"You two look comfortable," Kelly said.

He plopped down on the chair next to the sofa. They weren't cuddling or even sitting close. Bernard figured it was best not to flaunt anything. Sarah and John wouldn't care, but they didn't know how the other guests would react.

"Grabbed some snacks, something to drink, and now watching Michael Myers terrorize babysitters," Bernard said.

"Sounds like a great evening," Kelly said.

"What can I say," Bernard said. "I'm a simple date."

"Whatever works."

Rory curled up to Bernard. Bernard wrapped his arm around him as they continued to watch the movie. If Rory was comfortable enough to show affection, he'd oblige and to hell with anyone who disagreed, it wasn't about them.

"You two are such a cute couple." A voice came from behind them.

They looked up to see a woman dressed as a go-go dancer. Bernard looked closer.

"Emily?"

"Hi, Bernard," Emily said.

He stood and hugged her.

"I haven't seen you since Sarah and John's wedding," he said. "I'm sorry I couldn't make it to yours."

"It's okay, I understand."

It was a relief she understood. He missed her wedding because he was in the hospital. He'd drunk himself into unconsciousness after finding Tracy cheating on him. He was there overnight, but it took a week for him to find himself again. His stomach churned at the memory. He'd allowed Tracy to get under his skin and push him to drink his pain away.

"Hi, Rory, nice to see you again." She smiled.

"You too, Emily."

Rory hugged Emily.

"Is Chris here?" Bernard asked.

"No, he had a late shift at the hospital. They're short-staffed, so they called him in."

"That sucks," Bernard said. "It'd be nice to see him again."

"Maybe we can have you over for dinner sometime."

"That'd be great."

Emily said goodbye and continued to mingle with the other guests.

Bernard and Rory went back to the movie. Rory snuggled up close again and Bernard wrapped his arm around him. Rory curled his feet behind him.

"So, what would you say to a cruise?" Bernard said.

"A cruise?"

"Yeah, we get on a boat for seven to ten days and travel the ocean. Visit places and see the sights."

"I think that'd be fun," Rory said. "Where would we go?"

"I don't know. Devon's cousin is a travel agent. He might have a better idea. I just wanted to float it past you before I started looking into it."

"Yes, I'd like that."

"Great, I'll talk to Devon and get more details."

Bernard and Rory said their goodbyes when the clock hit nine. It was late and Rory had to get up for church.

They stood on the porch. "I'll see you tomorrow for our day at the park?" Bernard asked.

"I wouldn't miss it for the world."

They kissed. A hint of chocolate filled Bernard's mouth as he explored Rory's with his tongue. He wanted this to last. He wanted to spend the night with Rory. But long trips away from home would draw unwanted attention to Rory's family. Bernard understood, but his heart ached to hold him.

"I'll never get tired of kissing you," Rory said.

"I feel the same."

Bernard watched Rory walk to his car. He wanted to ask him to stay the night. He wanted to hold him in his arms.

"Rory?" Bernard called out.

"Yeah?" Rory said.

"I'd like you to stay the night," he said. "I want to cuddle with you, and I wish we could spend more nights together."

"Bernard." Rory's face fell. "If my parents decide to pick me up for church, how do I explain why I wasn't home?"

Rory walked back up the path to embrace Bernard.

"I understand," Bernard said. "I just wish it was more than Friday nights and an occasional weekday."

"I know." Rory put his forehead against Bernard's. "I'll come out when I feel it's right. It's delicate with my mother. I know I shouldn't worry so much, but she's a large part of my life. I don't want to hurt her."

"I know," Bernard said. "I'll see you tomorrow afternoon."

*

BERNARD DROVE HOME, tears threatening to fall. The relationship pushed him back into the closet. He couldn't be public with Rory. His mother controlled who he was. He wouldn't do anything without her permission. Dating him was defiance. If Mrs. Sinclair found out, it would be disastrous.

He sighed. Rory was endangering himself and his reputation at the church. He needed to take what he could get from this relationship. He'd do anything for Rory. That included hiding that they were a couple.

*

THE NEXT AFTERNOON Bernard met Rory at the park. They ate sandwiches and homemade pudding Rory brought and enjoyed the sunny day.

"How was lunch with your parents?" Bernard asked.

"Fine," he said. "My dad and brother know about us."

"They know?"

"Yes. My brother tried to force it out of me a few months ago."

Bernard watched as tears formed in Rory's eyes. He reached over and held him.

"My dad's the one who said I should come see you back in April. That first Saturday we spent together. I think he knew then but waited for me to accept it."

"Just like with me," Bernard said.

"What is just like with you?"

"Everyone else knew I was gay before I did."

His father told him as much. His parents waited for him to come out. He didn't come out to his dad until he was twenty-two. Sarah said she knew when he told her. He'd told Rory when he was twenty-four, right after his excommunication. They didn't speak for a year. Rory came back in time for Jason to break his heart. He stayed. He stood by him.

"Yup, seems that way," Rory said.

They followed the usual path. This time, Rory put his hand in Bernard's.

Bernard turned to meet Rory's gaze.

"Are you sure?" he asked.

"I need to be more comfortable in public with you. I can't keep hiding who I am. The more I do it, the more normal it feels. One day I will be so comfortable being with you that I can tell my mother."

Bernard leaned in to kiss him. Rory didn't back away. Their lips melded together. Couples passed, but no one said anything.

"You're so wonderful," Rory said.

"I think you are too."

They finished their walk and headed back to the blanket.

"So, since we both have to be up early tomorrow for work, I was wondering if I can stay the night at your place," Rory said.

"Of course, I'd love that."

A grin spread across his face. Bernard could hold and cuddle Rory on the couch and lay with him as they drifted off to sleep.

"Okay, let me go home and get a change of clothes and I'll meet you at your place."

"Great, I'll order pizza and we can cuddle on the couch and watch a movie."

"That sounds perfect."

They kissed goodbye in the parking lot, and Bernard got into his truck.

The drive home was invigorating. He was going to get the rare night with Rory, where they could be themselves and hide nothing from each other.

*

AFTER AN EVENING of movies and pizza, they climbed into bed together. Rory wrapped his arm around Bernard and held tight. Bernard breathed in his scent. They'd showered, but Rory had an odor he adored. The aroma that drew Bernard to him.

"I'm glad you asked to come over," Bernard said.

"I want to cuddle with you as often as I can."

"It's nice when you hold me," Bernard said. "I feel your love, your passion, and I know you're here with me. That you chose me."

"What we have is special to me. I want to be with you. I just wish I could be out. Not hide anymore."

Bernard shifted around and locked eyes with Rory.

"You can come out when you're ready. Not a moment sooner. You'll know when it's right."

"Thank you."

Their lips met, and warmth enveloped his body. Bernard moved his hands over Rory's furry body. Rory no longer wore pajamas when he slept over. The warmth of Rory's belly pressed against his own.

They'd only had sex twice, and both times were amazing. Rory was a passionate lover. He cared about what Bernard wanted. Just like Bernard cared about what he wanted.

"I've set the alarm for six, is that early enough for you?" Bernard asked.

"That's plenty of time."

"Okay. I love you."

"I love you too."

Bernard rolled over and pushed back until Rory's chest was against his back. Rory's big arm wrapped around his chest. He wanted this every night. He wanted Rory to stay with him. When Rory held him, everything felt right. They could face anything together. He didn't know if Rory would ever move in with him, but he hoped one day Rory would say yes.

Chapter Twenty-Nine

Rory

Friday, November 20

RORY AND BERNARD caught a matinee of *Enemy of the State*—a thrilling movie Rory enjoyed. Afterwards, they had dinner at a casual diner and headed home.

Rory stood on Bernard's doorstep. He looked into Bernard's eyes and smiled. He was in love, and there was no greater feeling. Bernard had been patient and kind. He was the person Rory had dreamed about finding.

"It's getting a little chilly. Let's go inside," Bernard said.

"I would love nothing more," Rory said.

They got into the shower and cleaned themselves up. Bernard

massaged Rory's back and shoulders. The tension in his body evaporated at Bernard's touch.

Bernard dried Rory off. His hands lingered on Rory's dick.

"You like to play with that, don't you?" Rory said.

"Why wouldn't I? It's a nice dick."

"Thank you."

"So, what shall we do?"

"I…" Rory stuttered. He looked away. He couldn't face Bernard.

"What, sweetie?" Bernard held his face. His warm fingers scratched his beard.

"I…I want to try anal." Rory's face burned.

He'd said it out loud. What would it be like to be inside Bernard? What would it feel like to have Bernard inside him? He didn't care which one, but he wanted to.

"Okay," Bernard said. "Do you want to top or bottom?"

"I don't know. I've imagined doing both with you."

"Well, we can do both."

"We can?"

"Of course, one tops, and then we switch before either of us comes."

"I've only ever seen it in porn. I think I know how."

"Come with me."

Bernard led him into the bedroom and laid him down. Bernard ran his fingers through Rory's hair. He found Rory's nipple and tugged it with his teeth. Rory gasped as Bernard nibbled the tip, his nipples hardening. He bit his lip when Bernard's fingers tweaked his other one.

"I'll top first, so if you don't like it, we can switch," Bernard said.

"Okay."

"Now, let me taste that cock."

Bernard wrapped his warm mouth around Rory's cock. He looked down to see Bernard swallow it whole.

Damn, he's so good at that.

Rory's cock was hard within seconds.

"Now that you're nice and hard, let's prepare your tight ass."

Bernard lifted his legs and buried his tongue deep into Rory's ass. He squirmed and moaned as Bernard's tongue explored his hole. Rory grabbed the back of his knees and spread his legs. Bernard's head bobbed up and down as he licked his ass.

Bernard's tongue ran the length between his ass and balls. Rory gasped as teeth nibbled on the tender flesh. It sent waves of pleasure up his body.

"That feels good," Rory said.

"You like it?"

"I like everything you do."

Bernard rubbed his facial hair against Rory's balls. Rory laid back as Bernard's mouth explored him. His cock, balls, taint, and ass experienced Bernard's touch.

"I'm going to prep you now," Bernard said.

He grabbed the lube and condoms from his drawer. Bernard made a show of lubing up his finger. He stared into Rory's eyes as his finger slid in. Slow. Gentle.

Rory closed his eyes. He let out a groan as Bernard hit his prostate.

Bernard continued, using slow, even strokes. Rory pushed against his hand. He wanted that finger deeper.

"I'm going to add another finger," Bernard said in a soft tone which eased the tension in Rory's ass.

Rory nodded.

Another finger joined the first, and a jolt of excitement ran down his spine. He'd only ever used one finger when he did it, and this was ten times better. He continued to push against the fingers. Bernard sucked on his cock while he fingered him. The combination was going to make him come.

"*Yes!*" he yelled as Bernard's fingers explored inside.

"Fuck, you sound hot."

"I want you inside me now."

"You want my thick cock in your ass?" Bernard said.

"Yes, please," Rory said.

"Are you sure your sweet, tight ass can take this enormous cock?"

"Yes, I want your fat cock in me and pounding me." Rory's eyes widened at what he'd just said.

"Well, someone has learned to talk dirty." Bernard grinned at him.

"You like it when I beg for your cock?"

"I like when you want me so bad you talk like that."

"Then get that condom on and get your dick in my ass."

Bernard put the condom on and put Rory's legs on his shoulder. He placed a pillow under Rory's ass. With his ass exposed, Rory held his breath.

"Be sure to breathe," Bernard said, "and relax the best you can."

"Okay."

"If it hurts, let me know. I'll be gentle."

Bernard was gentle. He eased his cock inside. A twinge of pain caused Rory to let out a cry. Bernard stopped and pulled out.

"Are you okay?" Bernard asked.

"Yes. Your dick is the biggest thing that's been in there."

"Okay, just let me know when to stop."

"Go ahead, try again."

Bernard added more lube to Rory's ass. He massaged it with his finger. Bernard's touch eased the pain in his ass. He relaxed. He wanted Bernard back inside him.

Bernard's cock entered him again. Bernard moved slowly, half an inch at a time. Rory appreciated the patience. Bernard wouldn't hurt him and wanted him to feel pleasure.

"I'm all the way in," Bernard said.

Bernard's balls hit his ass cheeks. He cherished the connection they had. He'd never been this intimate with anyone, and now his best friend was his lover, and he wanted this moment to last a lifetime.

Bernard moved and his cock hit Rory's prostate. It was like nothing he'd felt before. Rory jerked with pleasure and let out a moan.

"Yes," he groaned loudly.

"Do you want me to pump now?"

"Yes, slow though."

Bernard moved carefully in and out of his hole. They stared into each other's eyes. He loved looking into Bernard's eyes with him inside him. It was exhilarating to be so connected.

"God, you feel so good inside me." Rory reached up and pinched Bernard's nipples. Bernard let out a groan.

Bernard continued to stretch out his hole. His thick cock filled every inch of him. It made him groan. He moved his hands from Bernard's nipples to his throbbing cock. He stroked the foreskin over the tip and down again.

"I don't know if I can go much longer. I'm going to shoot my load,"

Rory said.

"Hang on." Bernard slowed down, slipping his cock out of Rory.

Rory immediately wanted to beg for that cock again. He loved bottoming. It was intoxicating.

"Thank you." Rory leaned in for a kiss.

"That was amazing," Bernard said. "You know how to take a cock."

"You were so patient and understanding," Rory said. "That's why I could take it."

"I'm glad I could make your first time enjoyable."

"Next time though, I want you to come inside me."

"I'll hold you to that, but for now, I'm going to make you shoot that load inside me."

"So, how do we go about this?" Rory asked.

"First, you're going to finger me like I did with you. Then I'm going to lay you on your back and ride that nice cock of yours."

Fuck, I'm going to be inside him. I want to know what his ass feels like wrapped around my cock.

"I want you," Rory moaned.

Rory moved to below Bernard and slid a lubed finger inside him. Bernard grabbed his cock and stroked it while Rory massaged his prostate. Bernard's hand on his cock excited Rory. He wanted Bernard's cock inside him again. He wanted to feel Bernard inside him, shooting his load while he jerked his cock to the sensation. Without a condom. He wanted to feel Bernard fill his ass with cum. Bernard was an amazing lover, and he never wanted to be with anyone else.

"Okay, another finger," Bernard said, desperation in his voice.

Rory obliged and slid a second finger in. Bernard let out a cry as he stroked his cock. The sound of Bernard's arousal caused Rory's cock to twitch. Bernard's ass squeezed around his fingers. His cock wanted that ass. He wanted to be inside Bernard.

"I want you to fuck me," Bernard said.

"You want this cock in you?" Rory pulled his fingers out and presented his cock to Bernard.

"You know I do."

Bernard laid Rory down. He slid the condom on and poured lube onto his dick and covered it.

"What do I do?" Rory asked.

"When I say so, you can start pushing against me."

Bernard straddled Rory and slid his cock inside. He took it with ease. A surge of jealousy erupted in Rory. He didn't know why he couldn't take it like Bernard did. It would make Bernard happy if he could slide into him with ease. Bernard had been doing this for years and he had more experience. But hadn't he not had sex in a while? He knew about Jason and Tracy, but who knows how many others he'd had sex with. Had he had sex with Sean? Another pang of jealousy hit him. Bernard was his first, but he wasn't Bernard's first.

It doesn't matter. Bernard chose me, not another man.

This was what Bernard wanted, he was who Bernard wanted. He smiled at the thought of Bernard choosing him over any other man.

"Damn, you can take that cock well." Rory tried to sound sexy.

"Because I love having your cock in my ass."

Bernard continued to move up and down on his cock. His hole clenched around Rory's dick, attempting to suck the cum out of him. It was fantastic. Bernard's ass surrounded his cock, eager for it.

"Okay, push back on me," Bernard said.

Every time Bernard pushed down, Rory pushed up against him. He moaned with excitement. Rory loved what he did to Bernard. This man made him feel special.

They continued to work. Rory didn't know how long he could last like this. Bernard's tight ass was warmer than his hand. It grasped his cock. He'd jerked off, but not with this intensity.

"I want to try from on top," Rory said.

"Anything you want, sexy."

Bernard slid off and lay down on the bed. He placed a pillow under his hips.

"I'll be gentle," Rory said.

"Not too gentle, just do what comes naturally."

Rory looked down at Bernard's waiting hole. He licked his lips. Rory wanted to fuck him. He wanted to look into Bernard's eyes as he shot his load inside.

Rory slid his dick into Bernard's ass. Bernard placed his legs on Rory's shoulders. Rory went in slow. He wasn't sure how fast to go. He didn't want to hurt him.

Rory pumped. "You like this?" He gazed into Bernard's eyes. His beautiful brown eyes.

"Yes!" Bernard begged. "Just like that. Fuck me."

Rory continued at the same pace. Bernard stroked his cock and didn't stifle his moans. The moans of pleasure excited Rory. He caused Bernard to moan, buck, and stroke his cock. Rory was in control, and Bernard lay there, submissive to what he wanted.

"Faster, baby. Fuck me," Bernard gasped.

Rory quickened his pace. Bernard pushed back at every thrust, his ass tight around Rory's cock.

"Yes, that's it," Bernard said. "Keep fucking me."

Rory put his whole body into it. He wanted to see Bernard come. A rush of adrenalin surged as he fucked Bernard. He watched Bernard's belly jiggle. Rory placed his hands on Bernard's chest and leaned into his thrusts. The momentum forced Bernard to gasp.

"Yes, harder, faster," Bernard said.

"I'm going to come," Rory said.

"Shoot that load, baby."

Rory shot his load. His cock pulsed with each spurt. He filled the condom.

"Keep going," Bernard said.

Rory continued to pump, still hard. Bernard's hand quickened on his cock. Rory watched as he convulsed. Bernard was about to come, and he couldn't wait to see him shoot.

"*Fuck!*" Bernard shot a load. It sprayed onto his belly.

Rory slid his cock out and collapsed next to Bernard.

"That was hot," Rory said.

"That was amazing." Bernard leaned over and planted a kiss on Rory. "You're amazing."

"I watched a lot of porn the last few months," he said.

"Well, it paid off."

*

THEY SHOWERED AND lay in bed, naked.

"I am so happy we're together," Rory said.

"I'm happy too."

Rory wrapped his arms around Bernard. He held him tight against him, his chest against Bernard's back. His soft cock lay against Bernard's ass.

Bernard grabbed his arm and pulled his hand to his lips. His soft lips brushed the back of his hand.

"I love you," Bernard said.

"I love you too," Rory said.

They lay there for a while. Rory escaped into the warmth of Bernard's body. He was soft and furry. They'd grown up together, and now they were partners. Rory's dreams of finding someone had finally come true, and nothing would pull them apart.

Chapter Thirty

Bernard

Saturday, December 5

BERNARD PULLED INTO his father's farm at ten in the morning. His father had insisted on having his birthday celebration there and had invited all his friends and family. Get-togethers were his father's specialty, and Bernard's birthday was one he looked forward to all year.

Someone had decorated the bench tables in the yard with green and blue placemats and streamers. Bernard's favorite colors.

Bernard's father rolled a grill out to the middle of his yard. Ginger bounded out of the truck and ran to the field to meet Bonnie. A cool winter breeze swirled around the dust and gravel.

"Dad, let me help." Emilio walked out of the house.

"I got it, son."

"Dad, let us help," Bernard said.

He walked up to the porch to meet his dad.

"Bernardo." He reached up to hug Bernard. "You're early."

While his father was distracted, Emilio moved the grill to the middle of the benches.

"I couldn't wait to see you." He wrapped his father in a hug.

"Rory's here," he said. "Came to prepare his desserts. The boys have taken to him. They think he's amazing. I told them he was your boyfriend."

"You told them?"

"Yes, it's fine. Emilio and Camila know about it. They think it's a great idea for the kids to get used to him being around and that love is love."

"That's great."

"Also, I told you he was gay."

"Yes, you did," Bernard said, "a few times."

"He's perfect for you."

"Thank you, Dad."

"*Uncle* Bernard!" Twin ten-year-old boys made a beeline for him.

"Duarte, Adão." He reached down and picked up the boys in his arms. "You guys are so big now."

"We're ten now," Duarte said.

"Yeah, last time you saw us, we were only nine," Adão agreed.

He didn't get to see his nephews as often as he'd like. He missed their last birthday because Emilio and Camila had taken them to the Azores for their birthday. They told him they loved the remote-control cars he'd sent them.

"Oh, you're all grown up now?"

"Almost. We are more mature," they said in unison.

"You sure are."

"Okay, we're going to go play now," Duarte said.

Before he could respond, the boys were off to the field to play with Bonnie and Ginger. They giggled and chased the dogs around the pen.

"They have a lot of energy," Rory said.

He wrapped his arms around Bernard from behind and kissed his neck.

"Happy birthday, sweetie."

Bernard held Rory tight against him. He inhaled his cologne. He couldn't get enough of it. Rory's touch and smell made him feel wanted. Loved.

"Thank you, sweetheart."

Bernard turned around and kissed him. He tasted raspberries on his lips.

"Why do you taste like raspberries?"

"I'm making raspberry custard tarts," he said. "I know you love them."

"You are more than I could have ever dreamed of."

They hugged, and Bernard gave him another kiss.

*

SARAH, JOHN, AND Kelly arrived at noon with little Mikey waddling along.

"You made it." Bernard jogged up and took the casserole dish from Sarah's hands.

"Why would we miss your birthday party?" Sarah wrapped an arm around Bernard.

"Besides, Kelly hasn't had your dad's food yet," John said. "He's in for a treat."

"They go on about it," Kelly said. "I couldn't pass up the opportunity to have some."

Once everyone was present, the air around the grill filled with the scent of burgers, hotdogs, buns, vegetables, and the spice of his father's secret sauce.

"Uncle Rory." Bernard's twin nephews came running, followed by two girls around the same age.

"Did they call me uncle?"

"Yes, they call any adult who is part of the family and is not their dad, mom, or grandparent uncle and aunt," Bernard said. "I forgot. You weren't around for that part."

"They think of me as part of the family?"

"Well, they know you're my boyfriend, so they don't see it as any different."

Rory smiled. Bernard loved his smile.

"I always wondered why you had so many aunts and uncles."

"Yup, pretty much any adult around us is an aunt or uncle."

"What's up, boys?" Rory knelt.

Bernard loved how Rory treated everyone, even children, with respect and gave them his full attention.

"Cousin Melissa and Mandy said you couldn't find all of us if you tried. But we think you can." Duarte spoke breathlessly. The two girls who followed nodded.

"I think I can. You all go hide, and I'll come to find you," he said.

"*One. Two.*" The kids screamed and scattered.

"I'll be back." His smile and wink warmed Bernard.

Bernard watched Rory play with the kids. They hid while he sought them out. The children were talented at hiding.

"So, how are things going with Rory?" Emilio slid onto the bench next to him.

"It's been amazing," Bernard said. "I've never been happier. Sarah said I fell in love with him years ago."

"And did you? Fall in love, I mean."

"Yes, I actually told him I loved him."

"He's great with the kids. They're having a blast with him."

"He really is a sweet man."

"Do you want children someday?"

Bernard thought about it. He'd wanted children for so long, but never found himself in a stable place to have children. Adopting was difficult for a single man, and impossible for a gay couple in California. He wished there was a way.

"I'd love children," Bernard said, "but there's no way for us to adopt. The state won't allow it."

"You never know what the future holds."

"True, we both want children. I hope it's something we can do. I know he'd make a wonderful father."

"You'd be a wonderful father too."

Would he be a good father? He'd wanted children but couldn't raise a child alone. With Rory in his life, they could raise a child together. They'd be great parents.

"Thank you."

"I've never seen you so happy, brother."

"Thank you," Bernard said, "it's just…"

"Nope, you're not doing this." Emilio cut him off. "You're not going into self-doubt mode right now."

"What do you mean?"

"You feel you're not worthy of love, but you are. That man over there is perfect for you. You love him and he clearly loves you. So, don't screw it up."

Bernard watched Rory chase Adão around a tire swing. He bent over to grab at him. Once in his arms, he tickled him. Adão screamed and giggled.

"Okay." Bernard held up his hands. "I surrender. I won't screw it up."

Emilio hugged him. "I know you're scared, brother. I know your past. You are a caring, loving, wonderful person who deserves to have someone who loves you."

Bernard squeezed his brother. "I know Rory is the right match. I have to get used to being loved."

"I understand."

Bernard continued to watch Rory with the kids. The twins avoided strangers but took to Rory. Something about him made them comfortable.

"Come eat," Bernard's father called out.

Everyone grabbed a plate, sat around on the benches, and conversation ensued.

"Rory, it's so nice to see you again," Aunt Antonia said.

"It's good to see you too, Antonia."

She smiled at him. Antonia always liked Rory. She even said he was one of Bernard's friends who mattered. He was grateful to have a family who accepted him, when Rory didn't. He wanted Rory to be surrounded by the love he deserved. He hoped one day Rory's family would accept him for the wonderful person he was.

Everyone enjoyed themselves. It was a wonderful afternoon. Bernard took in the scent of his father's cooking. It never ceased to amaze him how wonderful of a griller his dad was.

After everyone had their fill, they brought out the gifts.

Bernard sat on a bench. Gifts piled up in front of him.

His dad got him *Final Fantasy Tactics*—a strategy video game where you control a small army of soldiers on a chessboard-like battlefield against enemy armies. It took cunning, patience, and dedication to play.

"Thanks, Dad." He hugged his father.

"I know you like those games, so I went to the store, and this is the one the clerk said you might like. I didn't know if you had it."

"I don't, thank you."

He opened the rest of the gifts. Bernard received some ties, a watch, a coffee mug, a few board games, and a subscription to *Men's Health* magazine. The last was from his cousin Bella. They'd grown up together, and she always tried to get him to eat healthier and exercise. He didn't know if this was her way of hinting to get in shape or she thought he'd find the men inside attractive. Either way, her heart was in the right place.

Emilio, Camila, and the boys got him a new coffeemaker. It had a clock and brew timer and was perfect for him.

"This is fantastic. I can now prepare my coffee the night before. Thank you."

"We thought you'd like it," Camila said.

Bernard opened the gift from Rory. He lifted it. He smiled at the love

Rory put into this gift. Rory knitted him a sweater that matched the bear pride flag. It even had the bear's paw in the upper corner.

"Rory, this is beautiful." Bernard wrapped his arms around him. "Thank you so much."

"I'm glad you like it," Rory said.

"I love it."

Bernard kissed him. His lips were sweet from the punch.

"I'm so happy," Rory said. "I made it and was worried it'd be too much."

"Nothing you do for me could ever be too much."

The guests let out an audible *aww* as they hugged. Bernard didn't want to let Rory go. This man had done so much for him. Helped him learn to love and accept love again.

Rory brought out the cake. He'd baked a two-layer red velvet cake with cream cheese frosting, two dozen raspberry custard tarts, and an apple pie. Camila brought out vanilla and chocolate ice cream.

"Rory, the cake and tarts look amazing," Bernard said. "You didn't have to go to so much trouble."

"It was no trouble at all," Rory said. "I'm so happy I can share your birthday with you this year."

Rory had decorated the tarts with a raspberry on top. The raspberry swirl formed a bear's paw on the custard.

After taking in the aroma of the tarts, Bernard bit into one. The flavor of custard and raspberry swam in his mouth. It was divine.

The cake, decorated with the same bear's paw on top, tasted as good as it looked. Sweet chocolate and cream cheese melted in his mouth.

"Uncle Rory, are you going to marry Uncle Bernard?" Duarte asked.

Bernard looked into Rory's eyes. His future sat next to him. It didn't matter if they could legally marry or not; they were going to be together for the rest of their lives.

"Maybe one day," Rory said, "and we'll invite you."

"Awesome!"

After everyone had eaten their dessert, Bernard's dad strung up a piñata for the kids.

His dad pulled the rope on the piñata as the excited kids gathered around. It looked like a cartoon character he didn't recognize.

"Hit it," he called to Duarte.

Duarte swung at it with all his might. "Grandpa, I can't hit it," Duarte said.

"It, it…" His father stopped. He swayed on his feet. He dropped the rope. "I feel…" The words stuck on his lips. He collapsed to the ground in a heap.

"Dad!" Bernard screamed. He ran to his father. He shook him. "Dad, wake up." Tears welled in his eyes.

His heart raced. He looked around. He'd trained in CPR one weekend every year, and now it was gone.

"Move aside, Bernard." Bernard moved over and his cousin Bella began CPR. He was grateful she remembered. "Get the kids out of here."

Rory gathered up the children and took them inside. Camila followed.

Bernard stared down at his father's unconscious form. His eyes moved to each person, but nobody moved.

"We need to do something!" Bernard cried.

"I called nine-one-one. They'll be here in ten minutes." Bernard looked over to see Antonia.

"Give me space. He needs air. I need everyone to back away," Bella commanded.

The group moved back in unison. Bernard watched as Bella continued CPR on his father. She was a registered nurse and she would help him. Everything was going to be okay.

Bella got him breathing, though his breaths were shallow. She gave him an aspirin and took his pulse.

It was the longest ten minutes of his life. The ambulance arrived and two paramedics moved his father onto a stretcher. They lifted him into the ambulance.

"I'm going with him," Bernard said.

"What's your relationship?" one of the paramedics asked him.

"He's my father."

They motioned him in.

Bernard held his dad's hand. "It's going to be all right, Dad. They're gonna take care of you." He stared down at his father's glassy eyes.

"I love you, son," he whispered, then closed his eyes.

A rhythmic beeping sound echoed in Bernard's ears as he focused on his father.

"It's going to be okay," he whispered, softer this time.

Chapter Thirty-One

Bernard

Friday, December 11–Wednesday, December 16

IT WAS THE Friday after his birthday. Bernard sat in the pew with his family, Rory on his left and Emilio on his right. He fought back tears as the preacher gave the eulogy. The priest described his father as a powerful man and hard worker and talked about his dedication to his family. The usual garbage they said at a funeral.

The priest didn't know his father. He couldn't pronounce his name. He had nothing special to say about him. The man couldn't even translate the eulogy into Portuguese for his family. The church found a translator. The priest spoke too fast for the Portuguese and sign language translators.

The poor women couldn't keep up. It infuriated Bernard that they couldn't find a bilingual priest for a Portuguese funeral.

"Does the family wish to speak?" the preacher asked.

As the eldest, it was Bernard's duty to speak first.

He walked up to the podium.

He looked over at the Portuguese translator. "You can take a break. I can translate."

The woman smiled and sat down.

"Hello, My name is Bernardo Francisco Silva. My father, João Tomás Silva"—Bernard emphasized his father's name as he looked at the priest— "loved me unconditionally. He never judged me or told me my dreams were wrong. My father knew I was gay before I came out and accepted me for it. He took care of me and my brother after our mother passed away and saved up money to send me to college to follow my passion. He did everything for me, and now he's gone. I didn't have time to thank him for all he's done for me. I can never hug him or confide in him again. I'm going to miss my father more than anything in this world. I love you, Dad, and thank you for always believing in me, even when I didn't believe in myself."

Bernard repeated his speech in Portuguese for his family. He wanted to say more, but the words got stuck.

His brother followed with a heartfelt speech. Bernard registered his pain. Their father was close to both of them. Emilio followed in his footsteps and owned a small farm. His father helped him with startup money. They owed their father everything.

They buried his father in the family plot of the cemetery. Bernard and Emilio stayed behind as family and friends left.

"Do you want me to stay?" Rory asked.

"I...I'd like to be with my brother alone if that's okay."

"Anything you need." Rory leaned in and kissed him.

"I'm going to take the boys home," Camila said. "Take all the time you need. We'll see you there."

Camila kissed Emilio and walked off with Rory and the boys.

"I can't believe he's gone," Bernard said.

"Why didn't he listen to us?" Emilio yelled.

"Emilio, it's not his fault."

"Yes, it is," he said. "We told him to listen to his doctor and stop drinking and smoking. He didn't listen. Now he's gone."

"I..." Bernard couldn't answer.

His father went through two packs of cigarettes a day and drank far too much. He'd been that way Bernard's entire life. His beer drinking started when Bernard's mom died twenty years ago. Bernard was only sixteen. Emilio was fourteen. They had to get jobs to help support the family. Their father took on extra work to earn the money to give them what they needed. He worked twelve to sixteen hours a day.

Emilio put his arms around himself and fell to his knees.

"Why?" He choked back tears.

Bernard knelt beside his brother and wrapped his arms around him. His size engulfed Emilio's compact frame. Emilio laid his head against Bernard's chest. His brother convulsed with sobs in his arm.

"Shh," Bernard said, "we'll be okay. It's going to be okay."

"He didn't get to see you walk down the aisle," Emilio said. "He would've loved to see you in a suit getting married. It was all he talked about."

It wasn't legal for same-sex couples to marry. A ceremony would be something he and Rory could do. His father would've been there, so proud of his son, supporting and cheering him on.

They sat on the ground. Brothers bound by birth and held together by sorrow. They were opposites, but they loved each other just the same. Bernard knew his brother's pain just as his brother knew his.

The funeral reception was a blur. They held it at Emilio's house. He ran into family members he hadn't seen in years. They gave their condolences and brought food. He wasn't hungry.

"I think I'm going to go home," he told his friends.

They'd all come. Rory, Sarah, John, Kelly, and even Sean made it. It warmed his heart that all his friends were here for him.

"Do you want me to come with you?" Rory asked.

"I think I need to be alone."

"I love you, sweetheart." Rory wrapped his arms around him and kissed him. "I'll always be there for you."

"Thank you, sweetie. I love you too."

"If you need anything, call us," Sarah said.

"We'll be here for you," John said.

"Thank you, everyone."

Bernard got in his car and drove home.

He didn't remember the drive but found himself outside his house.

He walked through the house, let Ginger in, fed her, then sat on the couch while an infomercial talked about some new cleaning product.

"Ginger, let's go to bed."

*

THE NEXT MORNING Bernard lay in bed, still in his suit. Ginger lay next to him, cuddling under his arm.

"What am I going to do, Ginger?" He had no tears left to shed. "My dad's gone. I'll never see him again."

Bernard took Ginger out when she needed to go, made sure she had food and water, and lay in bed.

"He cared about me. We talked all the time. I'll never hear his voice again."

Bernard walked to the kitchen and played the messages. A message from his dad remained.

Hey, Bernardo. Happy birthday, son. I can't wait to see you today. I know it's early, but I couldn't wait to wish you a happy birthday. Love you, son.

Bernard replayed the message a dozen times before he walked back to his bed. He lay down and Ginger joined him. His tears fell again. Hearing his father's voice reminded him he was gone.

Ginger whimpered and curled up next to him.

*

ANOTHER DAY DRAGGED by. Bernard hadn't eaten. He couldn't eat. How could he enjoy food when this loss had drained the life from him? His father was his rock, the man who pushed him to be his best. He didn't have that support anymore.

He was napping when he heard voices coming up the stairs.

"I've never seen him this bad."

Is that Sarah? He concentrated, straining to hear.

"He can't be in good shape. He won't answer his phone." This was a man. John? Or Kelly?

"Well, we need to check on him," Sarah said.

The door opened. He didn't bother to sit up or open his eyes.

"Bernard." A soft voice came from the distance. "It's Sarah. Are you okay?"

"I'm fine," he said.

"Bernard. We're here to help." That was Kelly.

"Who's here?" he squeaked out.

"Me, John, Kelly, and Rory," Sarah said.

Great, more people to see the wreck I've become.

He opened his eyes to see them standing there. "I'll be okay. I just need time." He closed his eyes again.

"We know, we're just worried. When was the last time you ate something?" John asked.

"I don't know."

"We left some food in the fridge. You should eat something when you're up to it." Sarah said.

"I made a banana cream pie," Rory said.

"Thank you."

"Bernard. If you need anything, please let us know." Rory's voice came out soft.

Rory was scared. His voice revealed that much. He didn't want Rory to worry about him. He had other things to worry about than him.

"We're gonna let you get some sleep. Have you talked to Rich about your leave?"

He'd called the day his father passed away to let them know.

"They're fine with me taking the time I need," he said. "Rich said to take care of myself and to get some rest."

"That's good," Sarah said.

"We should let him get some sleep," John said.

"You're right," Sarah said.

Bernard felt Sarah's lips on his forehead, but he couldn't open his eyes.

"Bernard, would you like me to take care of Ginger for a few days?" Kelly asked. "She could play with Chester."

"I don't want to bother you. I think I'll be okay."

"It's no bother. You need to look after yourself. I'll take Ginger."

"Thank you."

The tears still couldn't come. His friends were by his side, helping him, and he couldn't shed a tear of gratitude.

"Come on, Ginger," Kelly called.

He opened his eyes to see Ginger leap off the bed after some coaxing. Kelly picked her up. He closed his eyes. The door closed.

"I love you, sweetheart." Rory pressed his lips against his. "Please take care of yourself. I hate to see you like this."

"I love you too, sweetie." Bernard returned the kiss.

"I'll let you get some rest and check on you soon."

*

THE NEXT FEW days were a daze. Bernard remembered going to the store but couldn't remember what he bought. He filled his days with sporadically eating, random TV shows, and sleep.

"Bernard," a distant voice called out. "I've come by to see how you're feeling and brought Ginger to see you."

Bernard looked over to see Kelly standing above his bed.

Ginger jumped up and curled up next to him.

"How are you holding up?"

"I'm okay, I ate something today," Bernard said.

"That's good, man." Kelly sat at the edge of the bed. "Everyone's worried about you."

"I know."

"Rory came by a few times, but you were out cold."

"I wish he'd woken me up so I could see him."

"I think he wanted you to rest." Kelly laid a hand on his knee. "He really cares about you."

"I know he does, but…" Bernard wanted to tell someone, needed to tell someone.

"But what?"

"But I don't deserve someone as sweet, kind, and wonderful as him."

Tears pooled in his eyes. Rory deserved to be happy, and he couldn't give him happiness. He was a wreck and couldn't even take care of himself right now.

"I think it's the heartache talking, I don't think you really mean that."

"How long has it been?"

"It's Tuesday the fifteenth."

"I've been like this for four days?"

"Yes, and we're worried about you." Kelly rubbed his knee. "If you need to talk, please reach out."

"I miss my dad. He's gone, and I don't know what to do. I could talk to him about anything, and now he's gone. I should have done more to stop him from drinking and smoking. I should have helped him when my mom died, I should have done so much more."

It all poured out of him. He was sixteen when his mom passed away, and he wallowed in his own emotions instead of helping his father and brother. He didn't try hard enough to protect them.

"It's not your fault," Kelly said. "You can only warn people so much. You can't force them to change. I know it's hard, I do. You need to take time to grieve your way. What happened back then wasn't your fault, and you were a teenager. I want to believe you did your best."

Bernard petted Ginger. She was a sweet dog who knew when he was sad. She was by his side with Tracy, and she was by his side with Sean, and she was here now.

Tracy, that arrogant asshole who is now with his other ex. Those monsters deserved each other.

Kelly broke the silence. "I'm gonna leave Ginger here with you for a little while. There's some food from Sarah in your fridge. I'll be back this evening to take her home."

"Thank you, Kelly. You're a great friend."

"I'm happy to help."

*

BERNARD SLEPT THE rest of the day with Ginger by his side. She refused to leave him.

He woke up in the dark. He reached to scratch Ginger's ears. She was gone.

"Ginger, here, girl," he called out.

Where is she?

Bernard ran through the house. He called her. He checked the laundry room, the backyard, the spare room, and even the closets. Panic set in. *Did she get out?*

There was a note on the fridge.

Hello Bernard,

I thought you might forget that I took Ginger, so I left this note. She's safe with me. You don't need to worry. Take care of yourself.

Your friend,

Kelly.

She was with Kelly. He breathed a sigh of relief. How long did he sleep? He didn't know what day it was.

Chapter Thirty-Two

Rory

Thursday, December 17–Monday, December 21

RORY PARKED IN Bernard's driveway and made his way to the door. Bernard had given him a key, so he let himself in. He'd stopped by every few days to clean and check on Bernard. He'd been asleep each time, and he didn't want to disturb him. Bernard needed rest.

Rory made his way to Bernard's bedroom. He opened the door and found Bernard passed out on the bed. Three whiskey bottles lay on the floor, one completely empty. The stench of vomit permeated the room.

"*Bernard!*" Rory said.

"Rory?" he asked. His voice was hoarse and weak.

Bernard's eyes fluttered open. Dilated pupils stared back at him.

Rory placed his hand on Bernard's forehead. His clammy skin was cool. Sweat pooled around his neck and covered the sheets.

"Did you drink all this whiskey?" Rory picked up an empty bottle.

"Huh?"

"There's an empty bottle, and another half drunk," Rory said.

"I think I drank it," Bernard said.

He looked around. Vomit filled half of his bedside trash can. Some had splattered onto the floor. There were dried crusts of vomit on Bernard's bed.

"Come on." Rory helped lift Bernard off the bed. They stumbled to his bathroom.

"I'm gonna be sick."

"Hold on." Rory lifted the seat as Bernard threw up. Tears rolled down his face.

"What have I done?"

Rory grabbed the cup from the sink and filled it.

"Here, drink some water." He pushed the glass of water to Bernard's lips. Bernard drank. Rory filled another glass and helped Bernard drink.

"Let's get you cleaned up." Rory helped undress him and sat him in the tub.

"No. I don't want you to see me like this. Leave me here."

"I'm not leaving." Rory turned on the taps. He filled the tub with cool water.

"You can't, you'll get wet."

"It's going to be okay."

Rory grabbed the soap and cleaned Bernard. He scrubbed his body and washed out his vomit-stained beard and hair. Tears rolled down Bernard's face as Rory cleaned him. An ache filled Rory's heart. Bernard's dad's death broke him. He needed him more than ever. He wouldn't leave him alone again.

He drained the dirty water and refilled it. Rory used the clean water from the spout to rinse Bernard's hair. His curls clung to his head.

Bernard continued to sob. His body convulsed with each breath he took.

"Shh. It's going to be okay, Bernard."

"Why are you washing me?"

"Because your bed looks like you haven't left it since I came by two days ago," Rory said. "Now, let's get you taken care of. Everything's going to be okay."

Rory drained the water and helped Bernard stand. He grabbed a clean towel and dried him off. Bernard shivered in his arms.

"It's okay," Rory said. "You're going to be okay."

Rory helped Bernard to the sink to brush his teeth. Two pills lay at the bottom of the sink. He looked over and a bottle lay at the bottom of the trash can. He pulled out the empty bottle. The label read *Paxil*.

"Bernard, what did you do with your pills?"

"My what?"

"Your medication. What happened to your medication?"

"I don't need it anymore. It isn't doing anything."

Rory stared at Bernard. He'd thrown out his pills.

"What did you do with them, Bernard?"

"I don't need them!"

"When was the last time you took it?"

Bernard stared at him with unfocused eyes. "The day after we buried my dad. The day I knew nothing would help."

"That was almost a week ago." Rory reached out and held him close. "Why did you stop?" he pleaded.

"They didn't help. I still got depressed when my dad died. They were supposed to ease my anxiety, not worsen it."

"That's normal. To feel like that. But you can't stop taking your medication." Rory hugged Bernard. "Once you get sober, we'll get you a refill. Everything's going to be fine. I promise."

"I just want it all to end."

Rory leaned away. "No, Bernard. That's not what you want."

"I'm sorry," Bernard said. His face contorted. Tears streamed down his face.

"It's okay. You don't need to be sorry."

Rory helped him get into his underwear, shirt, and shorts. He kissed him. Bernard needed to get better. This was temporary.

"Go ahead, cry. Let it all out."

Rory glanced around Bernard's room. He couldn't stay here. His bed was covered in vomit and urine.

Rory helped Bernard to the spare bedroom.

Bernard fell onto the bed. He curled up in a fetal position. His body convulsed with sobs. Rory grabbed his glasses and put them on the nightstand. He laid down behind Bernard and wrapped his arms around him. He pulled him in tight.

"No, this room is for guests," Bernard said.

"You need to sleep here tonight. Your bedding needs to be changed. I'll take care of it for you."

"Are you staying the night?"

"I can stay if you want me to."

"Please," Bernard said.

Bernard fell asleep.

*

RORY SPENT THE day cleaning the house. He washed Bernard's clothes and bedding and cleaned out the fridge. Some of the food had gone bad.

There was a knock at the door.

Kelly stood in the doorway, Ginger and Chester at his feet.

"Hey, Rory," he said, "how's Bernard doing?"

"Not too good, to be honest," Rory said. "I found him in bed with an empty bottle of whiskey on the floor."

"Shit, what happened?"

"Come in and have a seat."

Kelly let the dogs out back and joined Rory in the living room.

"So," Rory said, "he stopped taking his medication for anxiety and started drinking again."

"He did what?"

"Yeah, it was bad," Rory said. "I got him cleaned up, got him to drink a lot of water, and now he's sleeping in his spare room."

"Damn, I'm glad he's okay."

"I'm going to call the number and try to get him a refill."

"If you need anything, I'm ready to help."

"I think you've done a lot already," Rory said, "but if you can keep Ginger for just a few more days while we get him regulated on his medication and focus on getting better, that would be great."

"I'd be happy to. Chester's been happy and active with Ginger around. I might need to get him a dog."

They both laughed.

"Would you like some coffee?" Rory asked.

"That sounds good," Kelly said.

Rory busied himself with the coffee while Kelly sat at the kitchen table.

"Are you going to tell Sarah and John?" Kelly asked.

"I have to. They should know what happened."

They sat with the coffee in silence. Rory worried about Bernard's well-being.

"Well, I better let you take care of things here. You still have my number?"

"Yes."

"Great. Take care of him."

"I will."

"And call me if you need anything."

"Thanks."

Kelly got Chester and Ginger and headed out the door.

He has some amazing friends. I wish he could see it.

Rory called the number on Bernard's prescription and explained the pills had slipped out and fallen in the washbasin. The prescription had re-fills, so they filled it. He needed to take Bernard to get them tomorrow. He was in no shape to go anywhere today.

Rory went to the backyard. His team had set up a small shed with a generator for Bernard's greenhouse. They wanted to surprise Bernard for his birthday, but he didn't get to see it.

I hope he likes it when he's feeling better. I know how much he wanted to use it.

He called Sarah to tell her what happened to Bernard. The school was on a winter holiday, so he didn't have to work. Even if they weren't on break, Bernard was more important to him.

Rory showered and joined Bernard in bed. He held him tight.

"I'm never going to let you go."

Rory drifted off to sleep.

The next morning, Rory woke to groans from Bernard.

"Rory?"

"You're awake. How do you feel?"

"Like being hit by a Mack truck."

"That's to be expected. I'll go put on some coffee." He got out of bed. "You should take a shower. You've been asleep for a day."

Bernard stood and stumbled.

"Do you need help?"

"Yes, please."

"Do you want a bath or a shower?"

"I think I can take a shower."

Rory undressed Bernard and himself. He helped him into the shower and washed him. Bernard used the wall to steady himself. Rory steadied Bernard as he washed him. He was unstable, and he didn't want him to fall.

Rory dried and helped him get dressed. They shuffled to the kitchen, and Rory placed Bernard in a seat.

"I'll make some eggs, sausage, and toast for you, okay?" Bernard just nodded. Rory handed him some aspirin for his head.

"I've already called to get you a refill. We can pick it up this afternoon," Rory said.

"Thank you."

Why did Bernard do this to himself? He was cheerful, but then it all crashed down around him. Rory's mind raced. Anything could have happened to Bernard while he wasn't here. Bernard needed him.

They spent the morning playing *Chrono Trigger*. Rory didn't understand the appeal of video games, but it made Bernard happy. That's what was important. Bernard taught him the controls. It was fun to play with him.

In the afternoon, Rory drove Bernard around town to pick up his prescription, grab groceries, and get seeds for his greenhouse.

"You don't have to do this," Bernard said.

"I want to."

*

FOR THE NEXT two days, Rory cleaned, cooked, and helped Bernard wash up while his medication stabilized him.

Rory held Bernard at night while he slept. He loved it. He wanted to do this for the rest of his life.

Sunday afternoon after church, Rory showed Bernard the greenhouse. He explained how to work the generator and how to set the timers for the sprinklers.

"I love it." Bernard hugged him. "This is the best gift I could ask for."

"They all worked hard while we were out to get it ready for you. I just wish…"

"No," Bernard said. "This is a happy moment. This is so wonderful."

They kissed. He'd cheered up Bernard. He loved this man and would do anything to make him happy.

Rory helped Bernard plant and set up his greenhouse. They had fun working in the soil and planting carrots, green onions, and zucchini.

"This is going to be an amazing place," Bernard said. "I can't thank you and your friends enough."

"The smile on your face is all the thanks I need."

They kissed. The passion was back in Bernard's kisses. It was wonderful to have the man he fell in love with back.

"I should probably call Kelly and get Ginger back," Bernard said.

"Good idea."

They called, and Kelly agreed to bring Ginger home.

"Thank you for everything," Bernard said. He gave Kelly a hug.

"I'm happy to help," Kelly said.

"I'm going to make burgers for dinner. Do you wanna stay?"

"That sounds good."

They let the dogs out and ate burgers with chips. Bernard's appetite had returned. Rory smiled as he ate a third burger.

"So, do you guys have plans for Christmas?" Kelly asked.

"My family does a dinner and midnight mass on Christmas Eve," Rory said.

"I'm going to my brother's for Christmas Eve and then I'll stop by on Christmas morning for breakfast and presents," Bernard said.

"What about you?" Rory asked.

"I'm spending it with John and Sarah. Sarah's parents are visiting. So, that'll be nice."

"That's nice," Rory said.

Kelly glanced at his watch. "I have to head out. I'll see you guys later.

Thanks for dinner."

They all hugged goodbye.

Rory and Bernard spent the rest of the evening watching old movies and cuddling on the couch.

*

MONDAY MORNING, RORY said he needed to check in on Mina. She'd been alone a lot the past few days.

"I'll be back soon," Rory said. "I just need to make sure she has food and water and change her litter. I'm going to get some shopping done. Why don't you take a nap and I'll be home in time for dinner."

Rory placed a warm kiss on Bernard's lips. Rory parted his lips, eager for Bernard's tongue. Bernard's warm tongue entered his mouth. He sucked on it. He didn't want to let go. Bernard's mouth invited him in. They completed each other.

"I love you," Rory said.

"I love you too."

"I'll see you soon."

Rory drove home. The taste of Bernard lingered in his mouth. He wanted all of Bernard again. His heart, his body, and his mind. He didn't know how long this would last, but he wanted to enjoy it while it did.

Chapter Thirty-Three

Bernard

Monday, December 21–Thursday, December 24

RORY LEFT MONDAY morning. He told Bernard he needed to clean his house, take care of Mina, and run errands.

Bernard called and apologized for not being at work. Rich told him to take the week off since they'd be closed Thursday and Friday for Christmas.

Bernard rotated through multiple games. He couldn't settle on one to play. It wasn't even noon yet.

He made his way to check on his crops. The generator Rory's friends had set up continued to power the greenhouse. He and Rory had set it up to house all the vegetables he needed. The artificial light, heating system, and watering system kept it in perfect condition to grow what he needed.

Rory showed him how to change the timers, heating temperature, and lights if he wanted to grow different plants.

At one o'clock, he fixed himself a sandwich and chips for lunch. He missed Rory's cooking. He didn't have the energy to cook anything. He was grateful Rory bought supplies for simple sandwiches or he'd have to order out.

"I need to do something," he said to Ginger. "I can't sit in the house all day."

Bernard picked up the phone and called Kelly.

"Hello," Kelly answered.

"Hey, Kelly, it's Bernard. I was wondering if you had time to hang out at the dog park today?"

"Of course. Are you feeling better?"

"Yes, I'm doing a lot better. Thanks."

"Meet us at the dog park," Kelly said. "We can hang out while the dogs play."

"Sounds great," Bernard said. "I'll see you in ten."

*

KELLY SAT ON a bench when Bernard arrived. Ginger strained at her leash.

Bernard unhooked her harness and she bolted for Chester. The two dogs chased each other around the play area, nipping and barking.

"Hey, Kelly."

"Hi, Bernard. Good to see you out and about."

"Thanks," Bernard said. "I'm so glad Rory found me."

His heart ached at the thought of Rory finding him dead. He didn't want that. He didn't want to die, just numb the pain. If something had happened to him, it would kill his friends.

"Yeah," Kelly said, "from what I heard, it was close. I think a few more hours and you might have done some serious damage."

"I don't know what I would do without the friends I have. I've put you all through so much."

"We are here for you. So don't ever think you are inconveniencing us when you need help."

Bernard leaned over and hugged Kelly. Kelly rubbed his back.

"You're going to be all right," Kelly said. "You just need to take it one day at a time. It'll get better."

A man who'd faced so much hate and abuse was telling him it would get better. Kelly had overcome so much, and his words meant the world to Bernard. He would be okay. He needed to rely on his friends when he needed them and take care of himself.

They sat in silence as the sun shone down on them. The dogs seemed to have endless energy.

"Can I ask you something?" Bernard said.

"Sure."

"Do you think after what happened, you'll be able to love again?"

"I'd like to think so, but I'm more guarded now than ever. I'm afraid of what might happen. I spent eight years with that man, and that's time I can't get back. It's…" He stopped.

"I'm sorry. I didn't mean to bring this up. It was stupid of me."

"No, it's okay. I need to talk about it. I'm physically and emotionally scarred by him. That's not something I can erase. I'm more scared of what someone will think when they see my scars."

"I can see past them." Bernard placed a hand on his shoulder. "I see you for who you are. The scars on your chest and back are something you can't change. So, if someone judges you on them, that's on them. That's their issue, not yours. You're a gentle, kind man. You deserve love."

"Thank you. That means a lot."

"I won't rush you but try not to shut down. You've done so much for me and my self-esteem. I want to do the same. So, if you ever need someone to talk to, I'm here."

"You're a good friend."

Bernard glanced at his watch. It was four.

"Well, I better get home. Rory is coming over," Bernard said. "Thank you again for everything you've done."

"My pleasure."

They hugged, and Bernard headed home with Ginger.

Rory sat on the couch knitting when he walked in.

"I'm so sorry. I got caught up talking to Kelly at the park."

"It's okay, I busied myself with knitting."

Rory stood and walked over to Bernard. He embraced him and they shared a deep kiss.

"Can you stay the night?"

"Yes, of course. We're on winter break, so I don't have anywhere to be tomorrow."

*

A NIGHT CUDDLED up to Rory eased the tension inside his mind. Doubt crept in. How long would it be before Rory tired of him? Those thoughts had no place in his mind. He pushed it aside. Rory was here to stay.

Bernard and Rory spent the next day together. They watched a few movies and met Kelly at the park in the afternoon for Ginger and Chester's doggie play date.

Kelly and Rory got along well. Bernard grinned as they discussed *The Lord of the Rings*. Rory had read the books after finishing *The Hobbit*. The series was one of Kelly's favorites.

"I'm telling you, Sam is in love with Frodo," Kelly said.

"He regards him as a close friend. I don't know if he's in love with him."

"I don't know. I got the impression they're in love. Maybe it's wishful thinking. The secret love between two men, one that can never come to be because of societal norms."

"You might be right. I never thought of it that way."

Bernard agreed with Kelly but didn't say anything. Reading *The Lord of The Rings* series brought the idea of loving another man to the forefront of his mind. They were the books that made him question his own sexuality. Loving someone who society says you shouldn't. Did Tolkien intend to make the central relationship a secret of love between two men? No one would know his true reasons for having Sam being so close to Frodo.

They all said goodbye as the sun set and Bernard and Rory headed back to his house.

They ordered pizza and watched *Not Without My Daughter*. Rory loved the movie and Bernard had never seen it.

"So, she moved to Iran to visit his family, got stuck there, and now she has to find a way out?" Bernard asked.

"Yeah, that sums it up."

"That poor woman. What an awful thing to have happen."

"It's based on a true story."

"Really?"

"Yeah, I read the book. I think it's darker than the movie. She relies on a support group more than in the movie. You should read it. It's a good book."

"I'll have to check it out."

"You can borrow my copy."

Bernard couldn't help but smile. Rory was sharing his life with him.

They showered and got into bed.

Rory wrapped his warm arms tight around Bernard's chest. He squeezed him closer, not wanting to miss a moment. Bernard wasn't ready to be intimate so soon after his episode, but Rory's embrace helped him to relax each night. Although Rory's erection pressed against his back, he didn't push him or say anything about having sex. Bernard was happy that Rory gave him time. He'd been patient with Rory and now Rory was returning the kindness.

*

WEDNESDAY MORNING, RORY made a large breakfast of pancakes, eggs, toast, coffee, and bacon. It filled the kitchen with scents that made Bernard's mouth water. It was like breakfast on the farm when his mother used to cook every morning.

"This looks amazing," Bernard said.

"I wanted our last morning for a little while to be special."

Rory put a stack of pancakes on the table.

"Thank you."

They dug into breakfast. Everything melted in his mouth. It was perfect, just like Rory.

"So, what do you want to do today?" Rory asked.

"We should get out of the house. What about a trip to San Jose? Then we can see the lights at the park."

"That sounds great."

They made sure Ginger had food and water and headed to San Jose.

They spent the day window shopping, had lunch at a little cafe, and got gelato at a small parlor downtown.

They made it to the park at sunset, and the light shows started. They held hands as they walked through the lights. Houses shone with the season. Groups of people stared at the most elaborate decorations. One house had a light show, but people needed to be in their cars and tuned to the right radio station to hear it. Bernard was getting used to holding hands in public.

"Are you nervous?" Bernard asked.

"About what?"

"We're holding hands in public again."

"I think it's fine. I enjoy holding your hand."

No one noticed them, or if they did, they didn't comment.

They had dinner at a small restaurant before heading home.

"I'm sorry I can't stay tomorrow," Rory said as they got ready for bed. "I have to leave early in the morning. It's Christmas Eve and I have to spend time with my family."

"You don't have to be sorry. I'm going to head to my brother's for dinner. I haven't seen them since…" He didn't need to say more. He hadn't seen his brother, Camila, or the boys since the funeral.

"I understand. I know you'll have a wonderful time with your family. They love you, and I'm sure they miss you."

"You're right."

They embraced and shared a passionate kiss. Rory's lips invited him. His tongue explored Rory's mouth and wrestled with his tongue. Bernard's cock stiffened. The desire to undress Rory surged through his body, but his mind wouldn't allow it. He wasn't enough for Rory. Rory had watched him fall apart, and he deserved a man who could hold it together, not him.

Why is Rory staying with me? I can't give him what he wants. I waited for him, but now that he's given me his body, I'm the one who can't perform. I'm broken.

"Damn, you're a great kisser," Bernard said. "I can't get enough of it."

"You are too," Rory said. "I love kissing you."

They changed into bed clothes and climbed under the covers. Bernard put on his mask. Rory held him tight against his chest. It was nice and warm. He wanted to ask Rory to move in with him. Rory stayed here often enough that it felt right. The answer would be no. His mother didn't approve of them even being friends. There was no telling what she'd say or do if she discovered they lived together. It was impossible. No matter how much he wanted it, he couldn't ask Rory to make that leap.

Chapter Thirty-Four

Bernard

Thursday, December 24–Friday, December 25

BERNARD SAT AT the table with Emilio, Camila, and Penelope for Christmas Eve dinner. They were the only family he had left, and being with them was wonderful. He wished Rory could join them, but his family had a tradition, and he needed to stick to it.

"So, how is everything with Rory?" Camila asked.

"It's fantastic. He was there for me when Dad died, and I couldn't have asked for anything more."

They talked about having Rory over for dinner after the holidays. It'd be nice to have a meal with his family and Rory, who was now part of his family.

After dinner, Bernard headed home to finish wrapping the presents. They had a tradition of opening gifts on Christmas morning, and he was behind on wrapping.

He sat in the living room wrapping while reruns of *I Love Lucy* played.

"Ah, I love this show."

He finished wrapping at a quarter till midnight.

"Ginger, why did I wait until the last minute to wrap gifts? I have to be at Emilio and Camila's by seven tomorrow. Those boys will be prompt."

He walked into the kitchen and noticed the red light blinking on his answering machine.

He pushed the button.

"Listen to me, you perverted sinner." It was Maeve Sinclair's voice. "Mr. and Mrs. Carmichael saw you two at the lights in San Jose holding hands. I told you to stay away from my boy. This is your last warning. If you come near him again, I'll get a restraining order. Your kind can't be trusted. Never contact him again."

Bernard took deep breaths to prevent him from yelling at the phone. *Who does she think she is? She has no right to keep us apart.*

He picked up the phone and called Rory. It went to his answering machine.

Bernard looked at his watch. It was midnight. Rory and his family would be at midnight mass at the church. He wouldn't wait. He needed to confront this head-on. That woman had done everything in her power to keep them apart. He had to do something. Rory had to do something. They'd kept it a secret for months, but it was out. Rory's mother knew. She would watch Rory like a hawk from now on. If he stepped out of bounds,

Bernard was sure she'd be there to pull him back. He hated to think about it, but Rory had to make a choice. What did he want?

Bernard pulled into the parking lot of his former church at midnight. They decorated the church with poinsettias and a nativity scene. The church lights glowed white and lit up the sign, Saint Michael's Roman Catholic Church. Baby Jesus was now in his crib, as the tradition called for. Bernard circled the parking lot for ten minutes. Cars packed the parking lot.

Typical. No one comes to church until Christmas midnight mass.

He parked across the street at the convenience store parking lot. It was closed, so he was confident the owners wouldn't tow his car.

He made it to the large church doors. He took a deep breath and opened the door. Inside, he heard those who gathered singing the praises of Jesus.

When the song ended, the preacher looked up. "That was beautiful, we're blessed today to have such a large turnout."

The preacher looked out and his eyes locked on Bernard's.

"Mr. Silva, you don't belong here," he said. "Unless you've come to repent for your wicked ways."

"I've done nothing that warrants being kicked out of the church."

"I would call attempting to corrupt our son enough to have you removed." Mrs. Sinclair stood.

"You see." The priest pointed. "Corrupting others in the church is grounds to uphold your excommunication."

Bernard winced at the words. It'd been twelve years since they'd excommunicated him, and the words still stung. He knew the risk but came to the church.

"He didn't corrupt me," Rory called out.

"Dear, you don't know what you're saying," Mrs. Sinclair said. "He's filled your head with evil homosexual thoughts."

The entire church watched the conflict unfold, but nobody moved to assist either side.

"You called me and told me to stay away from him," Bernard said. "You have no right."

"You called him?" Rory said to his mother, looking appalled.

"I have every right. You have evil thoughts and have given those thoughts to my poor sweet boy."

"They're not evil thoughts." A voice next to Rory spoke up.

Mr. Sinclair stood and put his hands on Rory's shoulders. Mrs. Sinclair stood speechless.

"Ronan, what has gotten into you?" Mrs. Sinclair asked.

"I will no longer sit by while you berate our son. I should've said something a long time ago."

"How dare you," she said. "Our son will be an abomination if he continues down this wicked path."

"I don't think he's an abomination," Ronan said.

"Neither do I," said Duncan.

"I don't either," said Catherine.

"What's an abominabilation?" their daughter Penelope asked.

"It means he is an evil sinner," Mrs. Sinclair found her voice.

"Uncle Roro is nice. He's not evil," Penelope protested.

"You're too young to understand, sweetheart. You'll understand when you're older," Mrs. Sinclair said.

Penelope screwed up her face. "I know Uncle Roro likes that man Barnyard."

"Who told you such bad things, angel?" Mrs. Sinclair asked.

"Mommy and Daddy said that Uncle Roro was in love with Barnyard and that they should be together, but Grammy doesn't like it."

"What filth have you been filling my granddaughter's head with?" Mrs. Sinclair glared at Duncan and Catherine. "I should have her removed from your care."

"From our care?" Duncan said. "You have no right to her. She's our daughter. You think because you're her grandmother you know best?"

"I know what's best." Mrs. Sinclair stood at her full height.

"Also, we never mentioned Rory and Bernard to her," Catherine said.

"She must have overheard us talking after she'd gone to bed," Duncan said.

"Enough," the priest bellowed. "Mr. Silva, the Church has excommunicated you, and I require you to leave this holy temple. If you refuse to leave of your own accord, I'll have you removed."

Bernard shared a glance with Rory. He stood there hoping Rory would say something, anything.

"Rory, I love you," Bernard said.

"Filth like you don't know what love is. Only lust and sodomy," Mrs. Sinclair said.

"I'll go then." Bernard turned away, defeated.

He'd come here hoping Rory would see he loved him. He wanted to be with him for the rest of his life. Bernard had tried to escape the pain of Tracy for seven years. He sabotaged all his dates and potential relationships for nothing. He'd reconnected with someone who loved him as much as he loved them. It was all for naught. Rory was a good Catholic man who would put his religion above anything else. That included his own happiness.

Bernard had to face the fact that after this, their friendship was over. Maeve Sinclair would see to that.

Bernard placed his hand on the door.

"*Wait!*" Rory said.

Bernard turned around in time to catch Rory in his arms.

"What?" Bernard said.

"I love you too, Bernard Silva." Rory placed a soft kiss on his lips.

Bernard wrapped his arms around Rory and held him tight. For this moment, no one else existed. Bernard and Rory stood in an embrace, lips pressed together. The world stopped.

"You're the one I want to be with," Rory said. "No, you're the one I *need* to be with. You have always treated me with kindness and love. You have never pushed me to do anything I wasn't comfortable with, and you'd let me choose my religion over you if you thought it would make me happy."

"I…"

"You don't have to say anything. My heart belongs to you. I know deep down it always did. I just wish I'd figured it out sooner."

"This is unforgivable," the priest said. "Repent now, or you too, Mr. Sinclair, will be excommunicated."

"No, please Father, we can work this out," Mrs. Sinclair begged.

"He can't change how he was born," Mr. Sinclair said.

"Men are not born to be in love with men. It's sinful lust that draws them to the path," Mrs. Sinclair said.

"It is not, because I once loved a man beyond lustfulness," Mr. Sinclair confessed. His hands flew to his mouth. Everyone in the church gaped at him.

"That's simply not true. We have been married for forty years. I would know if you had lust in your heart," Mrs. Sinclair said.

"You were not my first love," Mr. Sinclair said.

"What?"

"I loved another before you, his name was Angus Stewart." Mr. Sinclair spoke softly. "We fell in love, but we knew the village wouldn't accept our love. I'm attracted to both men and women, so I knew I could build a life with a woman. I never forgot him though. He was and always will be my first love."

"You are not the man I married," she said. "I can't believe you've had these immoral thoughts, and I never knew."

"Having thoughts is not a sin," he said.

"You've probably cheated on me," she spat. "You faggots are all the same." With that, she pushed past everyone in the pew and moved toward the door. She grabbed Rory by the hand. "I can at least save you."

"No, Mother, I'm not going with you."

"Don't you 'no, Mother' me, I am still your mother…"

Rory cut her off. "You're my mother, not my keeper. I'm tired of following your rules that have made me miserable for so many years. I know what happiness is, and that's being with Bernard." He pulled his arm from his mother's grasp and looked up at the priest. "You can excommunicate me, I don't care. If this is how the church runs, on hatred and vileness, I'm better off finding a more accepting church."

"You are no longer…"

"Yeah, we get it. No longer welcome," Bernard said.

Bernard and Rory moved through the doors and headed for the parking lot.

"I brought my car," Rory said. "Can I meet you at your place? I don't want to be alone tonight."

"Of course, I'd love nothing more than having you at home with me."

*

BERNARD DROVE HOME. His pulse quickened at the thought of Rory lying next to him again. He remembered the first night they spent together. It was a passion he hadn't felt in years. He wanted that again.

Bernard sat on his couch as the seconds ticked by.

At one o'clock there was a knock on his door. Rory stood on the other side, tears streaming down his face.

"What's the matter?"

"They…they…they're going to excommunicate me." He collapsed into Bernard's arms. Bernard helped him onto the couch. Rory sobbed into Bernard's chest.

"Shh, it's going to be okay," Bernard said. "I'm here for you."

Bernard stroked Rory's hair as he sobbed. Bernard understood his fear. He'd faced this when the church excommunicated him and thought the world would collapse around him. He needed to be there for Rory. Rory faced this because of his love for him. He wouldn't let him face it alone.

"What…if…I…made…a…mistake?" Rory sobbed.

What could Bernard say to this? Rory made a decision that would change his life forever.

"Love is not a mistake," Bernard said. "I love you with all of my heart. I'll always be here for you."

Rory looked up. "You mean that?"

"Of course I do, I've loved you for so many years. I never thought you'd feel the same."

"I love you too." Rory leaned up to kiss him. They embraced on the couch, Rory's sobs subsiding.

Rory fell asleep in Bernard's arms. Bernard continued to stroke his hair.

"I hope I can make you as happy as you make me right now," he whispered.

Bernard didn't know what time he fell asleep.

*

RORY GROANED AWAKE. "What time is it?"

Bernard stretched and felt the stiffness in his joints. He'd never found the couch a comfortable place to sleep, and this position didn't help.

Bernard looked at his watch. "It's seven-thirty."

Rory sat up and stretched. "I'm sorry I fell asleep."

"You needed the rest," Bernard said. "Do you want to get some breakfast?"

"It's Christmas Day though, who's open?"

"My brother invited me to Christmas breakfast, and I'm sure you're more than welcome."

"I don't want to impose."

"You could never impose." Bernard leaned over and kissed him.

"What's the plan?"

"You head home to shower and change while I do the same here. I'll make sure Ginger has everything she needs and then I'll head to your place to pick you up."

"Okay, sounds good."

They kissed goodbye, and Rory left.

Bernard called his brother. They were thrilled to have Rory join them for breakfast. He showered, brushed his teeth, and changed. He was excited to have Rory in his life. The past few months had been hard on them both.

Chapter Thirty-Five

Bernard

Saturday, December 26–Thursday, December 31

BERNARD SPENT HIS days the next week at work and evenings with Rory. He would have Friday off for New Year's Day but had to work New Year's Eve.

He'd asked him to move in on Sunday, and Rory said yes. Rory still had to pay the rent for January, so that gave them time to move at their pace.

They introduced Mina to Ginger on Sunday so they could get used to each other. Bernard wanted to be there the whole time to see what would happen. It surprised them at how well Mina took to Ginger. Ginger always loved to play, but she'd never been around cats.

They chased each other through the house, playing tag. Bernard's back fences were high, but he was still worried that Mina would get out. He'd hired a contractor who specialized in pet enclosures to build a ceiling in his backyard that would prevent Mina from escaping. In the meantime, he kept Ginger inside or outside but didn't keep the doggy door open. They didn't need Mina getting loose.

"Well, that was easy," Bernard said. "I thought Ginger would try to eat her."

"She's feisty, but it seems they understand this is how it's going to be and they should just get used to it."

Every day, Rory went to his apartment to pack up as much as he could. Kelly and John helped when they weren't working. It made the work easier.

Each night they went through boxes and sorted them. They reminisced about their childhoods. Rory had two picture albums full of photos of them in high school and when they were in their twenties.

"Look how muscular I used to be," Bernard said. "Leaving the farm did a number on me."

"I was always a chunky kid."

Bernard looked at him and saw tears form in his eyes.

"What's the matter?"

"It's just...I was always the fat kid. I never fit in anywhere until I met you. You never made me feel bad about my weight. You were always my friend."

"I didn't see your weight as anything but part of you. I liked you for you."

"Thank you."

"I'm the one who pushed you away when I came out. Thinking you wouldn't accept me, and here we are, boyfriends."

"Boyfriends sounds so middle school," Rory laughed. "What if I called you my partner?"

"I'd like that."

They hugged.

"I'm sorry I pushed you away in grad school," Rory said. "That wasn't right of me."

"I understand why. You did what you thought you had to. I'm just glad you came back to me."

They continued to flip through the photos. Rory pointed out people he hadn't seen since high school. They had a group of eight people who hung out together. Two moved away, leaving six in their early twenties. Bernard, Rory, and Sarah were the only ones who kept in touch. The other three stopped talking to Bernard when he came out. Although he thought he pushed them away like he did Rory. Sarah was the only one who refused to be pushed away. She became his rock. Bernard did not know where any of the others were.

Bernard walked into the spare room to see a dozen extra boxes stacked in the corners of the room.

"You have a lot more than I thought," Bernard said.

"Well, I've collected things over the years," Rory said, bringing another box into the room.

"It's okay, we have the space."

Bernard didn't use his third bedroom. He stored a few things he didn't use anymore, so Rory's boxes could fit while they arranged them around the rest of the house.

"I'm so glad you said yes," Bernard said. "I know it's a big step."

"We've known each other forever. I don't see any reason not to move in."

Bernard pulled him into an embrace. He inhaled Rory's musk, his cologne lingering in his nostrils. Everything about Rory made him quiver.

"You're everything I've ever wanted in a partner," Bernard said, "and I'll do anything to make you happy."

"Can I set up a small work area here? I just need a portion. It won't take up much space."

"This is your room now, for all your work. We can set it up any way you want it."

"Really?"

"Of course. I don't use it for anything. I'll get a storage shed for things I might want to keep but don't use. We can put some things in there for you too, if you'd like."

"That would be great." Rory kissed him again.

Rory's kisses were sweet, passionate, and everything he ever dreamed of.

"I want to make love to you," Bernard said.

"Are you ready?"

They hadn't had sex since Bernard's dad passed away. And Rory had been distant since leaving his mother behind. His father and brother still talked to him, but his mother refused. They hadn't been in the mood to have sex.

"Yes. I want to feel you inside me," Bernard said.

Rory led Bernard into the bathroom and they showered. He laid

Bernard on the bed and kissed him.

Rory's tongue traced a path from his neck down to his erect dick. Rory took it all and sucked. Bernard shifted, the sensation echoing through his body.

Rory pulled Bernard to the edge of the bed. He lifted Bernard's legs and ran his tongue around his entrance. Rory hadn't done this to him before. Rory's tongue entered and Bernard squirmed.

Bernard leaned down and lifted Rory's head. They gazed into each other's eyes.

"I want you to fuck me without a condom," Bernard said. "I want you to fill me up."

They'd gotten tested in October and both came back negative. They hadn't had sex without condoms yet.

"Yeah, is that what you want?"

"Yes."

Rory prepped Bernard with two fingers and lots of lube.

"You're so tight," Rory said.

"It's tight for you," Bernard said. "I want to feel my ass wrapped tight around that cock."

"Are you ready for my cock?"

"Give it to me."

Rory lubed up and placed Bernard's legs on his shoulders and eased in. Bernard helped guide him. Rory was gentle with his entrance. Bernard knew he was afraid of hurting him, which made him an amazing top.

Bernard gripped the bed as Rory's cock entered.

"Fuck," Bernard said.

"Are you okay?"

"Yes, it's just so big."

"You can take it, big guy. I know you can."

Rory's belly pushed against him and he moaned as his cock filled Bernard's hole. Rory's uncut cock eased inside his ass. Their bodies connected on a new level, without a condom to separate their flesh. He could lie here all day with Rory's cock in his ass.

He breathed deep as Rory moved in and out, stretching his hole. Rory kept a slow pace.

"Fuck me," Bernard said.

"You want it?" Rory said.

Rory had gained confidence in the bedroom and it excited Bernard. He moved his legs to wrap around Rory's back and pulled him in.

"Okay," Rory said.

He pounded into Bernard. Each thrust sent jolts from his ass to his cock. He grabbed the lube and dripped it on his cock and stroked it.

"I want you to come first," Rory said. "I want to see you come."

"You want me to come?"

"Yes, I want to see what I do to you."

"Fuck, that's hot."

Bernard grabbed his balls in the other hand and pulled. He reared at the pressure.

"Keep going. I'm going to come," Bernard growled.

"Come for me, baby."

Bernard let out a groan and cum shot to his chest. Three more followed and hit his belly.

"Keep fucking me," Bernard said. "I want to feel your cum inside me."

Rory continued to pump, his dick swelling inside. He was close, and it was going to be explosive.

Rory let out a loud moan as he thrust one last time. Rory's cock throbbed as cum shot out. Each pulse elevated Bernard's ecstasy. Rory had come inside him.

Bernard squeezed his ass as Rory pulled out and rolled over next to him.

"Fuck, you're good at that," Bernard said.

"I just did what you taught me," Rory said. "You showed me how."

Bernard leaned in and kissed him. "Some of that is just you."

"Well, I guess when you want to please someone, you learn."

"Well, I'm glad you learned. I love it when you fuck me."

"Next time, you top. I want to feel you fill me with your cum."

"I'm happy to do whatever pleases you, sexy bear."

"I love when you call me that." Rory smiled.

"Then I will say it as often as you want me to, sexy bear."

They kissed. Sweat mingled with the mint of the toothpaste. Bernard licked Rory's lips and drank in the sweat.

They cleaned up and went to bed. Bernard still had to work, and Rory had more packing to do. Bernard fell asleep in Rory's arms. This was how it would be from now on. He would never have to go to sleep alone.

*

BERNARD GOT OFF work early on Thursday due to the holiday. He drove over to Rory's to help him pack.

They moved most of his furniture to a rental trailer to take to a donation center.

They donated Rory's bed, dresser, and other furniture he didn't need. He insisted on holding on to the nightstand his brother made him, so they set it up on his side of the bed. He wanted to keep a recliner his grandfather gave him. The chair fit perfectly in the corner.

They'd unloaded most of Rory's apartment by Thursday evening.

Kelly, John, and Sarah joined them with little Mikey.

"Well, you guys have officially moved in together," Kelly said.

"We have." Bernard kissed Rory.

"How does it feel?" Sarah asked.

"It'll take getting used to," Rory said, "since I left home, I've lived alone. This will be a pleasant change."

They watched Mikey run around with Ginger. She'd run and hide from him. When he found her under the table or a chair, she'd scoot off to another location.

"We're having a party tonight," Sarah said. "You're welcome to join us."

"What do you think?" Bernard asked Rory.

"I think I'm exhausted," Rory said.

"I think we're going to stay in tonight," Bernard said. "We've had a lot happen over the last month."

"I don't blame you," John said, "but if you change your mind, you're more than welcome."

"Thanks," they both responded.

They said goodbyes, and both collapsed on the couch.

"I don't feel like cooking," Rory said.

"How about we order out?" Bernard said.

"Sounds good. What's open?"

They ordered pizza and watched *Naked Gun 33 ⅓* on ABC.

"This movie is hilarious," Rory said. "I mean, what's better than a comedy?"

"I have to admit, I prefer romances, but this is great."

Rory fell asleep in his arms. Bernard stroked his hair as the end credits of the movie ran. It was only ten-thirty. He turned off the TV and enjoyed the silence. He had his partner in his arms.

As midnight approached, Bernard shook Rory.

"Hey, sexy bear," Bernard said. "It's almost midnight."

Rory got up and stretched.

"How long was I out?"

"About two hours," Bernard said.

"You stayed there for two hours while I slept?"

"Yeah. I liked it."

Bernard changed the channel to the countdown. They watched as the crowd in Times Square shouted down from ten.

Five...four...three...two...one...

"Happy New Year, sweetie," Bernard said.

"Happy New Year, my love," Rory said.

They kissed as the ball dropped.

This was the beginning of their life together. As a loving couple.

Epilogue

One year later

BERNARD FACED THE mirror. His fitted blue suit enhanced his physique. He liked how he looked. He loved himself again.

He continued to adjust his tie, trying to get it perfect. He finally gave up and tossed the tie to the side.

"I'll go without."

Sarah walked in behind him, dressed in a floral gown.

"You look amazing," she said. She picked up the tie. "You forgot this."

She created a beautiful wrap for his tie and adjusted it.

He turned back to the mirror and smiled. "Thank you."

"How are you feeling?"

"I can't believe it's happening. I'm finally getting married, or at least as close to getting married as I can."

"The love you and Rory have for each other is beyond a piece of paper. I know it's important to have legal protections, but one day you will."

He wrapped his arms around her. Sarah's friendship had never wavered. She was always there for him. Tears welled up in his eyes. He'd made it. He'd found love when he thought all was lost.

"No crying," she said. "You're going to make your face all red and puffy. That won't look good in pictures."

"You're right," he laughed.

He grabbed tissues and cleaned up his face.

"Now," she said, "I'll meet you out there."

*

BERNARD ENTERED THE main space of the Portuguese hall. He and his brother used their standing in the community to rent the hall for his ceremony. A few of the older members disapproved, but the younger, more open-minded members outnumbered them. A wedding at the hall was his dream, and he'd be damned if anyone would stop it.

They had erected an arch for their ceremony. A woman in priest garments stood under the arch.

On Bernard's side of the arch stood Emilio, Sean, John, Sarah, and Kelly. On Rory's side stood Duncan, Davi, Nicolas, Sophia, and Jeff. Neither of them wanted to have a best man or best woman. They just wanted their closest friends in their wedding party.

Bernard stood next to Rory at the end of the rows of seats. Dressed in a gray suit, he looked as handsome as ever. He was going to spend the rest of his life with the man standing next to him.

The guests stood as they walked up the aisle together, hand in hand.

Love filled the room as their friends and family wept tears of joy for their union.

Bernard's family sat on the right side, two empty spots for his mother and father. Camila and the twins sat smiling up at him. Camila held little Mikey in her lap. He reached for his mother, but she cooed for him to relax.

This was his family. The family who always believed in him. His Aunt Antonia and his cousins, Bella and Carlos, sat in the next row, beaming.

On Rory's side, Catherine and Penelope sat with Rory's father. His mother refused to attend. After the incident at the church, his mother filed for divorce. It was a blow to his father, but he'd recovered. He said it had been a matter of time before it would end. She said she never truly loved him.

Eddie's son, Parker, sat next to Penelope. They were best of friends. She'd mentioned she was going to marry him one day.

It was a small gathering, but a powerful one. He and Rory didn't have many friends, and even fewer family members who truly accepted them, but those who did were here. That was what mattered.

"We are gathered here today, to unite Bernardo Silva and Rory Sinclair in a commitment ceremony," the priest said.

Rory and Bernard insisted on a female priest from their new church. They attended an inclusive church, dedicated to the support of love. Michelle Xiong was more than willing to do the ceremony. She loved it.

"Do you, Bernard, take Rory as your life partner, and the man you will marry when the day comes for legalization of same-sex marriage?"

"I do." Bernard smiled.

"And do you, Rory, take Bernard as your life partner, and the man you will marry when the day comes for legalization of same-sex marriage?"

"I do." Rory beamed.

"Then with the power vested in me that we all have the right to love as we choose, I now pronounce you life partners. You may kiss."

They shared a deep kiss. One they knew would last forever.

Acknowledgements

I would like to give a warm thank you to Colin Dereham and Kate Munro. The best beta readers any writer could ask for. None of this would be possible without their help.

About the Author

Jole Cannon is a high school math and math programming teacher. When he's not shaping the mathematical minds of tomorrow, he's playing video games with his partner, watching television, doing math for fun, and working on his master's in history.

Email

JoleCannonWrites@gmail.com

Facebook

www.facebook.com/profile.php?id=100088973277082

Twitter

@JoleCannon

www.ninestarpress.com

www.facebook.com/ninestarpress

www.facebook.com/groups/NineStarNiche

www.twitter.com/ninestarpress

www.instagram.com/ninestarpress

bsky.app/profile/ninestarpress.bsky.social

www.threads.net/@ninestarpress